*In the Name of God,
the Merciful, the Compassionate*

First edition, October 2014

This work is licensed under the Creative Commons Attribution-NonCommercial-ShareAlike 3.0 Unported License.

ISBN 978-1-500-72980-6

*In the Name of God,
the Merciful, the Compassionate*

Tim Parise

The Maui Company
Maui, Hawaii

1

    Twilight settled on Georgetown, a golden hour between that time when the civil servants had knocked off work for the day and the time when they would go out again to dine, dance, drink, and wait for the sunrise. Traffic slowed, the sidewalks emptied, the cafes closed their doors with worn velvet ropes for a little while. But they left the doors themselves open to catch the sea-breeze that had blown in from the Atlantic. The air was cool and moist where the rays of the sun did not fall. It was an uncommon reprieve from the warmth that was already submerging the capital. Soon summer would come down on the former swamplands and slowly steam their current residents like an old-fashioned federal agent opening an envelope. So the few drinkers out before sunset pulled their chairs onto the patios and clustered around the largest windows. Staffers walking their dogs in the Dumbarton Oaks Gardens smiled and exchanged greetings. Third floor residents sauntered out onto their balconies, or at the very least opened their double doors wide to welcome the breeze.

    Major Martin sampled the air without opening his eyes. Sea and earth were better smells than human flesh, and tonight the wind at least smelled of the sea, with only faint hints of gasoline and soot and plastic. The contrast sharpened the effect of the fumes from the incense that crumbled, glowing, on a burner in the corner. The last traces of the damiana leaves he had burned earlier disappeared completely. He sensed the sudden change in temperature, but it failed to shock him. His regular breathing continued, smooth and even, without showing a break as the fine hairs on his exposed skin responded automatically to the chill.

A few minutes later, his brain reacted as his body had, and in his concentration he was once again aware of the noise in the background, which he had ignored as if it did not exist. All because his mind knew semi-consciously that a series of words had been spoken which he would consciously want to hear. He listened.

The CNN reporter was reading a dull piece about the economic crisis in Dubai and the attempts its fellow emirates were making to repair the damage. Then something else about a trade agreement with India. Then a lengthy commercial break. And only then the bit of information with which the Major was concerned:

"The Supreme Court of Iran has confirmed the death sentence passed against Arash Kadivar and Feroze Jan and has scheduled their execution for three weeks from today. Kadivar and Jan, who were convicted of sodomy eighteen months ago, have been imprisoned since then in the city of Tabriz, in northern Iran, awaiting the outcome of their appeal to Iran's highest court. Chief Justice Sadeq Larijani, known for his connections to the country's military establishment and his hostility towards Islamic moderates, rejected a complaint from the defendants' lawyers that the court had deliberately delayed proceedings until both of the defendants had reached the age of eighteen in order to minimize potential criticism from Iran's political allies.

"While death sentences for consensual homosexual activity have become less common in Iran, with none having been carried out since 2012, the conviction of the two teenagers, who admitted to a three-year relationship, is believed to signal the beginning of a new campaign by religious hardliners to respond to the ongoing political shift in the United States. Sandra Donaldson of the Human Rights Campaign said…"

The sound ceased. The Major cut it off with a thought. The force of will was stronger than a volume control, and he had no interest in listening to a bureaucrat prate about a tragedy she was incapable of feeling.

Of course the Iranian court had delayed final confirmation of the death sentence. With both boys over the age of eighteen, it would not have to make a legal exception to its own laws. Larijani had doubtless enjoyed making them wait. Not to mention that he had given his colleagues in the security services ample opportunity to identify anyone who protested or spoke out in favor of the condemned. And in the meantime, the only thing the American activists could think of to do was to make televised statements deploring the sentence and conflating half a dozen distinct issues every time they spoke.

The Major felt his anger growing. He controlled it, monitored it, was in some degree pleased to note that it did not interrupt his steady breathing or raise his heart rate. But it didn't go away. It didn't retreat. He examined himself, searching for the source of the rage, because it was rare that he felt moved enough for his emotion to threaten to become physical. Do I resent Larijani? he asked himself. No, that was not the answer. He resented the Iranian judge for being an oppressor, but so many men were oppressors. The abuse of strength and power were more common than restraint. It was a recognition broad enough to take personal hatred out of the equation. What, then? The Iranian had power and used it as he saw fit. But the woman who was speaking into the void, or had been--she also had power, or at least access to those who had power. And she as their mouthpiece had as good as told the world that they would do nothing.

She was the one he was angry at. Her, and those behind her. It was not a new feeling for him.

He opened his eyes and rose from the half-lotus position in an unhurried movement. Outside the window, the sun was almost down.

* * * * *

The cab deposited him beneath the rainbow-colored streamers that hung over the entrance to the club. It was too close. He had to turn and walk away from the building before reaching the end of the line that stretched away from the door.

He was unfamiliar with the scene in general and this club in particular. But tonight the Major felt curious. He knew that most of the gay community, prosperous and increasingly content, had been neutered for all practical purposes. He wanted to see it in action though, to give color to the words on the page. The line moved up. The Major paid the cover charge--a mark of the owner's confidence in the popularity of his establishment--and went in.

Vitality, he thought at once. The crowd was young for the most part, which was a surprise in a city filled with professionals who were required to have certain degrees and a certain amount of age before they would be considered qualified for half the civil service jobs that accounted for most of the available employment in Washington. The boys were reasonably pretty, not as beautiful and abundant as those in Florida, but not as tired and worn as those in California, either. He recognized a well-known local Marine reservist behind the bar. The music had moved on from what he remembered. It had become pure movement, all synthesizers and electronic algorithms, all beat. Not much remained of the divas whose voices had formed the original basis for the songs. Vocals had been washed out in search of more energy.

Undirected energy, the Major realized. Completely undirected. The opposite extreme from Quantico.

He moved on, up the stairs to the second floor, inconspicuous among the strobe lights and neon clothes in his dark shirt and jeans and espadrilles. It was less crowded than the level below, and, from the sound of it, much less crowded than the one above. Couples and groups lounged about on leather sofas around low tables. Small white shorts rode up and revealed gleaming glimpses of smooth legs tucked into combat boots. The shifting light here was softer and more subtle, the byproduct of plasma screens rather than lasers. The Major glanced up at the screen nearest to the end of the bar as he made his way across the room. Unlike the others, which were flashing the latest music videos, it was tuned to ESPN, which had seen fit to show football replays in the middle of the summer.

Football! He could have controlled the sudden sneering tilt of his mouth, but he chose not to. The Major loathed football. It was an idolization of the worst kinds of group behavior, a scaled-down but nevertheless complete metaphor for everything he and some of his fellow instructors at the Marine Corps University were fighting against. Deployment in line. The confining of a conflict to given boundaries. An obsession with taking and holding physical territory. The use of players for specific roles without flexibility. The love of carefully worked-out plans made before an action. The omnipresence of armor plate and defensive thinking. A set of rules that gave preference to winning fairly over winning. American football was the military tactics of the First World War with an audience. And yet much of the military doted on it, especially the academies. No maneuver, no unconventional war, just a straightforward conflict with everyone accepting the outcome when it was over. A complacent fantasy. Play by the rules and you'll be okay no matter what happens. Martin knew he was probably reading too much into a simple choice of channel. But he couldn't help feeling that there was something wrong when the gay community, which argued that it was fighting against discrimination, had so lost its sense of being at war with mainstream society that it could lap up the same oversimplified platitudes beloved by the mainstream. There were staffers in the club tonight who would be back on the Hill on Monday making speeches about equality and human rights. They apparently felt right at home in this atmosphere. He looked around. No one showed resentment towards the programming or looked outraged at its subtle rejection of the original principles of their cause.

None of the Major's irritation showed on his face, either. He waved the bartender over and ordered a White Russian. The drink was strong, almost too strong. The club circuit was still on the same vodka kick it had been going through the last time he stepped into a bar, several years earlier.

He started circulating, listening for scraps of conversation. Trivia, all of it. Boyfriends, Atlantis cruises, petitions, bills, upcoming pool parties, legal challenges, the new and fascinating subject of gay divorce. The personal and the national colliding on a level that failed to strike any kind of a balance and seemed petty to an outsider. At the other end of the room an obviously straight girl was showing off her bosom to three excited twinks, who appeared to be congratulating her on something. The Major listened in for a minute. Ah, plastic surgery. He shut the crowd out and wondered what it might have been like to walk into a real gay bar, decades ago, when the war for gay liberation was still called a war and there was fire in the eyes of the men and women who fought it.

Someone tugging on his sleeve brought him back from those reflections. He looked down at a short, dumpy woman, fortyish, with greasy hair and a distinct lack of balance.

"…and we can cater to any scene you like," she was saying. He couldn't place her accent, although he decided she was probably from somewhere in eastern Europe. "We have private rooms available or we offer group rates. Slings, chains, whips included…"

"Excuse me?" the Major said crisply.

She thrust a card into his hand. It showed a picture of a woman in a leather corset next to the words "Controlled Pleasures", typeset in a font that would have disgraced a Dutch brothel.

"Have you ever considered that a gay bar might not be the best place for a straight dominatrix to tout for clients?" the Major asked her. He looked her over and decided that she wasn't any such thing herself. Probably just an habitual drinker who picked up extra money referring other drinkers to a wide range of establishments once their inhibitions were gone.

"You might want to try it sometime," she simpered at him.

"Unlikely." He dropped the card down the front of her blouse and handed her his drink before she could react. Then he turned and walked away.

He didn't stop until he reached Stead Park. P Street was busy with cars and pedestrians. The sidewalks of 17th Street were crowded with the dressy and the not-so-dressy heading from one club to the next. The city was noisy again, the reprieve of the afternoon gone. Minivans bearing taxi signs cruised by him as often as middle-aged men looking for bedmates did. The Major decided to walk home instead.

He crossed Dupont Circle and went on past the boutique restaurants, the smaller hotels, the embassies of Indonesia and Portugal. Luxembourg and Niger, he recalled, were just to the north. To the north as well, standing in the shadows on a narrow little triangle of grass, was the statue of Taras Shevchenko. It had an inscription on the base. "Dedicated to the liberation, freedom and independence of all captive nations." Captive nations! The statue's erection had been nothing more than a cheap shot at the Soviet Union a lifetime ago. No one cared about the captive nations. At the time, the United States had been doing its best to acquire as many captive nations of its own as possible. It had even gone to the length of absorbing one of them into the union as an excuse for its retention. Now Ukrainian protestors gathered there to lay flowers at the feet of the dead poet and demand that their nation be rescued from its captors--by which they meant that it should be allowed to reappropriate the Crimea regardless of what the Crimeans thought on the subject.

The Major wanted to shout at the empty square, "Liars! You are all liars!" But the only sound he made was a soft sigh that died in his throat.

On impulse, he stepped off the sidewalk and took one of the trails that turned aside into Rock Creek Park. The darkness, and the splashing of the token trickle of water from below, helped him focus his thoughts. The birds and squirrels slept, and the night was still early. No ardent young things would be copulating in the bushes just yet. He let himself drift while his eyesight adjusted to the shadows.

The captive nations--nations in the sense of peoples, his own included--could not be free if they would not fight. Granted, more and more of them were fighting, but the ideal that mocked him from the granite plinth of the statue went unrecognized in those wars. They were battles over the concrete, not the abstract.

He moved so quietly as he walked, and his dark clothes were so inconspicuous, that he was almost on top of the scream when it exploded from a pair of frightened lungs and was cut off with the audible sound of flesh striking flesh.

The Major took two rapid steps and turned the corner in time to see three burly men throwing a fourth, less substantial figure into the bushes.

"Is he out?" one of them growled.

"Looks like he hit his head on a stump." All three of them were staring into the underbrush. The silver chains on their leather clothes tinkled in the faint ambient light reflected from the clouds.

"Serves the fucker right." The third man moved forward but the previous speaker jerked him back. "My turn first, and don't you forget it."

Just then the Major coughed. His canvas shoes had silenced his footsteps, and their preoccupation had done the rest. They jumped back from the bushes and saw a single man grinning at them. Grinning in a way that by itself was infinitely more barbaric than either their playacting or their true intentions.

"What the fuck?" the leader of the pack shouted. One of the other men tried to tackle the Major. He was half a foot taller than the officer and outweighed him by at least half as much again. But a good light infantryman is built to be mobile, not brutal. The Major shifted his weight from one leg to the other and lunged before the charging bear could extend himself all the way. He struck him in the throat with the palm of his hand and his attacker tripped on his own feet, choking and squealing as he fell.

And then he turned and caught the second man between the legs with a kick that produced a scream louder than the noise their victim had made.

That left the leader of the trio. The alpha bear, the Major supposed he was called. He circled, his face pinched, angry and afraid at the same time. Afraid enough to realize that the man opposite him was dangerous; angry enough at the interruption and the threat of prison that he would stay and fight.

He didn't throw punches. He tried to grapple with the Major, to seize him and crush him through superior strength. The Major could see at once that the only experience this man had ever had with striking a blow had taken place in a dungeon, not in any kind of combat, not so much as a street brawl. He moved like an actor, trying to intimidate his enemy with exaggerated body language. It didn't work on the Marine officer, who could still remember the feel of a pesh-kabz tearing into his thigh, the splatter of burning powder on his shoulder. Each time the bear came at him, he shifted his ground and let the attack pass by.

Finally, the Major hit the man. Not with his fist, but with the back of his hand. A contemptuous blow. a painful blow rather than a disabling one. The bear's head twisted to the side under the impact. When he looked back at the Major, blood was trickling from the corner of his mouth, where his teeth had sunk into his lip. He knew the significance of the slap. He'd used it often enough himself.

The Major saw his recognition and chuckled aloud.

His attacker grabbed at him again. He turned, quickly, between the outstretched arms and hit the bear in the sternum. Without fat to absorb it, the man's ribs and lungs took the force of the punch. He staggered. His legs wobbled, then gave out for a moment, and he fell flat on his backside.

Now it was the Major's turn to circle, still laughing that quiet, sarcastic laugh which said clearer than words, *You tried to hurt someone. How does it feel?*

He grabbed at the Marine's legs, but the Major declined the gambit and simply walked away, disdaining to kick the scrabbling, bleeding, sweating hunk of flesh. The bear scrambled to his feet, uttered a gurgle, and swung at the Major, a halfhearted, wild punch. It missed completely.

The Major turned and began to punish him. His blows were all delivered with an open hand, and they all landed on the bear's head, with the exception of the few he used to block his adversary's blows. The number of defensive strikes he used diminished. The thug was showing less and less fight. Instead of taking the offensive, he was cringing away from the Major, from the pain and disorientation and humiliation of being treated as he had treated others. He tried to cover his face with his hands; in an instant, his forearms and wrists tingled with the agony of skin trapped between bone and an external force. He dropped them, howled in anger, and made one last run at the Major.

Who stood there serenely waiting for him. He opened his mind to the events of the day, and extended his arm.

A bystander could have heard the bear's jaw shatter under the impact. His two friends, recovering from their own pain, did, and shivered. They hadn't planned for the night to end this way. At least, not with them on the receiving end of the assault.

"Come here," the Major said. His voice carried without being raised to a shout. One gasping, one still crouching, they obeyed him.

"Take your filthy friend and get out of here." The berserker grin had disappeared from his face, but his lips still quivered in an approximation of a smile. The bears didn't dare argue with him. Half carrying, half dragging their leader, they stumbled away down the trail as fast as they could go, back to their superficial respectability.

The Major watched them go. Then he walked back to the bushes and looked down into the gap. All the humor of release was gone from his expression.

"You bastards," he said into the night.

2

Asim slouched back in his chair. The cheap corrugated blue plastic yielded and creaked. Up at the counter, the proprietor snored on undisturbed. Outside it was eighty-five degrees, and the little air conditioner that served the shop was broken again. And there probably wasn't power available for it anyway, not with five generators out in the past week from sporadic rioting and rationing in effect. Sleep was the easiest way to escape the heat of an early summer, especially for an old man.

The arrangement suited Asim. The cafe owner was garrulous when awake, and he preferred not to be distracted. He had gone so far as to shut down the other three battered Dell computers that sat next to him on the long table. If a customer came in at this time of night, he could start one back up if he wanted it that badly. As for the owner, he would thank him for saving electricity if he ever realized the machines were off.

Apart from the noise coming in from the street, the only other sounds in the room were the buzzing of the fluorescent lights and the steady rattle of the keys on Asim's keyboard. In spite of their plastic construction, modern computer keyboards rattle just as much as their cast-iron counterparts of the nineteenth century did. And Asim was keeping up a steady pace, flicking back and forth between browser tabs, monitoring the conversations on nine different Facebook pages and two

Twitter accounts. A few of the pages had been set up by his fellow students at the University College of Bahrain. There was one from Dubai, and one from Syria. The rest were Egyptian. Their common subject: the Arab Spring, or the Arab Spring 2.0, as the computer science majors insisted on calling it. Asim was trying to keep the conversations from growing too personal. Not out of any reverence for civility, but personal slurs had a way of giving the police information which they could potentially use to identify the writers and jail them under the new decrees.

    The feeds were busy tonight, the Bahraini ones in particular, and busy in a way that underlined the need to keep them clear of personal information. A Bahraini judge had decided to round off his work week by sentencing two students to life in prison for committing an act of terrorism and inciting violence. They had driven their car--their car, it was noted--down the King Faisal Highway, parked it in front of the Bahrain Financial Harbor, overturned it with the help of some friends, and set it ablaze to protest what they termed "the government's shameless pursuit of foreign business at the expense of true local development." In handing down the sentence, the judge had drawn a parallel between the case and another involving the destruction of a Formula One car some years earlier. "It is not permissible," he had written, "for individuals to destroy their own property in such a manner as will bring the Kingdom and its financial interests into disrepute. By doing so, they are directly causing harm to the population of the nation as a whole, regardless of whether the property destroyed is theirs to dispose of or not. The sentence for this act is well-established in regard to the property of others. It should be no different when property belonging to the perpetrator of a treasonable act is involved."

    The protestors were seething at the precedent the judgment had set. Protest now equaled defamation, and defamation now equaled treason. The breadth of the ruling indicated the judiciary's increasing willingness to interpret royal decrees more and more broadly. Other judges in other ongoing trials would doubtless use it as an excuse to expand the definition of treason still further. Already social media users were speculating about how long it would take for the government to rule that use of a computer or phone to post political criticism online fell within the new standards for abuse of private property. Life in prison for a single tweet was suddenly a very real possibility. Now and then, a pro-government commentator would stir the pot by arguing that individuals had a responsibility to society and that any behavior which disrupted society was a crime warranting punishment. They pointed to the British institution of anti-social behavior orders and American hate speech laws as examples of similar reasoning in so-called democratic nations.

It was Asim's job to moderate this discussion to some extent. He added his own summaries of conversations, deleted spammers and the occasional agent provocateur--the Bahraini police were inept internet users. Their institutional culture viewed the electronic world as the domain of revolutionaries and malcontents, which made it difficult for their special investigative teams to blend in with the ordinary traffic flow. And he headed off any line of argument that seemed to support the government's position. There was no need to give the more conservative Bahrainis an online platform, he reasoned. They had Al Jazeera and the papers to make their views known. Those outlets would no longer risk publishing anything that was the slightest bit reformist.

His computer made a noise that was the digital equivalent of a stone being dropped into a pond. An electronic gurgle. That meant a new message from someone he actually knew. He scanned the tabs and flipped back to the one that was blinking an alert. A chat window had popped up in the bottom corner of the screen and his classmate Khalil was typing into it.

"Remember that my sister got married last month?"

That was a bit random, Asim thought. "Yes, what about it?"

"At the wedding I met a guy who works in Al-Mouwda's office." Adel Al-Mouwda had been a member of the Chamber of Deputies for a good quarter of a century, despite having been dismissed from the leadership of his own party years ago. Somehow he managed to stay in office without any organized political support while calling for the expansion of the government's powers, a stance that hadn't yet alienated his constituents for reasons that remained obscure.

"I thought you said he wasn't useful."

"He wasn't. But he's been thinking about it."

"Wondering if it's going to be him next?"

"That, and he came across a memo that Al-Mouwda's written for the prime minister." Khalifa bin Salman continued to cling to the top government job regardless of his advancing age. Some Bahrainis claimed he lived on merely to spite his great-nephew, Crown Prince Salman, who was first deputy prime minister and his probable successor--and who was seen by the public as being more sympathetic to political reform than his great-uncle.

"Something that Al-Mouwda wrote personally?"

"It sounds like it."

"You haven't seen this yet?"

"He snapped a picture of it. He's sending it to me in a few minutes."

"And you want me to spread it around."

"I can't get to a computer right now." Trying to use proxy addresses and secure protocols from a smartphone was a cumbersome exercise at best, and for distributing filched government documents, those were necessary. That made it faster for Khalil to pass the letter on to Asim, who could post it online without leaving a trail.

"Well do you know what it's about?"

"He says Al-Mouwda wants to loosen gun ownership restrictions."

"That can't be it. Not with riots in the streets he doesn't."

"Hang on a second." There was a pause, then the picture itself appeared in the window. Asim started reading.

Unbelievably, Khalil's first impression was correct. One of the most conservative, pro-government deputies in the chamber was asking the prime minister to loosen arms control requirements at a time when dozens of protestors and dissidents were being jailed every day and thousands more went free only on sufferance. All firearms licenses in Bahrain had to be approved by the Minister of Interior. The process could not be carried out at a lower level. As a result, few Bahrainis who were not members of the police or the royal family owned weapons. Al-Mouwda wanted to change that. He proposed that the Minister be directed to delegate his authority to selected police officials so that more licenses could be processed "in this time of crisis."

At the same time, the criteria for receiving a permit were to be tightened. Police officers, as a condition of their exercising the authority to issue licenses, would be required to verify that an applicant was loyal to the king and the government. Applicants would be required to take an oath to that effect. The offices responsible would also have instructions that licenses were to be issued only to applicants whose backgrounds revealed them to be hostile to the pro-democracy protestors. In short, Al-Mouwda wanted to get weapons into the hands of those most likely to be opposed to reform, to give them the ability to stop it. As if that wasn't enough, he also suggested that the holder of a firearms license be treated with special leniency if he did kill a protestor, since "the possession of a permit indicates that the licensee had already demonstrated both loyalty to society and social obligations, namely his obligation to support his rulers, and reasonable cause that he feared aggression on the part of the dissident minority." Al-Mouwda finished up by remarking that the measure would strengthen the government's position among Bahrainis who were hostile to the reform movement but also personally distrustful of the ministers for their perceived corruption.

"Wow," Khalil typed.

"The prime minister won't take this seriously. No chance."

"He will if he gets scared enough."

"It'll backfire. The police can be tricked. We're doing it now."

"Even if it does it won't help us. So what if a few of us could slip through the cracks? Most of the ones who get licenses will be our enemies. Extreme case, the plan does backfire and the good citizens the government armed end up overthrowing it one day, but they're not any more sympathetic to us than Al-Mouwda is. No change."

"The king won't see that eventuality as a good thing."

"He won't have to if the prime minister can convince him there's no chance of the program getting out of control."

"And if he doesn't do something with it Al-Mouwda will take the proposal to the chamber and make it public."

"So we get there first and make sure that everyone hates it before he can win any allies."

"You take care of it. I have to go meet this guy now. He wants to see that the info gets used." The light next to Khalil's name in the chat window blinked off.

Asim opened an email anonymizer and attached the picture to a new message. He typed the addresses of ten different recipients into the form. Each address was a random jumble of letters and numbers located at a free hosting service. Those accounts were never checked, but had been set up to automatically forward any messages they received on to another set of unpredictable addresses. And the second set of recipients would do the same, and the process would be repeated several more times, expanding at every repetition, until the information landed in the hands of thousands of real people. It wasn't as secure as encryption, but it would be a nightmare to trace, and should the Bahraini police ever get the necessary subpoenas, the most they would find out was that the message had been dispatched from a computer somewhere in the Czech Republic. Which was where the internet thought Asim was at the moment, thanks to the way he had rerouted his IP address.

He sent the email off and went back to patrolling the newsfeeds until his phone vibrated in his pocket with the arrival of a new message.

There was no name on the screen, just a number he recognized. The two lines of text read, "The police are on their way."

Out of the corner of his eye he saw a reflected flash of color in the darkened windows of the shop across the street. It moved closer. It was the blue light of a police cruiser.

Asim reached behind the tower and flicked a toggle switch on a heavy little metal box he had installed weeks ago, when he first started coming to the cafe on a regular basis. It gave off a reassuring dull purr, and the monitor in front of him turned black, flashing "No signal" in large letters. The box was a demagnetizer, and the magnetic field it poured out disarranged, overwrote, or cleared every sector on the computer's hard drive. No forensic lab in the world could put the bits back together after the digital structure of the drive had been destroyed.

He slipped his feet back into his sandals and stood up. The police car was still not in sight, and there were no loiterers in the street to see him leave by the back way. Behind a tall shelf stuffed with decades-old magazines, an unpainted wooden door opened into a janitor's closet, where there was another door giving on the main hallway of the apartment building that housed the cafe. Asim eased through both and bolted the first door behind him from the inside of the closet, to give the impression that it had never been opened at all. Ten more seconds and he was outside, walking away from a bare rear wall pierced with small windows, its lack of features somehow recalling the mud-brick forts of an earlier era. He moved quickly, but he didn't run.

Either the police had managed to trace at least some of his activities back to him--which he doubted, he was always very careful about operational security--or one of his classmates had talked. The latter seemed more likely. Most students opposed the government crackdown, but there were always a few who sided with the status quo, perhaps in the hope of securing well-paid jobs from which they couldn't be fired after graduation. And during the last uprising, the "moderate" crown prince had gone so far as to terminate scholarships and funding for students who expressed revolutionary views. That could well happen again on a larger scale, given the economic strain Bahrain was feeling. If there was a spy reporting on him, which Asim assumed there was now, it wouldn't be hard to find a motive. Loyalty, careerism, simple need…

Pinning the motive to a known person was more difficult. He'd taken a number of his friends to that cafe on previous occasions. It was a good place for a chat, and a good place to hack from since the sleepy old man at the counter never asked questions, only opening his mouth to express his own thoughts. One of them could have had a change of heart and reported him. Or one of them could have mentioned the place to a third party, and that third party might be the tipster.

It didn't matter. He was a known quantity to the police now, and if he didn't have a masochistic streak, his wisest move would be to go underground.

Except, Asim realized, with the sudden shock that comes when a theory turns into a threat, that there was someone following him.

He stopped and looked at the menu in a restaurant window, scanning his surroundings as best he could while pretending to read. There were few people on the street and he spotted his tail at once. Another young man, T-shirt, jeans, nondescript. He was walking straight towards Asim but not looking at him.

I am not trained for this, Asim thought as he began moving again. He wanted to know where that plainclothesman came from. Didn't he get out of the building in time? One of the officers must have suspected the closet door and sent a man around through the alley. If that was what had happened, why didn't the spy arrest him on the spot? The answer was immediately obvious, of course. They wanted to see where he was going. They wanted him to run to some of his fellow activists for protection. Then there would be a raid and a new batch of dissidents for the courts in the morning, and a decade of torture to follow.

The hacker tried to keep his thoughts ahead of the panic. He didn't have a refuge without compromising others, and unless he shook the policeman soon, he wouldn't have the opportunity to come up with an escape plan, either.

The streets of Muharraq were so numerous and contorted that most of them went unnamed. Numbers were the best the city planners had managed to do. Road No. 633, Lane No. 337--the list of monotonous designations went on for pages. Most of them appeared only in the official lists. Street signs were a rarity in the best-maintained districts and nonexistent in others. Added to the numbered routes were thousands of unmarked, unlisted, unofficial alleys and corridors that ran pell-mell through the piles of three-story cinderblock buildings. No two structures in Muharraq faced exactly the same way, although they were all an identical shade of pale tan. When dust storms drifted in from the mainland, it was impossible to tell at which point the sky became blue, because the ground blended into it without a clear break. The city was old when Alexander conquered Persia and ancient when the Prophet was born, and oil wealth and a population boom had multiplied its tangles without unraveling them.

Asim tried to put the confusion to work for him. He ventured up and down random alleys, favoring the ones where he knew beggars and the unemployed came to sleep. The reposing figures would confuse his pursuer, he hoped. He was tempted to lie down and play indigent himself, but decided it was too much of a risk. If the spy caught him, he doubted he would be able to get away. Bodies with holes through them had been turning up in the streets at an increasing rate lately. He would shake his tail in the usual way.

But he couldn't. The undercover man was too good, and he was too inexperienced. His meanderings became less elaborate as his fear grew stronger. He wanted to get away, and that idea possessed him, pushing away his attempts at reasoning out a new course of action. He wanted to feel safe-- he knew he needed to feel safe to be able to cope with the threat.

That touched off a chain of recollection. Khalil had another friend, Ameera, who was more than a little paranoid and went in constant fear of an Iranian invasion. Asim remembered the day when she had pulled out a worn old Soviet revolver--luckily they had been the only ones in the cafe at the time--and announced that she had bought it from a smuggler, just in case there were foreign troops in the streets tomorrow morning. Khalil had stuffed it back into her bag and spent the next two hours persuading her not to carry it around with her unless she wanted to be attacked by someone worse than an Iranian soldier. Eventually he persuaded her to let him cache it with a supply of spare flash drives and burner phones their group kept for emergencies. Asim could still see her handing the bag over to him with an obstinate expression on her face. He remembered her hounding Khalil about whether it would safe enough from a random search, and his assurances that yes, the cache was well-concealed and outside the usual scope of a police investigation.

And Asim knew where that cache was.

He turned away from the lights of Sheikh Isa Avenue and headed west and south. The policeman was still following him, waiting. If I can scare him off or at least make him take cover, Asim thought, I have a better chance of getting away.

He swung right into one of the city's broader alleyways. At the far end, two or three figures could be seen moving about in the dim light.

Perfect, Asim whispered to himself. He darted off to the right again, into a side street hardly wider than a doorway, and began running. This one curved away from the other, hiding him from the eyes of the plainclothesman. He hoped the spy would go all the way down the wider street before realizing that it ended there and that his quarry was not among the pedestrians moving in and out of the little shops and tenement buildings. At that point he would either concede defeat or come back up the street to check the narrow side corridor. And if he did that, the pursuit would resume, because Asim would have lost the lead he had gained while looking for the cache.

He skidded to a stop opposite another blank concrete wall and looked around, panting. The cache was somewhere above eye level, marked in a way that was unmistakable--there! An empty oil drum with the lid still on it leaned against the side of an adjoining building. Asim clambered up on it. In front of him was a decaying sign advertising the services of a seamstress who lived upstairs. He punched the sign, and his fist went right through the papier-mache and plaster that had looked like painted wood an instant before. Behind it was a hole let into the side of the old wall. His fingers fumbled around in the space, slipping over hard plastic everywhere, all too modern for his needs. Then he touched metal, warm and still retaining a small portion of the day's heat. He jerked it out through the plaster shards. It was Ameera's Russian revolver, all right. Khalil had kept his promise even if he didn't believe her. He checked the cylinder, awkwardly due to a lack of practice. It was still loaded.

He stepped down from the barrel and looked around. The spy was nowhere in sight. Asim turned and walked down the alley that led out into the next part of the maze. Ten yards along, it took a sharp turn, and he found it blocked by the wreckage of a collapsed balcony.

He raced back to the street where the cache was, hoping he still had time to get up it to the next turn--and nearly fell on top of the spy as he hurtled back around the corner.

The policeman jumped back, startled, then reached behind him.

"Hands!" Asim yelled, the panic in his voice carrying conviction. He'd been given no chance to hide the revolver and it pointed so easily at the plainclothesman now that he needed it.

They stood there, both of them waiting.

The policeman moved first, slowly reaching for his own weapon again. Asim took a step closer. He froze.

"Stop."

Asim flinched, but fought back his curiosity and fear. He kept the revolver trained on the spy. Out of the corner of his eye, he saw a man crawl out of a broken packing case nearby. The intruder took in the scene, then very deliberately walked across the alley and planted himself between the two armed men.

"Get out of my way!" Asim yelled, shifting his ground to keep the policeman in his sights.

"Stop," the newcomer repeated. "You are more useful to us and to your friends alive and without a price on your head for a capital crime than you are dead or in prison." He moved with Asim, still obstructing his view. The latter's ears pricked up at the word "us." He was sure the spy's had as well.

"Go away," Asim growled, still fighting for a good firing position. "Help me or go away."

"If a man kills a believer intentionally his recompense is Hell, to abide therein forever," the man in the middle quoted with complete composure, "and the wrath and curse of God are upon him and a dreadful penalty is upon him."

"I don't need a sermon right now! Get out of--"

Blood burst out of the man's chest as the policeman's gun roared in the echoing canyon between the walls. He fell. Asim pulled the trigger of his own pistol automatically. The first shot took the spy in the shoulder and his second bullet, intended for Asim, flew wild. Asim's next three shots caught him in the torso. The policeman dropped his weapon and joined his victim on the cracked pavement.

Asim gasped for breath, feeling as shocked as if the bullets had hit him instead of passing him by untouched. He knelt by the side of the man who had tried to stop him. His breathing was ragged, but at least he was still breathing. The spy he had to check for a pulse, which was there as well, however faint.

In the distance, a siren called to its fellows.

3

Another teacher plodded up to the podium and droned out an introduction for the next video. The Major shifted in his seat, masking his annoyance with a neutral expression.

The vice-principal he had found waiting outside his office two weeks ago had been very eager to secure him for Eastern High School's first anti-bullying event. "I can't tell you, Major Martin, how much our students would appreciate your contributing to the discussion," she had gushed. "Not only as an openly gay Marine officer, but also as a distinguished educator with expertise in the study of violence and conflict resolution. The public affairs office was very enthusiastic about your record in the field." Privately, the Major wondered how the public affairs office had become acquainted with his existence, let alone his sexuality, but he'd accepted the invitation anyway. The students, he felt, would enjoy what he had to say. The teachers would not, but that was their problem. They'd invited him; they had thereby welcomed his comments as well. He thought, as always, of the late Colonel Boyd, whose legacy was treasured by certain members of the Corps, and Boyd's habit of shouting "Let the record show that you asked the question!" right before telling his interrogator something unpleasant. Well, if they didn't like his speech, he hadn't liked the videos he was forced to watch from the platform, either. Fair is fair.

The first one had been awful. Four teenagers talking over one another from about the least optimistic, most defensive script he'd ever come across. "I've been bullied my whole life," the speakers said in unison. "For my decisions, for my opinions, for my size, and for my looks. All I ever wanted was for someone to stand up for me. I've been in situations where I was being bullied and people just kept walking by me. Not doing a thing, completely ignoring what was happening." Did they really expect a disinterested third party to come rushing to the rescue? the Major wondered. Apparently so. "You can be the change!" the video exhorted. "If you see someone in the hallway being bullied, find a trusted adult, tell them everything you saw to help the victim. You can also try creating a distraction to divert the focus of the bully." The Major closed his eyes in pain at that. If the Department of Education's only advice to witnesses of abuse was to pass the buck, it was never going to solve the problem and its anti-bullying efforts could be discounted as infantile gestures, nothing more. Direct action was apparently off limits. "If you know of someone who's being bullied, you can spend time with them. Even just talking to them. Let them vent about anything they're experiencing or have recently experienced. It'll make them feel so much better about themselves!"

It will make people feel better about themselves to relive their humiliation and be reminded of their defenselessness? the Major asked an imaginary education official. The lack of a response didn't bother him. He would have gotten the same blankness if he had spoken the question aloud to any of the educators sitting next to him.

The next video had showed an old man talking about the psychiatrist who he credited with helping him to understand his sexuality in his youth. "I owe him my life, I really do." After him there was a pretty twink up on the screen, saying "I joined my school's gay-straight alliance and things got so much better!" Peer review in academia, the Major reflected, was only a specialized development of the human urge to socialize, to gain approval from organized groups.

He was still wondering about what element of the human character made individuals so willing to defer to groups in matters of judgment when the next video started. The voice was faintly recognizable and he glanced back at the screen, away from the crowd. It belonged to that blonde, floppy-haired screenwriter who had tallied up an impressive resume as the creative force behind a series of failed art-house films. And yet he continued to be hailed as a gay icon for the one timely, successful project he'd been involved with, in spite of the fact that his own personal views couldn't have differed more from those of his subject. The Major smiled as he remembered the critic who had evoked a picture of the writer hoisting the pride flag aloft with his perfectly manicured hands while trying his best to ape the behavior of mainstream, middle-class society. Nowadays most of the man's notoriety came from his ongoing relationship with a beautiful young British gymnast half his age. He was asking the assembled students, from the safety of a thumb drive, whether things had gotten better for them, whether society had done enough to become more tolerant and open.

I can tell you that, the Major said to himself. It hasn't. Not even close.

The last video clip featured a girl who described in detail all the things her classmates had done to her while remaining startlingly upbeat and cheerful about it. She kept assuring her audience that "it absolutely does get better. And I know you're like, oh, I've heard that so many times already, but I promise you that that is true and I'm not just saying it." The Major saw it as making promises without planning. And why, he wondered, is this anti-bullying project being conceived of, for the most part, as something which should focus on sexuality? Why is the connection assumed?

He realized that the same vice-principal who had waylaid him in the hall had finished speaking and was staring in his direction. She'd just introduced him to the students. Half-hearted applause was still dying away in the more sycophantic sections of the audience. "Time for a change of pace," the Major said under his breath, and he stood up and walked across to the podium.

He looked out across the assembly, over a thousand students in all, and let them look back at him for a minute. Silence built suspense. He was glad again that he had not worn his uniform today.

"'Down these mean streets a man must go who is not himself mean, who is neither tarnished nor afraid. He will take no man's money dishonestly and no man's insolence without a due and dispassionate revenge. He is a lonely man and his pride is that you will treat him as a proud man or be very sorry you ever saw him.'

"Well, are you that proud?"

He let Chandler's words, phrased as a direct challenge, bounce around the auditorium.

"When you're being punched, kicked, abused, your teachers and parents aren't going to come running to save you. All they can do is scold and punish after it happens--and that's not going to help you. It's too late. You'll still have the pain. You'll still carry the scars. And neither your suffering or the delayed reactions of a few adults are going to protect you in the future.

"Sure, maybe a few of your friends might rush to your defense, but what if you don't have any? Or what if they're too scared to act?

"In that moment, when you are being attacked, the only person who can save you is you. But you have to be not only willing to save yourself, but determined to do so as well.

"The only way to stop bullying is for you to fight back.

"Let's think for a minute about why people are bullied. Your school seems to think that most of the time it's because of their sexuality. Or at least that's what your teachers' choice of videos says about what they're thinking." He heard the teachers stirring uncomfortably behind him, but none of them were willing to confront him just yet. "In the real world, people get bullied for much less than that. They're bullied because something sets them apart from the rest. Any difference, however small, will serve as an excuse.

"If you don't protect your differences, if you're not proud of them, and if you don't keep anyone else from trying to suppress them, that's as good as saying you're ashamed of yourself as a person.

"Are you ashamed of yourself?"

"If you're not ashamed, then fight back against anyone who tries to hurt you.

"If someone slaps you and knocks you down, get back up and punch him in the gut. Do not yield to force. Do not wait for someone to come save you. It's not their responsibility. It's yours, to demonstrate that you are a strong and courageous human being. If you're strong enough to fight for others as well as yourself, that's excellent. But if you're not, then at least fight for yourself. People become victims only through their own inactivity.

"You cannot trust others to help you. You couldn't trust your classmates not to bully you, after all. Your teachers' assurances didn't do you any good when you were face down in the dirt crying. If you ask for outside help, you won't get it. If you go on thinking that outside help can save you, you become dependent on that hope and unable to act on your own. And hoping that one day you'll grow up and things will be better isn't going to stop a blow or a curse.

"You must recognize that you stand alone. You must take pride in that fact, in everything that sets you apart, and you must assert it. Not aggressively, not proactively, but if someone tries to take your pride from you, then you must make them afraid to ever try it again.

"If you want a peaceful solution without violence, where everyone wins, there's not going to be one. The only way to protect your rights is to fight for them. Freedom isn't a group thing or a national thing, or an abstract idea. It's the actions we take every day, as individuals, to make sure no one takes advantage of us. It's something that must be lived.

"If someone attacks you, defend yourself."

* * * * *

"What exactly did you think you were doing in that auditorium?"

"Passing on the lessons the Corps taught me, sir."

"By telling teenagers to beat each other up?"

"By telling them that it was a good thing to defend themselves and a better thing to defend others."

"You said 'If someone knocks you down, get back up and punch him in the gut.'"

"Yes, sir."

"And how do you think a bunch of sixteen year-olds felt about that?"

"If they'd ever been attacked by a bully, I imagine they felt like it was a much more useful piece of advice than being told to run for a teacher or wait for adulthood."

"Major, you were encouraging them to be violent and aggressive towards their fellow students, for God's sake!"

"Sir, if you were walking down the street and saw someone being mugged, wouldn't you run to their assistance, even if it meant beating up the attacker?"

"I would. But then I'm trained to use force. High school students are not. Besides, I'm a Marine. It's my job to protect others. It is not the job of a teenager to be a vigilante for perceived injustices suffered by his friends."

"There's a difference between revenge and self-defense."

"Neither of which a student is entitled to act in, or capable of acting in."

"Why? Because they're too young? Colonel, these kids are suffering and no one is capable of helping them but themselves. No one can be there to protect them every minute of their lives. If they don't learn that, they will continue to be abused."

"There are alternatives to violence as you know very well. The Department of Education has a program in place to decrease the amount of bullying that goes on in schools--"

"I saw that program in action yesterday. It's created a culture of cowardice and evasion."

"Language, Major!"

"Yes, sir."

"You can't call people cowards just because they don't defend themselves. Is that hard for you to grasp?"

"No, sir. I agree that in specific cases a lack of action is not necessarily a sign of cowardice. But in general, when you see an entire persecuted group sitting down and letting itself be hurt, and the people who are supposed to be helping them are advising them to go on doing that, it's fair to say they're missing something important. Something like courage, or maybe honor."

"Major Martin, you have to stop thinking that all of life is one big ongoing war of liberation. It's not. Clamber on up from among your papers on South American guerrillas and Pashtun warlords and African rebel movements and realize that you live in a stable society where people don't fight on a whim just because they think they're at a disadvantage. You cannot keep bringing discussions about war into discussions of social problems. That's not going to make us look less threatening to the rest of society or help our cause."

"Us, sir?"

"The gay community as a whole." The Major let his eyes drift down to the framed photo on Colonel Lamoreaux's desk. It showed the colonel, his new husband, and their two adopted children grinning stiffly at the camera. On the whole, he thought that that little display of homonormativity was a trifle over-emphasized.

"What we look like to the rest of society doesn't affect the human rights we have and shouldn't affect their recognition of our rights. In any case, I wasn't speaking to those kids as a member of the gay community."

"Oh, that's right, you were speaking to them as a United States Marine and an expert on conflict resolution!"

"I made it very clear to the staff at the school that I was not speaking for the Marine Corps. I did not mention the Corps at all during my address."

"No, you were happy to stop at passing along tips and tricks from our martial arts program so these kids would find it easier to hurt each other if they felt they were being attacked. Fill me in on this: what's going to happen if one of them thinks he's going to be assaulted in the near future and decides to strike first?"

"What happens when the United States decides that a foreign power poses a potential future threat to its safety?"

"Major, that is not the same thing!"

"In the abstract, sir, it's exactly the same thing."

"Humor me. Forget about your abstract cases for a fucking minute and think about a kid in school who's afraid he's about to get beaten up. So when the prospective bully's back is turned, he grabs a rock and bashes his possible future attacker over the head. That guy ends up in the hospital with brain damage and suddenly it's the victim who's the bully. Whose fault is it?"

"No one's."

"Excuse me?"

"If the kid was genuinely afraid for his safety, it's regrettable that he overreacted, but it's understandable. The difference between bullying and self-defense is intent."

The colonel's eyes bulged. He started to say something, then cut himself off and drew a deep breath.

"If you were living in the same world with the rest of us," he said in a quiet tone, "you'd realize that it was your fault. You're the one who put the idea into his head, and by association, the entire Corps shares your guilt. At least that's what the press would say--will say, if it happens.

He rose, made a circuit of the room, and came back to his desk.

"You may be a brilliant instructor, but you don't seem to grasp that certain kinds of instruction are best suited for specialized audiences."

"No, sir, I don't."

"You admit it."

"Of course. There's no such thing as a student who's unfit to learn."

"Well, you're going to have to do something about that." Colonel Lamoreaux leafed through the papers in front of him. "This isn't the first time this has come up, either. Your previous fitness reports have mentioned this tendency of yours to go off the rails and stray from the curriculum that the Corps has approved for your classes. In fact, you were counseled on the subject by my predecessor."

"Yes, sir."

"Hopefully you learn your lesson better this time. I'm going to speak to the school administration to arrange for you to apologize to the staff and students for your remarks, and for you to explain to them that your lessons for officers about to deploy to a war zone aren't appropriate for teenagers, whose problems are best solved through mediation and reliance on adult authority. If they're satisfied with that, you will receive a letter of admonishment and the matter will end there."

"I'm sorry, sir, but an apology is something I can't give the students."

The colonel suddenly looked very ugly. "Major, you have an obligation to the Corps to protect its reputation and image."

"Sir, I have an obligation to the Corps not to lie."

"It's not lying to tell a high school kid that he can't beat up his friends!"

"It is lying to tell him that someone else is going to keep him safe and that he doesn't have a right to defend himself!"

There was an uncomfortable pause. Colonel Lamoreaux sat back down.

"Major Martin, you are relieved of your duties immediately pending a full official investigation of your actions at Eastern High School. Dismissed."

* * * * *

"Busy?"

"Not in any way that counts," Emily Goldstein said, looking up from her papers with a benevolent smile. "Aren't you supposed to be in class this afternoon?"

"Yes--and no." The Major drifted into the office and settled down in one of the worn chairs opposite her government-issue desk.

"I know that look of yours," the surgeon said. She frowned slightly at him. "Why aren't you teaching today?"

"I've been fired," the Major said.

"Colonel Lamoreaux is trying to get rid of you?"

"At the moment his thoughts are probably drifting more in the direction of court-martial."

"For your speech at that high school the other day."

"He offered to stop at reprimanding me if I went back and told the kids they don't have a right to defend themselves."

"That man has an inferiority complex that would be dangerous if he was in charge of anything important. I should have Barbara put together a psychological profile on him for the fun of it."

"Inferiority complexes are how most officers get promoted, because they make subservience to generals who are barking mad much easier."

"So your theory is that we're the odd ones for not feeling burdened by other people's decisions."

"Pretty much. Doubly queer. How is Barbara, by the way?"

"Tired. Minds don't heal like arms and legs. We're still going to be treating these same PTSD cases ten years from now. And her department just lost another therapist to private practice."

"The Navy could recall their shrinks in a reserve capacity if they really wanted to."

"They're talking about it, but it could take years for them to make it official. In the meantime, she has to take on extra patients and all the extra paperwork that comes along with them. She's not happy lately. She did like that Venetian wine you sent us, though."

"Well, she was getting bored with those Australian imports." The Major stared out the window while stroking the silver figurine of a peacock that stood incongruously on one corner of Dr. Goldstein's desk.

"Did you come here just to vent, or was there another reason?"

"It's not all venting. I need to talk something through and you're the only person I can talk about it with. And I thought you might take a look at my hand, too."

"He loves me only for my surgical skills. Very well, pass it over."

"I'll forgive you that jab because you refrained from saying 'hand' it over."

She gave him a wise and weary smile. "In my profession, you learn not to pun around sharp instruments." The scissors she extracted from a drawer glittered in the afternoon light, matching the shine of the silver oak leaves peeking out from under the collar of her lab coat. "You've been trying not to use this hand too much?"

"Except for gesturing to make a point, yes."

"That won't overstrain it, even in your case." The doctor peered at the tender flesh the bandage parted to reveal. "Seems to be healing well, although I think we should wait a few more days before taking the stitches out. The X-ray didn't show any bone splinters to worry about." She fetched a roll of gauze and began to wrap his knuckles up again. "You never told me how this happened."

"I broke a man's jaw."

"How do you know it was broken?"

"I heard it snap."

"So I take it you two didn't kiss and make up afterwards."

"Given that he and two of his friends were about to rape a kid, no."

"What happened to the friends?"

"They went down first. One in the throat, one in the balls."

Dr. Goldstein sighed. "One day someone is going to come along and interfere with one of your crusades."

"You think so?"

"That, or you'll be outnumbered and end up getting killed."

"I'm already outnumbered." The Major's face twisted in a grimace.

"Did that hurt?"

"No. I was thinking of something Lamoreaux said."

"Hmmm. What happened to the kid?"

"He wasn't hurt very much, only a few scrapes. They dropped him and he lost consciousness for a bit before I came along. He woke up in time to see me using his chief assailant as a punching bag and then all three of them slinking off bloody into the night. I think that helped him more than any amount of counseling ever could."

The doctor put her medical supplies away and leaned back in her chair. "And by extension you think the same response would help teenagers who are being bullied. That they would be better off, psychologically speaking, if they could see the bullies getting the tables turned on them."

"It would be more useful if they themselves were the ones to turn the tables. Seeing someone else triumph over your enemy isn't always satisfying. Sometimes it's deeply unsatisfying. You feel cheated."

"What did Colonel Lamoreaux say that put you off so much? You're not usually affected by his ravings."

"He played the us card."

"The us card?"

"He tried to appeal to me as a fellow gay man. Said that it would hurt the gay community if we were perceived as being belligerent and aggressive."

"And your position has always been that it wouldn't hurt for us to be more aggressive for the first time in decades."

"We're surrounded by weaklings. If I wanted to be melodramatic, I'd say we live in an age of weaklings." The Major shrugged his shoulders in irritation. "Don't fight for human rights, ask your abusers politely for them and give excessive thanks if they condescend to make concessions. Don't stand up for yourself, run to someone in authority if you feel threatened. Don't stand up for someone else, make your voice heard but don't do anything, because as long as you speak out, that absolves you of blame. Don't use your personal grievances as a launching pad for a true liberation movement, be content with gaining the same limited privileges that the mainstream has. Don't rock the boat, emphasize that you're the same as everyone else, not different."

"You can't compensate for the failings of an entire community through your individual actions."

"I can lead by example. That's what I'm supposed to do."

"Beating up three rapists is laudable, but it's not a sustainable form of leadership."

"Is there a shortage of rapists in the world?"

"You'll run out of yourself before you run out of victims. Petty vigilantism won't accomplish anything. You're the strategist. Think about it."

"Emily, I know I shouldn't be indulging in violent emotional outbursts, but I'm not a drill instructor with the luxury of a steady supply of people to shout at! Redressing abuses when I happen to stumble across them is the most I can do! And it's gotten worse and worse for me lately. Every time the Human Rights Campaign cries victory, my stomach turns. So much vanity and such paltry results! These activists have power, potential power, and they don't use it! They don't have the intelligence to use it, and if they had the intelligence, they wouldn't have the motivation! There are human beings suffering while they make banners and call themselves heroes, and they don't give a damn. Their minds grow in tiny boxes like fancy Japanese vegetables and--"

The Major abruptly pitched forward onto the edge of his chair, half standing, half balancing on his hands. His fingers were clenched tight around the plasticized metal bars.

"Boxes," he almost whispered. "Power. Intelligence. Motivation."

Very gradually, he let himself sink back into the cushion.

"What are you thinking?" Dr. Goldstein demanded. She looked alarmed. "That's another expression of yours I don't trust. Spill it!"

"I have intelligence," the Major said, half to her, half to himself. "I have motivation. Those together are power. Better than power."

"In other words, you think there's a way for you to do something that your mortal foes in the HRC can't and won't. Something worth doing."

"There was once an imam who threatened Genghis Khan with a terrible curse if the Khan spilled a single drop of his blood. Genghis, exhibiting a sense of dark humor, had his men stitch the imam tightly into a leather sack and then trample him to death with their horses. He was just as dead, but technically his blood was never spilled, so the curse didn't work."

"And the moral of that charming medieval tale?"

"There are always loopholes."

"Which loophole are you planning on jumping down this time, Alice?"

"One that I can now that that idiot Lamoreaux has deprived me of my usual occupation." The Major smiled a smile filled with hunger and excitement. "I may need to find a few extra resources to make it happen, but that's a minor detail."

"Are you going to get hurt?"

"I hope not."

"Is someone else going to get hurt?"

"Possibly, but that's not my intent."

"Are you going to help someone with this?"

"Two people directly, more indirectly."

Dr. Golstein stared at him for a few moments. She shook her head. "You'll have to tell me a lot more to convince me, but I might--might--be able to put you in the way of finding the resources you need."

4

The gun was hot in his hand. He hadn't expected that. He could feel the energy still radiating away from the emptied chambers.

If he was found with a weapon that had been used to kill an undercover agent of the government, he would be dead before they got him to a police station. His corpse would be found on the street in the morning, and his death would be put down to the rioters, the dissidents, and the pro-democracy activists. In death the police would use him against his own friends, maybe going so far as to charge one or two of them with his murder. He drew back his arm to throw the revolver up onto the roof of one of the neighboring buildings, where it might not be found for weeks.

"Stop."

Asim spun on his heel again. The wounded man had dragged himself up on one elbow and was staring at him.

"You like to tell people that a lot, don't you!" The words came out bitter and almost hysterical.

"Only when they should stop and think." The man was wheezing heavily, and his voice was weaker and less commanding, but he looked no less determined for all that he was lying on the ground in a puddle of his own blood.

"And what should I think about?" Asim wanted to know.

"Wipe it first. Your prints--they might be found."

The stranger had a point. Asim pulled his shirt off and rubbed out every smear he could see on the metal surfaces of the pistol. The checkered bakelite grips grated against the cloth; they wouldn't hold a print in any case. He took the gun by the barrel, still covering his fingers with the shirt, and threw. It soared up over the parapet of the building and disappeared, clattering against the concrete. But no one looked over to see where it had come from.

Asim saw that the stranger was trying to stand up. The sirens were getting louder.

"Will you tell the police as little as you can about me?" he asked, desperation showing in his voice again.

"I will tell them nothing." The man had scrambled to his knees. He was sweating from the pain. "But you must help me. Help me stand up."

"But if you wait for the police, they will call an ambulance--"

"If they find me here, they will kill me on the spot. Just as they would kill you. We must go."

"The alley is blocked," Asim said in frustration.

"We have time."

"For what?"

"To go around."

Asim doubted that very much, but he didn't have many alternatives. And it would be a relief to have someone else making the decisions now. "All right."

He put his shoulder underneath the man's arm and lifted him gently. He wasn't heavy. In fact, he was slimmer and smaller than Asim, and from a foot away, he appeared to be about the same age.

They hobbled back up the alley, the stranger biting his lip to prevent himself from screaming.

"There are lights ahead," Asim pointed out, whispering for no clear reason.

"Just a little farther," the man said. "A few steps…now to your right…here!"

He heaved against Asim as best he could, pushing him into the shadow of a small alcove in the wall of the old building. Asim felt rough wood under his hand. "A door?" The jingle of keys answered that question.

The sirens were almost at the entrance to the alley now. One car screeched to a stop, then a second, then a third. Shouts and the tramp of boots filled the empty passages.

"They're coming," Asim hissed. The bolt on the door turned. He forced it inward and pulled the stranger after him. His fingers slipped on the edge. To his surprise, the heavy panel jerked away from his grasp and reseated itself. The bolt clicked automatically into place.

"Go," the stranger said, tugging at Asim's sleeve.

The passage ahead was dark and narrow. Given the former condition, the latter was an advantage. It kept them from straying. Some yards further on, the hall opened into a foyer that was almost as dark.

"Right," the stranger said with a nudge.

The right passage turned sharply several times and ended in another door. This one was unlocked. Asim pushed it open and stepped out into another alley. Cold air hit him in the face. The desert night had finally come.

"Where is the nearest hospital?" The wounded man was bleeding all over his clothes, but he managed a weak smile at that question, one that was both ironic and gentle.

"The nearest police headquarters would be the same as a hospital to me. I cannot go there. You must take me to my friends."

"But--"

"If it helps, I was sent to find you. I regret that you did not arrive without a tail, but we did not think the police would manage to track you."

Asim sighed. "How were you sent to find me?"

"We know a few people who share the same goals." By that he could only mean the Bahraini hacktivist community.

"All right. What's your name?"

"Shadi."

"You tell me where to go, then."

The alleys of Muharraq twisted around them as they staggered onwards. Asim wanted to stop at least a dozen times, but Shadi refused to halt. Some part of Asim's mind agreed with the judgment on a rational level. He needed medical care, and he could only get it in the safety of his friends' company. A delay was worse than continued activity. But he was beginning to cough up blood. It spattered black and foreboding in a fine mist on the dusty tan of a wall that he leaned against for a moment.

"How did you know where to find me?" Asim finally asked him.

"Khalil told a friend of his who passed the message on to us. He thought you might need a new phone. He didn't mention that you might start sharing that crazy Ameera's ideas." Shadi tried to chuckle and went into a coughing fit.

"My phone! I didn't ditch it!"

"No…no…you don't need to," Shadi grunted, swallowing his pain. "That's your emergency line. That network has not been compromised." He was trying to walk faster and kept tripping over himself.

"You need to slow down!"

"We're almost there."

Almost meant two more turns and a detour through a crumbling ruin into another nondescript alleyway.

"Up those stairs," Shadi panted, motioning at a set of steps that led halfway up the face of a much older building. There was no railing, and he was rapidly getting weaker. Asim had to strain to get him up onto the landing. No door barred their passage at the top. A curtain of worn beads hung limp beneath the elegant arch that served as a lintel.

Inside, the room was empty and deserted. A faint clicking in the background, like that of insects patiently eating away at the fabric of the structure, was the only noise.

"Here," Shadi said with greater insistence. He stumbled in the direction of the opposite end of the room. Asim caught him and helped him.

The clicking was louder there. Shadi reached out, groping with both hands, and part of the wall bulged away from him. It was a curtain, Asim realized, a heavy woven curtain.

It slid away to reveal another large, unfurnished room. In the middle of the floor, a young man sat cross-legged, typing on a small netbook.

He looked up at the two newcomers. "You found him. Were you injured?"

"He had a tail, and the tail stung me," Shadi said. "But I'll live."

"I'll tell them." The watcher went back to typing.

"Is that all?" Asim asked, but Shadi was pulling at him again, urging him towards a third curtain on the far wall. This isn't safe, the hacker thought. Anyone could walk right through here. The curtain parted on either side of them and Shadi's legs gave out completely. Two men stepped forward and caught him.

Asim gasped with relief as the weight was taken from him. He stretched his shoulders, working the muscles loose to relieve the strain. He realized that Shadi had disappeared and someone else was standing next to him.

"He said he would live. Will he?"

His escort shrugged. "I'm not trained in medicine, but I think he will. They said it was only a clean hole through the lung. That will heal, as long as the wound doesn't get infected."

"Are you his friends?"

"We are the underground. Would you like something to eat?"

* * * * *

"I thought I was already part of the underground," Asim said, wiping his bowl with a piece of flatbread.

"There are different levels to the underground. As there should be. A distributed network survives more easily than a centralized one. But we do something here that is out of the ordinary."

"You're very well organized."

"For our purposes we have to be. Still, it's easy since there aren't many of us."

"Could you use some extra help?"

"Meaning you?"

"Yes. I was almost arrested tonight. I don't want to repeat that experience, and you all seem to have stayed out of danger so far."

"Don't be fooled. What we are doing is dangerous. We are safe so far because we remain unknown, unlike the more visible protest groups. When the government does realize we exist, then we will be under threat every minute."

"I'll be under threat if I leave, too," Asim pointed out.

"That is true. And you are a hacker. You could be useful."

"That's what Shadi said when he tried to stop me from shooting that policeman."

"He was right. You shot his attacker?"

"Yes."

"Will he live?"

"I don't know, I've never shot someone before. But the police got there almost at once. Someone with pull must have called them."

"I hope that he will."

"Why? Why care? He's probably killed before. He'd kill us if he could find us."

"That's still not a good reason to kill him. Either morally or practically."

"In practical terms, it doesn't matter. The police see an assault on one of their own as reprehensible whether the attacked officer lives or dies. They would murder me regardless if they could find me."

"Perhaps in this case, although the general principle is up for debate. And morally--"

"Morally I have no strong views on the subject."

"Our imam would differ with you on that, but it's your decision, not his or mine."

A look of wariness entered Asim's eyes. "You have an imam here?"

"Yes, he's one of us."

"How can you be certain? Every religious scholar I ever met ended up siding with the government sooner or later. He could be a spy."

"He runs our network. In fact, he created it. It was assembled to carry out his plans."

"I don't like this," Asim said, standing up. "Either he's going to sell you out to the authorities when he thinks he's snared enough pigeons in his distortion of the net, or he's got some aggressive agenda that he's using you to push. I'm sorry, but I don't feel safe enough to stay here under those circumstances."

His guide chuckled slightly, under his breath. "Okay," he replied. "As I said, it's your decision. But please make it after learning all the facts. I want you to meet him first and hear what he has to say."

"Not a chance!"

"Why not? Afraid he'll convince you?"

"Not likely! But I don't want him seeing me just so he can give me up to the police later on!"

"He already knows as much about you as any of us do. As for recognizing you, he won't ever be able to do that. And if you decide to leave after all, even if he was tattling to the police, he couldn't tell them more than that you were here and left. They have more to charge you with than being in the company of fellow subversives."

Asim hesitated. "I suppose you're right. But what if he calls them while I'm still here?"

"Look at it objectively. Would your capture tonight be important enough for him to justify bringing down the entire network he's built up?"

"Well, no."

"Then come on. The sooner you meet him, the sooner you can decide once and for all and get out of here if you still think it's unsafe."

The house, or rather the complex of adjoining houses that sheltered the underground, was old, musty, and dark. No lights showed in any but two of the rooms, apart from the occasional white radiance of a computer screen in a corner or the green blinking of a router diode. Asim's guide felt his way through the building by touch and experience. Asim found it tricky to follow him. The houses had been thrown together awkwardly at an earlier date, with no coherent plan. There were steps and doors and passages in odd places, and the floors of one building were not level within a room, let alone with those of the adjacent structure.

They went down into the basement. No windows at all pierced its thick mud-brick walls, a relic of an earlier age. The stairs, of the same material, were steep and narrow, and had no railing.

It was as empty as the rest of the house, save for a burning oil lamp, a worn carpet, and a man seated on that carpet.

"This is our imam," the guide said softly. He motioned for Asim to take the last few steps.

"May the peace of God be with you," said the imam. "Please come closer."

Asim felt uncomfortable, not only because of the semi-religious nature of the encounter--although there was nothing explicitly religious about the scene before him--but also due to the imam's ambiguous appearance. He sat down on the hard floor and studied him. If Shadi and his guide were of his own age, the imam must have been younger still. His face, and the skin of his hands and forearms, was unlined. His voice had not rasped or strained to make itself heard. His gaze extended off into an unmeasurable distance and did not shift to accommodate Asim's presence. So self-possessed, and yet he must have been less than twenty years old. Behind him, Asim heard the guide leaving the room. He was left alone.

"You are studying me," the imam said. His mouth smiled. His eyes did not move.

"You look familiar," Asim said. He hadn't planned to say that, but it was true. He did recognize the young man in front of him, though he couldn't place him.

"You may have seen me before, a long time ago. My name is Ra'd bin Mazin."

Asim's mouth dropped open.

Ra'd bin Mazin had been a legend in Bahrain not so long ago. At four he had known the Quran by heart. At ten he had known the books of the hadith, both the six Sunni books and the four Shia books, from start to finish. And he had understood them. At twelve he was famous as a preacher. He had delivered a sermon at the Al-Fateh Mosque which twenty thousand worshipers had attended, packed into the parking lot as well as the building, eager to see the child who had mastered so much and could speak to them with such simplicity. To the annoyance of the senior scholars, his sermons had dwelt entirely on the individual's personal relationship with God and the need to discount the conclusions of any claimed authority on religious matters. When he disappeared from public view, rumors went round that the government, or his rivals, or both, had conspired to put him out of the way. Some said openly that it was for the best. He would never rise to the higher ranks of Islamic scholarship. He would never be able to study the writings of the masters and identify the hand and brushstrokes of each, a requirement for advancement in the field. Ra'd bin Mazin had been blind from birth.

And now he had reappeared and was sitting in the dusty basement of a tumble-down house in a crowded suburb, a node on an electronic web woven around the entire Arab world.

"I did see you. My father took me to Khamis when you spoke there."

"I am glad that you remembered. I am sorry that we were not able to bring you here with less trouble. You were afraid then, and you are afraid of the same thing now. Is that not so?"

"How do I know you won't hand me--and all of us--over to the police?" Asim demanded.

"You remember my sermons. Do you think from my words that I would be willing to do so?"

He looked away from those sightless eyes. "No," he said.

"I would not. But I will not swear that to you either, because I do not think you would believe me if I did so."

"Right again. I wouldn't."

"From what I have been told by your fellow hackers, you do not trust any of the ulama. Why?"

"Since you ask me straight out, I'll tell you. You're all on the side of the government. Limit our freedoms in the name of tradition and a higher law is your recurring theme."

"Your fear is a reasonable one. But the basis for it should not exist."

"I don't think that I'm--"

"No, I was not referring to what you believe or are afraid of. As I said, your fears are justified. It is the reason you are forced to fear that is at fault. You see a connection between Islam and the state which persecutes you. Because other Muslims have joined the state in its persecutions, you associate Islam itself with the abuses the people of Bahrain have suffered. That connection exists, but it should not."

Asim snorted. 'Tell that to the Islamic State of Iraq and the Levant, which is running wild in the desert. Tell that to King Hamad, who approved a constitution which says that we're an 'independent Islamic Arab State,' that 'the religion of the State is Islam,' and that 'the Islamic Sharia is a principal source for legislation.'"

"The only truly Islamic government is no government at all."

Asim had been in the process of standing up to leave. He sat, or rather, fell, back onto his heels with a thump. "Excuse me? Would you mind repeating that?"

The imam did so.

"How can an Islamic government not be a government at all? That's a contradiction in terms."

"Islam does not make provision for government. The two concepts cannot be joined."

"Ha! Tell that to the king and his ministers!"

"The king is an idolater."

"I've had too many surprises tonight," Asim moaned after a short pause. "How can you come to that conclusion? Not that I would argue with you about it for the purposes of our common cause," he added hastily.

"It's self-evident, is it not?"

"Not to me. Okay, you've dismissed the concept of an Islamic state, which millions of Muslims would be willing to argue with you over, and you've dismissed the king on personal grounds. What about sharia?"

"Sharia is the law of God revealed to us by the Prophet, nothing more. It is not man's law."

"But man is supposed to obey it."

"That is so."

"Then there's your government."

"Not at all."

"I still don't see how you can acknowledge the law but not the government."

"Where in the law does it say that man may enforce those laws?"

There was another break in the conversation while Asim thought about this.

"I don't know," he admitted at last.

"The answer is nowhere."

"Are you certain of that?"

"'The guidance of God, that is the only guidance.' 'He is the One to decide, the One who knows all.' 'He sent down the criterion of judgment between right and wrong;' 'is it not His to create and govern?' 'I ask you, are many lords differing among themselves better, or God the One Supreme and Irresistible? If not Him, ye worship nothing but names that ye have named, ye and your fathers, for which God hath sent you no authority; the Command is for none but God; He hath commanded that ye worship none but Him; that is the right religion, but most men understand not.' 'Who is it in whose hands is the governance of all things, who protects all but is not protected of any? It belongs to God.' 'What God out of His Mercy doth bestow on mankind there is none can withhold: what He doth withhold there is none can grant apart from Him.'

"It is a fundamental article of our faith that the authority to rule, to make and enforce laws, rests only with God, and cannot rest with man. The Prophet himself was rebuked for making laws that God had not revealed to him."

"But God has given authority to men before," Asim countered, becoming drawn into the discussion in spite of himself.

"Yes; to certain men. Who were they?"

"The Prophet, of course. And Moses and Abraham."

"And who beyond those?"

"Solomon? And David."

"Yes, they were among those to whom God delegated his power on occasion. And who else?"

"I don't recall."

"The Quran is quite specific. In addition to those you have mentioned, there were Adam, Isaac, Jacob, Aaron, the judges of the children of Israel, and Zul-qarnain."

"Well, then…"

"Is King Hamad one of those men?"

"I should think not."

"Is King Hamad the Prophet?"

"No!" Asim said, horrified, his cultural sensibilities shocked even through the layer of indifference he'd built up over the years.

"A final question, then. Is King Hamad God?"

Asim could only stare at such a question from an imam.

"I cannot see your expression, but I can imagine it. We will assume that your lack of response indicates a negative. The king is not among the men to whom God granted authority, and if he was, that in itself would not constitute a complete claim to rulership. It was said to the Prophet that 'before thee also the apostles We sent were but men to whom We granted inspiration.' And the king is not himself God. Therefore he has no claim to authority."

"But what about the Prophet's successors?"

"It is written in the Sahih Muslim, in the Book on Government, that the Prophet said all men would be subservient to the tribe of the Quraish, and that the Caliphate would remain with their tribe. However, it also records that the Caliphate would come to an end after twelve caliphs, and it further relates that the Prophet absolutely declined to appoint a successor, knowing that his authority was not his to transfer."

"If not the king, what's your solution? Is democracy acceptable? Representative government?"

"No. 'Who doeth more wrong than such as forge a lie against God, or deny His signs?' Any attempt by one man, or a group of men, to make laws and govern others is a usurpation of divine authority. 'Thou art not one to manage men's affairs, but if any turn away and reject God, God will punish him with a mighty punishment. For to Us will be their return; then it will be for Us to call them to account.' The King of Mankind does not require human assistance in enforcing the only laws that can exist. 'Thou art held responsible only for thyself.' 'Who goeth astray doth so to his own loss; no bearer of burdens can bear the burden of another.' 'Admonish thy nearest kinsmen; then if they disobey thee, say "I am free of responsibility for what ye do!"' We may advise our fellow believers, but we were created as individuals, to serve God, not to rule in his place."

"That doesn't leave anything."

"In the most literal sense of the term, yes."

"You mean no government at all?"

"Yes. That is what I first said."

"You mean anarchism."

"Islamic anarchism."

"And you believe this conclusion you've come to is warranted?"

"I can see no way in which a government can exist or be supported that does not defy the will of God," the imam replied.

"This is a bit much to comprehend. It's more than I was looking for. I wanted the current government purged of corruption and oppression, not the concept of government as a whole destroyed!"

"But it must be for any Muslim who wishes to remain logically and theologically consistent."

"I'm not sure that I am that consistent," Asim stated.

"You do not have to be. I and my friends do not ask that you share our convictions, only that you share our common goal. Which I believe you already do."

"What are you trying to do here? To bring the government down altogether? You can't."

"I know. It is a task beyond our powers and it would be painful to everyone involved even if we could accomplish it. But there is so much energy loose in the Arab community and the Muslim community today. Sometimes that energy manifests itself in calls for democracy and human rights; sometimes it makes itself known in calls for the destruction of the United States and the West. In either case it is wasted. It is not a specific government, corrupt, Western, or otherwise, that is the true enemy of Islam; it is the very existence of the state. That idea is what I wish to spread. Islamic anarchism is not a new conception, only a neglected one. Now we have a social media network at our disposal that can bring it to public attention. There is revolution in Egypt; there is dissatisfaction here at home; there is war in Syria; there is terror in Iraq; there is hardship in the Emirates; there is internal rivalry in Saudi Arabia. Rulers have lost the trust of the people. Those people are, for the most part, Muslims. Would they not be encouraged to hear an explicit connection being made between their faith, their strongest-held beliefs, and their political and social goals? Would it not strengthen the revolution?"

"It probably would," Asim admitted.

"That is what I wish to accomplish."

"So you're not likely to turn us over to the police. One, you need us, and two, you see the police as blasphemers."

"You think quickly. Yes."

"Why have I never heard your arguments before?"

"My arguments are the words of the Quran. But even a close student of the Book who studied it in an ordinary madrasa, under the guidance of a scholar, might not see them because he was not looking for them. Human beings are accustomed to rulers. In their short-sightedness they assume that what has always been must be right. They overlook those parts of the revelation that contradict their habits. And the ulama, as they need the power of the state to maintain their precedence, are unwilling to put forward speculations that would question the state's legitimacy. Several Iranian theologians have tried it. They were killed."

"Will you stay?" Ra'd bin Mazin asked eventually.

"For now." Asim stood up and moved in the direction of the stairway. "You've convinced me that you won't betray the movement. I'll need time to think about the rest of what you've said."

"You will learn more about it as you work with your friends. Your tasks will require that you express the ideas as well as provide the technical capacity to deliver them."

"There are two more things I don't understand," Asim said. "You want to dissolve all governments, yet you seem to be a pacifist."

"What gave you that impression?"

"The man you sent to bring me down here expressed surprise that I would have been willing to kill the policeman who tailed me from the internet cafe."

"'If a man kills a believer intentionally his recompense is Hell, to abide therein forever, and the wrath and curse of God are upon him and a dreadful penalty is upon him,'" the imam quoted.

"That's what Shadi said when he tried to stop me, too. Isn't there a contradiction there? You can't destroy a government that maintains stability without invoking destruction and murder as well."

"You can if you are a true believer. Someone who believes that God has forbidden him to kill his fellow man does not require a government to force him to be peaceable. Faith resolves the contradiction."

"But by your own argument, if the state is illegitimate, someone who supports it, such as the policeman, can't be a true believer."

"Perhaps. But the validity of his belief is something that he alone is competent to judge. You and I are not able to make that conclusion."

"That's the other thing. You said the king was an idolater."

"I believe that is a fair term to use given the circumstances."

"Why?"

"What is the unforgivable sin?"

"The setting up of partners with God."

"The state assumes the right to govern men and make laws, powers which are reserved to God. It is thus an idol even if it does not take visible form. And the king, who defers to the concept of the state rather than to the words of God, worships a false god by doing so."

5

The Major let his rental car drift to a stop behind an old man whose vehicle must have been inching into its fifth decade as well as into the intersection ahead. He didn't care for the car the agency had stuck him with, which was bright red and handled, in his opinion, like a cube of cheese. But it was invisible in suburbia, among the old two-story houses and the new two-story houses that stood in neat rows, each on its own patch of ground that was too large for the structure it supported and too small for a decent garden. The houses got bigger as he drove. Even Kansas had its high-rent districts, well outside the city center, where new paint and plywood reigned supreme over areas better measured in acres than square feet. The few genuine mansions were far behind, clinging on with mortar to the sides of office buildings downtown. These new buildings represented new money and could only be described as large houses, not mansions.

He kept an eye on the numbers that peered out from the shrubbery. There was the combination of digits he was looking for. A twist of the wheel--well, more like two full revolutions--brought him into an elegantly groomed driveway that went on for less than ten yards before looping beneath a vast porte-cochere and going back the way it had come. The Major parked carefully off to one side and stepped out. The front door of the house flew open, exhaling a pretty blonde girl who was busy jabbering over her shoulder in a language and accent that were pure Parisian. As she passed him, he noted the traces of cat hair that festooned her blouse. That must be the help Emily mentioned, he thought.

A boy was standing in the open doorway looking at him. The Major returned the stare. Wild, but not so wild as to be out of control, he concluded from his observations.

"You're Major Martin?" the boy asked. The Major nodded. "I'm Josh Cranford. Come and meet Andy." He disappeared into the foyer. The Major followed.

Three rooms later, they came across another boy who was playing with a kitten. The second boy, like the first, was twinkish and reasonably good-looking. The kitten was a tabby.

"Andy!" Josh shouted across the remaining distance. "This is Major Martin."

"Hi there!" He held up the kitten for the Major's inspection. "This is Silk. Amelie just brought him over today. We love him already!" The kitten, knowing itself to be flattered, nuzzled the Major's hand.

"He's already learning how to work people over," the Major observed.

"Yeah, he's really good at that. So we got a call from Emily Goldstein saying that she had someone we might want to meet. You know her well?"

"For the past few years. She and her girlfriend are the only people I can talk sense to these days, or that's what it seems like more and more."

"She's always been level-headed."

"How do you two know her?"

"She worked on the same research project as my dad did years ago," Josh said. "They've kept in touch. At one point he and my mom wanted her to talk to me about my sexuality, but I think she figured out pretty fast that I was as comfortable with it as she was with hers." He sniggered.

"That couldn't have been all that long ago."

"Hey! We're both nineteen!" Andy said in mock outrage.

"She might have mentioned that. And married a year, too."

"Well when you've been giving head to the same boy ever since seventh grade…" Josh began before the two of them burst into laughter. The Major smiled.

"So what did you want to see us about, anyway?" Andy asked when they had calmed down.

"Emily thought you might be able to help me with something," the Major said. He was watching the boys carefully now. "She showed me a music video the two of you made. About bullying victims fighting back against the bullies, and about their friends taking--not exactly vengeance, but shall we say preemptive action--against them."

"No one ever liked that video much," Josh said.

"It was Josh's idea to start with. He's a black belt. Taekwondo," Andy added by way of explanation.

"What did you think of it?" Josh asked.

"You two are not Pavarotti in terms of your vocal abilities. But apart from that, I agree with you."

"Welcome to the minority," Andy said, shaking hands with the Major with an overdone air of solemnity.

"It's still small, and it's getting smaller," the Major retorted. He got up and began to circle the room. The kitten, breaking away from the caresses of the two boys, followed him. "I think I should give you two a brief explanation of how I came to be here. I teach at the Marine Corps University. A few days ago, I was invited to give a talk at a high school in Washington about appropriate responses to bullying, in my dual capacity as a gay military officer and an expert in conflict studies. I went up on stage and said much the same thing that you did in your video."

Josh whistled. "The teachers must have been pissed at you."

"They went howling to my commanding officer, who suspended me from duty until he can make up his mind as to how much whitewash will be required to cover me and any stain I leave behind. So now I have some time on my hands to do something that actually matters."

He reached into the folder he was carrying and drew out a creased piece of newsprint, a single blurry photograph taken from a distance, which he handed to the boys.

"Feroze Jan and Arash Kadivar. A couple much like yourself. Except that they're going to be killed for it in two more weeks."

"We've been following the case," Josh said, handing the photo back to the Major.

"Then you know nothing has been done. Amnesty International has made a statement and gone back to typing up reports. The Human Rights Campaign--God, how I loathe that organization!--has made a statement and gone back to holding benefit dinners to raise money to pay its lawyers. No one has done anything--and yet they could have. It's so easy."

"Is that what you're going to do?" Andy asked.

The Major turned back towards the two boys on the sofa.

"I study low-intensity conflicts," he said, his voice quiet. "I have tried to understand why people start wars. Not how they're fought, but why they start. I've learned that wars start, without exception, when someone feels threatened or oppressed. Even a military dictator can fear the mere existence of a group that does not appear to be a direct threat to him, because its existence is a flaw in his ideal vision for his society. Is that sort of fear objectively justifiable? Perhaps not. Is it any less real for that? No.

"And when you understand that humans revolt out of fear, you begin to sympathize with them, especially if you've ever felt fear yourself. The right to revolution stops being an academic issue and becomes a personal one. You can understand from your own experiences how simple, how satisfying it is to take action against someone who has made you afraid, so they can't ever do it again. The more oppressive they are, the more they have degraded you, the more hostile you feel towards them and the more willing you are to fight. Fighting back is not an extraordinary measure, but a reasonable one--one that you are entitled to take.

"The problem is that this understanding is not widespread. The right to revolution remains something expressed on paper only, and, most importantly, something that is not expressed evenly across oppressed or disadvantaged communities. An American president created the concept of self-determination of peoples, and the United States government has an official policy of promoting representative democracy--and yet it recognizes the independence of Kosovo but not that of the Crimea. One group is judged to have the right to assert its principles through direct action, and the other is not. But that is irrational. If one oppressed group has the right to revolt against its enemies, then all oppressed groups must have the same right as a matter of principle."

"You want us--the gay community, I mean--to go to war against Iran?" Josh asked in astonishment.

"Not at the moment," the Major said. "But I do want to go into Iran and bring those two boys out alive."

"Is that doable?" Andy wanted to know. The Major had stopped pacing and was facing them, and the kitten jumped back up into Andy's lap and started purring.

"Yes," the Major replied. "Such an expedition would come as a surprise to the Iranian government. They're not prepared for incursions aimed at rescuing political prisoners. They're certainly not prepared for opposition from a foreign minority they despise and deny."

"But you couldn't do this by yourself."

"No. I'd need a team."

"Can you find the men?"

"I already have two in mind who share the same motivation and would be glad to help out in a worthy cause like this one."

"Will it be expensive?"

"Not on the scale of what wars usually cost, but it will be beyond the reach of a Marine officer's salary. That's why Emily recommended you two."

"Our large disposable income?" Josh said. He wasn't offended by the Major's blunt remark, only interested.

"That and your sympathies."

"There are other rich gays who are active in donating to--"

The Major made a noise similar to the sound a walrus washing up on a very hard and stony beach would give off. "Yes, there are other rich gays--and every single one of them is useless for all practical purposes! Billionaires who are lauded for giving ten thousand, or a hundred thousand, or a million--insignificant in comparison with what they could do. And they use it wrong. They drip it down to the same organizations that have become apologists for homosexuality and campaigns for the normalization of variant behaviors. Thiel, Geffen, Hughes, Bradley--none of them have put a dollar into any form of direct action to get what they claim to want. They say we should be able to get married, and to further that, they throw parties and run ads and line the pockets of beltway attorneys. Did it ever cross their minds for a single second that the easier way to get it, not to mention the cheaper way, would be to bribe a few congressmen and judges? Their minds are incapable of grasping the concept of direct action, either that it's justified or that it can succeed. They've betrayed our cause, which was built on direct action and riots and protests and all-out assaults. No, I need backers who have courage."

"And you think we have courage?"

"I'm guessing you at least have more of it than the average. You two are not, in any sense of the word, conventional."

Andy looked a trifle guilty. "Well, we have been major contributors to some of these campaigns you hate so much in the past--"

"Until one of them sent us a letter asking us please not to show up at any of their events because of our stance on bullying and our well-publicized public displays of affection while we were on our honeymoon in Dubai," Josh interrupted. "They said we were damaging their reputation and making it look as if they were encouraging dangerous behavior. Oh, but we weren't to let that stop us from sending checks." He didn't look happy about it at all.

The Major grimaced. It was an amused grimace and yet not pleasant to witness.

"You find that funny?"

"Actually I was remembering the words my commanding officer used when he relieved me," the Major said. "They were very similar to the ones you've just quoted."

"He's gay too? Hypocrite!"

"Gay and recently married to a much younger man. They're both busy ensuring that their relationship comes off as being as normal and non-threatening as possible while they worm their way into Washington's polite society."

"But is it a bad thing for us to be accepted? To be called normal?" Andy asked. "We are, after all."

"Are we?" the Major retorted, raising an eyebrow. "And if we weren't, would it matter?"

Andy looked at him, puzzled.

"I'll explain. Every social movement which aims at liberation, at increasing human freedoms, eventually ends up being co-opted by the same values of the society it originally opposed. A culture of liberty becomes a culture of limits. It happened with the civil rights movement. It happened with feminism. And it's happened again with gay rights. The initial enthusiasm for doing away with oppressive laws, and sympathy for those engaged in similar struggles, gives way to an acceptance of the existing system in return for the extension of certain limited privileges and freedom from persecution.

"The 'born this way' argument was the worst thing to ever happen to the gay rights movement. It made the debate about norms, not rights. Gay people are normal; therefore, they should enjoy all the normal rights of citizens. Except, of course, the right to choose abnormal or deviant behaviors. It disconnected from and overshadowed the argument that individual choice, regardless of whether or not it runs counter to the will of the majority, is itself a human right far more important than government recognition. And so the gay rights movement has ceased to be a human rights movement at all, because it now values peace and cooperation and privileges over the concept of liberation.

"By its very definition it is cowardly. It strives for acceptance? Only a coward, a weakling, or an idiot is eager to be accepted by someone who despises him or by a culture which demands that he change to accommodate it. The gay rights movement has not demanded acceptance on its own terms, but has tried to achieve it on the terms of mainstream society. They have not asked for laws to be removed in order to abolish discrimination, but for new laws to be created that include them within existing privileged categories. They don't want to redefine or improve society; they aren't courageous enough to celebrate their differences, which are the key to individuality; they seek the safety of the group."

"Let me see if I follow you," Josh said, leaning forward. "You admit that existing laws are discriminatory?"

"Yes."

"But you are opposed to new laws that would remove that discrimination."

"Because the discrimination is in the existence of the laws themselves."

"I'm sorry, I still don't quite understand."

"I'll give you an example. Remember all the sign-waving outside the Supreme Court when United States versus Windsor was being heard?"

"Hard to forget it, given the coverage it was getting."

"The single image that lingers in my mind from that day is a protestor outside the court holding up a plain white board with rainbow letters on it. They spelled out 'Happy monogamous marriage for all.' And that one sign gives it all away. AFER and the HRC and the ACLU don't want equal rights. They want the current narrow definition of marriage, as a privilege, slightly enlarged to bring one more protected class within its scope. Members of the five out of every six human societies that practice polygamy were not intended to be included. Either because multiple marriage is 'abnormal', because it's antithetical to American culture, or because it's just plain icky. Those people aren't going to be allowed to share the privilege."

"Whereas a response that didn't involve privilege would be--"

"Striking down all laws regulating marriage and leaving it up to individuals to decide who they wanted to marry and how they wanted it done. True equal marriage, unlike that farce of an act that Congress just passed."

"That's a lot to swallow," Andy said, frowning.

"It underscores the point. They didn't get rid of a limit on our freedoms, they created a new one."

"But aren't all civil rights limited by law?"

"Civil rights, yes. Human rights, no."

"Wait--you're saying two different things, aren't you? One is that the things we can do because we're human are more important than the things other people tell us we can do."

"That's correct. Humanity comes first."

"Well that's the second thing, isn't it? We can't just think about our own social group, we have to think about all other groups as well."

"Yes. A general principle of liberation."

"Which brings us back to where you started. The right to revolution. If one group has the right, all must have it."

"Including us, the gay community, wherever we are threatened, especially when we are threatened with violence."

"And going into Iran to rescue that couple would be a way of asserting that right over the cowardice of the existing advocacy groups."

"Not to mention that it would give you a chance to irritate them," Josh added.

"I admit it," the Major responded. "I despise these people who talk about equality when all they really mean is a different form of discrimination."

"But putting arguments over principle aside for a minute," Andy persisted, "don't you think we're better off than we were?"

"What's the point?" the Major said. "I will accept nothing as a gift that is mine by right."

"Do you like fighting?" Josh suddenly wanted to know.

"No. But I recognize its necessity."

"To protect the weak?"

"Not to protect or assert anything. Its existence is an indication that individuality and personal freedom are being exercised, because individuals, left to themselves, constantly come into conflict with one another. These gay rights organizations would like to outlaw certain forms of discrimination, but preventing discrimination is itself discrimination. They'd like to ban hate speech, but hate speech is a form of free speech. They try to eliminate conflict, but they only cause new conflicts. Until they accept that we live in a world permanently full of contradictions, where everything can't be made nice and smooth and shiny, they're going to be unhappy."

"If conflict is natural, then there's no reason to hold back from it."

"If it's the most effective solution to your problem, then yes, that statement is true."

"And holding back where a confrontation could be effective--it's fair to call that cowardice."

"Cowardice or weakness or stupidity. Take your pick."

"Okay," Josh said. "In that case, we won't hold back. You're certain you can pull this off?"

"I was an infantryman before I was a teacher. I can do it."

"And you think it will be effective in breaking the illusion that we have to be nice gays, good gays in order to be given human rights that we should have already?"

"It will at least show there are feasible alternatives to asserting our rights that don't involve our going begging, hat in hand, to someone no better than ourselves."

"And these two Iranians are going to die anyway?"

"The sentence has been finalized. Yes."

"All right, then." Josh looked at Andy. The other boy nodded. "You can go ahead and put the revolution on our Centurion card." He snickered. "Now--just how are you going to get them out?"

The Major took a map from his portfolio and unfolded it before them.

6

Asim's face glowed in the dark, shining with reflected light. His fingers traced the fragile keys of the Eee PC, turning the commands of his brain into digital impulses as he switched between tongues. The imam's essays had to be translated into at least three languages before they could be released: Arabic, English, and HTML. And the differences between Gulf Arabic and Egyptian Standard had to be accounted for, and with Asim's arrival, one of the other hackers, a languages major before the police caught on to his activism, decided that he might as well start partial translations into Persian and Punjabi. His participation had ended up increasing their total workload, not lessening it as they had hoped. But hackers enjoy certain kinds of challenges, as long as they aren't required to leave their silicon friends behind while rising to meet them.

To his surprise, Asim found that the work was beginning to fascinate him. It frightened him, too. As he had told the imam, he had aspired to government reform, not government disassembly. He was a logician, not a man of faith. As a logician he could understand that the absence of a state was unlikely to produce worse effects than the presence of one. But he also understood that it was a very difficult goal to accomplish, and that the effects would have to be widespread and multiplied across the region if it was to stick. Without a guiding faith, an internal conviction that his actions conformed to God's will, the risks were more obvious to him than the rewards. That didn't stop him from continuing to type even as he considered those risks. The fear he had felt when the policeman had chased him across the city had turned to anger. He had been victimized by his own people, his own nation, for trying to help them. He sensed the threat, but reached forward to meet it at the same time that it made him tremble with aversion.

And the imam's arguments were persuasive. Asim had never been an especially devout Muslim, even less so by the growing rigor of the standards that Saudi-trained and Saudi-influenced scholars were attempting to impose on Bahrain. As such, he was in the same position as many other Bahrainis his age: disillusioned by the state and by their faith, both of which had ceased to give and only demanded without a break. In that atmosphere, he'd never thought of Islam as revolutionary. Instead, it was something old and traditional, something imperial, something hypocritical that ordered and bullied.

The imam's words had conjured up a different picture. Now Asim could see the Prophet wandering the desert, cast out by his fellow Meccans for his unorthodoxy, rejected by the local Jews whose ancient faith he had hoped to restore. He spoke of revolution to wild, proud, disdainful tribes. His speeches were directed against the one constant and conservative point in their otherwise malleable culture: their ancient idols. When he was attacked by men who hated his faith, he escaped them. Then he defeated them and took their towns and forts to be his own. At last he came back to Mecca and destroyed the idols and made the city the center of a faith so ephemeral that it could have no concrete symbols, because those symbols posed a danger to its existence as a thought, a concept.

The Apostles of God, Asim was beginning to understand, were all revolutionaries. Moses, who had set the children of Israel free from foreign rule; David and Solomon, who had united the tribes over their own traditional jealousies;

Jesus, who had come preaching faith alone when Judaism had degenerated into a mere bickering over details of ritual.

His fingers stopped moving and hovered over the keyboard. In the blackness of the room, staring into the backlit display of his computer ruined his ability to see anything of his surroundings. All the same, he was certain there was a shadow in the corner that was new. A shadow moving in the direction of the doorway, and no footsteps to accompany it.

Which was doubly odd, because the hackers were careful to make audible amounts of noise in the dark when they moved around the buildings, to prevent their fellow workers from being startled.

Asim strained to see if there really was movement out there. He sensed, rather than heard, the curtain in the doorway part.

At that moment, whoever was in the adjacent room must have adjusted the brightness setting on his screen, because light flickered through the gap for a second before the curtain closed. Asim caught a glimpse of a blue shirt sliding through it.

He stopped his work and went methodically over his recollections of the day. The only one of the hackers who had been wearing a blue shirt was Faruq. Asim wondered why Faruq would be sneaking around the building. He could have come and gone as he liked and no one would have cared, or noticed at all if they were busy.

Something else was poking at the back of his mind. He knew Faruq from somewhere. Not in the same way he knew the imam's face, not the way you remember a public figure. He'd been in close contact with him at some point.

Contact. That was it. Faruq had been in a transistor design class that he had taken a year ago. At least he thought Faruq had been in the class, hiding among the sea of faces in the rear of the lecture hall. About to graduate, in his last term. And hadn't he heard something about the older student having snared one of the coveted and increasingly rare government jobs that most of the students aspired to in spite of their professed revolutionary principles?

His suspicions of betrayal came flooding back. But this time they had a more definite object than his original mistrust of the imam had found.

Asim swiped his finger across the touchpad and opened a new tab. Khalil was offline right now. But if anyone would know, he would. That's why he was a middleman. He could remember faces and names and put them together and make the faces think that he empathized with them in every way possible. Maybe that's why he was never very good at coding, Asim reflected. He typed a message into the box: "Do you remember a student called Faruq, who had that transistor class with us that we used to go have halwa after? Didn't he go to work for the Ministry of the Interior when he graduated?" With any luck, he'd know for sure in a few more hours.

And if it was true? Then what? Run again without asking questions? To where? Ask Faruq himself if he was a spy or a double agent? Insult him or expose him, either way? Get arrested? Get killed? Expose the operation? Offend a valuable asset? Trust the imam to be able to tell between a genuine double agent and a smooth liar?

He felt no fear now, only anger. Someone was threatening him again, and he was beginning to tire of it.

* * * * *

When he woke up and rolled over on his pallet, the morning was already hot, and there was a message light blinking on his screen.

He opened it. It was from Khalil:

"You mean Faruq al-Uthman? He didn't go to Interior, he went to Justice & Islamic Affairs. Funny, isn't it? Not sure how he ever got his degree in the first place, he didn't know anything about computers. I checked with someone I know in the ministry and he hasn't been seen in weeks. Supposed to be seconded to the prime minister's office, but no one there has seen him either. Why? Has he popped up again?"

Asim didn't want to reply to that message just yet. He needed to think.

There was spiced lamb at lunch that day as a compliment to Shadi, who was recovering well. No infection, and he was able to sit up, carefully cushioned, and enjoy the meal with the rest of them. He tried having Asim fetch his tablet for him, but Fihr al-Masri, who had stitched him back together, refused to let him have it. Shadi appealed to the imam as arbiter. The imam told him to wait a few more days. Attempting to use his right arm would prevent the wound from healing properly. Shadi protested that he could type with his left hand only, that it wouldn't be a problem, but when he demonstrated, he discovered that his typing speed was far too slow for him to tolerate and settled down amicably to eat.

The tablet incident was a welcome distraction for Asim, who couldn't seem to keep his eyes off Faruq. Twice the latter caught him staring and he jerked his gaze away.

* * * * *

"Did you want to talk to me about something?"

Asim started and twisted his head around to see who had spoken to him. It was Faruq. His chest tightened.

"No, not that I can think of," he said.

Faruq didn't seem willing to accept that answer, but didn't press the subject right away, either. Instead he sat down on an old crate and looked out over the parapet with Asim. The dusty roofs of Muharraq spread out all around them. In the distance, the afternoon sun made the new commercial towers along the Manama waterfront shine like pillars of pure energy.

"You keep staring at me, though," he eventually said. "All this morning. All through lunch. And now you sneak away and claim you have nothing to say? You weren't doing that yesterday."

"If we're talking about sneaking, why were you sneaking around the building last night?" Asim demanded, nettled by Faruq's insistence on returning to the topic.

"I wasn't."

"You came through my room with your shoes off, deliberately trying to not make a sound!"

"It must have been someone else."

"No one else was wearing a blue shirt last night."

"I'm not the only one here who owns a blue shirt."

"No, but you were the only one wearing such a shirt an hour before you snuck through my room, trying to be clever."

"My, but aren't you observant!" Faruq teased him. "You sound like a detective out of a spy novel!"

In spite of his words, his left cheek twitched slightly. A muscle spasming under the effect of nervous tension. That told Asim nothing he didn't already know. Faruq was hiding something, he was certain. What that was remained unclear.

"Anything else against me?" Faruq asked in an ironic tone, as Asim remained silent. "Have I been swiping your flash drives? Trying to steal your phone? Hacking your wireless connection?"

"I doubt you could do that."

"Why not? I'm a hacker too."

"You were at the bottom of your class."

"Now how would you know that?" Faruq's voice lost its overtones of sarcasm.

"Because we had a class together a year ago."

Faruq leaned forward and peered at Asim, his eyes squinting. "Yes, we did. Now I remember you. You weren't at the bottom of the class. And for that reason I'm surprised that you remembered me."

"It took me a while," Asim admitted.

"To remember? Or did you have to ask someone about it?"

"I remembered it," Asim lied. He thought it was convincing enough. Faruq's stare was getting on his nerves. Fortunately, he appeared to have something else on his mind.

"I wouldn't have thought you'd end up here, of all places," he mused. "You were never very religious, at least from what I saw of you."

"I'm not here because I'm religious."

"Oh, so you're a secularist in it for the momentary safety and satisfaction it provides you?"

"I don't know. I was here and there was work to do."

Again, Faruq drew back from a line of questioning that Asim sensed he would have liked to pursue. "How did you get here, anyway?"

"Why would that matter? I think the more interesting question is how you ended up here. I heard that when you graduated you got a government job and a pension for life."

"I was fired," Faruq said blandly. "Also the Ministry of the Interior was not a very moral place to work. I wanted a job where my faith was woven into the fabric of my duties."

So he is a government spy! Asim concluded. *He wasn't fired. He's still working for the Ministry of Justice--not Interior. If he was fired, Khalil would have known about it. And if he was a double agent for us, he wouldn't be hiding it.*

The everlasting peril of being a deep cover agent is that you will eventually come across someone who knows about your past or is able to check on it, and that he will be able to discover a discrepancy in your account of yourself.

"That's very noble of you," was all Asim said aloud. Faruq stared at him, trying to decide if he was serious or making fun of him.

"It's more noble than running from an anonymous text message."

"And an unmarked car pulling up outside my window?"

"I thought you said they sent regular police cars after you?"

"They did. But I never said that to anyone here. Just that I saw the cars coming."

Asim stood up. Faruq pushed him back. He was angry now.

"Sit down," he said quietly.

"No." Asim got to his feet a second time.

Faruq shrugged, then reached behind him and pulled a gun out from underneath his shirttail. It wasn't an old, pitted Soviet reject like the one Asim had grabbed in desperation. It was a gleaming new PPK. Further testimony to the fact that in Bahrain, only the police have easy access to weapons.

"You've given yourself away now," Asim said. This time, he wasn't panicking.

"As if I hadn't before?"

"Well--not conclusively."

"I could have passed it off as an assumption?"

"Maybe."

"Maybe. But in combination with my nocturnal activities and that look on your face when you said you recognized me and remembered I had a government job--too much of a risk. Besides, I prefer it this way."

"You prefer to kill me?"

"Actually I prefer to have you as an ally. Say no, and I will kill you now. Say yes, and I'll arrange for a full pardon for you after the ministry arrests the remainder of the underground. You can't sabotage this fool's translations; I can't either. Too much checking involved. But we can keep tabs on his planning to prevent them from going out and causing chaos. You have no emotional stake in his scheme. You came here out of desperation. Well, that reason's gone now. Working with me, you can go back to your normal life. No criminal record, no threat of arrest."

Asim said nothing. Faruq became impatient.

"Well? Yes or no?"

"Yes," Asim finally said.

* * * * *

"And why should ye not fight in the cause of God and in the cause of those who, being weak, are ill-treated and oppressed?"

He put the Quran down and turned back to his computer screen. The imam had dictated the references for the commentary from memory, without a single pause or hesitation. Every verse Asim had checked so far was correctly chosen and reinforced the essential message of the essays.

"If two parties among the Believers fall into a quarrel, make ye peace between them; but if one of them transgresses beyond bounds against the other, then fight ye all against the one that transgresses until it complies with the command of God; but if it complies then make peace between them with justice and be fair: for God loves those who are fair and just."

In the second decade of the twentieth century by Western reckoning, it was commonplace for radical scholars and imams to tell Muslims that it was meritorious for them to fight and conquer unbelievers. It was much less common for a scholar to tell his coreligionists that they had an obligation to fight in defense of their fellow Muslims who were being oppressed, even if the oppressors were themselves Muslim. Certainly no one had mentioned that to the contract labor agencies which imported workers from India and Bangladesh and then starved them while they died by the thousands. "O ye who believe! Stand out firmly for justice as witnesses to God even as against yourselves or your parents or your kin and whether it be against rich or poor: for God can best protect both."

Ra'd bin Mazin had noted that scholars and interpreters who would object to these exhortations being used in the context of rebellion against an unjust government would doubtless cite a verse in Surah 16: "God commands justice, the doing of good, and liberality to kith and kin, and He forbids all shameful deeds and injustice and rebellion."

"But what is rebellion?" the imam's commentary asked. "Resistance to justified authority and disobedience of the law. The only justified authority is that of God; the only law is that of God. 'Truly the command is with God in all things!' Disobedience of human laws and resistance to human authority is therefore not forbidden."

And would actually be rewarded, the commentary went on to say. "Those who strive and fight hath He distinguished above those who sit at home by a special reward."

The weaker argument that leadership was traditional and necessary was also attacked on a Quranic basis: "When it is said to them, 'Come to what God hath revealed; come to the Apostle,' they say, 'Enough for us are the ways we found our fathers following.' What! even though their fathers were void of knowledge and guidance?" "When they do aught that is shameful they say, 'We found our fathers doing so,' and, 'God commanded us thus.' Say to them: 'Nay, God never commands what is shameful; do ye say of God what ye know not?'" "Wert thou to follow the common run of those on earth, they will lead thee away from the Way of God. They follow nothing but conjecture; they do nothing but lie." "Therefore expound openly what ye are commanded and turn away from those who join false gods with God."

False gods. The recurring motif of idolatry that the imam was so keen on stressing in his talks. Asim was not sure that it was strong enough to catch on with the general public, but revolutionaries and reformers across the Arab world were increasingly well-informed on political theory. It might take hold, and if it did...

A shadow fell between him and the window, blocking out the light. Faruq was standing there, a frown on his face.

"I need to talk to you. Come in here," he said. There was no use arguing about it, Asim knew. He put his laptop down and followed the spy.

In Faruq's own chamber, or at least the room he most often used, he turned and confronted Asim.

"I've been thinking," he said. "And watching you work. And I've realized that you are a computer geek through and through. You weren't likely to have recalled me from one class a year ago, not to the extent where you would know what I was doing now. You don't notice people. Did someone else tell you about me? Did you go looking for information when you got suspicious?"

Asim hesitated.

"I'll take that as a yes," Faruq snapped. "I need the name of your contact."

"If there is someone--"

"There is. You as good as told me just now. Who is he?"

"Why do you need to know?"

"Because the ministry needs to know, of course. Who is he?"

"What are you going to do, recruit him, too?"

"No, he'll just be arrested. We want the names and connections in his head. Having him unable to use those connections will be more helpful to us than having him use them on our behalf. Now give me his name."

"You're going to kill him."

"Arresting someone doesn't mean killing them, idiot!"

"In this country it does. To your police pals it does."

"You don't have a choice. Who is he?"

"I'm not going to tell you," Asim said, crossing his arms and staring back at Faruq without any remaining trace of submission in his bearing.

Faruq chuckled. "Are you deaf? I just said you don't have a choice. Tell me now."

Asim spun on his heel and walked away.

Three steps later, Faruq's gun went off behind him.

He stopped, then turned around.

Faruq stared at him, puzzled. There was no bloodstain on Asim's shirt. He looked in succession at his pistol, at the little golden case it had ejected, and back at Asim again. Still no blood. He shrugged, steadied his grip with both hands, and let off three more rounds into Asim's chest.

The bullets did nothing.

Behind them, the curtain in the doorway parted, and the imam stepped through it, followed by Fihr and Junayd.

"Why are you trying to shoot him?" the imam asked. His voice was as calm as if he was reciting the Book in a mosque, not watching--or rather, listening to--one of his helpers attacking another.

"I caught Asim texting our location to a number that I recognized as one assigned to the Ministry of the Interior," Faruq said without a pause. He was good under stress, Asim realized.

"Killing is not an appropriate response to treason."

That threw Faruq off his stride for a moment. The imam went on:

"In any case, I have been listening to your conversation. Asim is not the one at fault here. Why try to kill him to compensate for your own misreading of the situation?"

Faruq's back stiffened. "Because killing is an appropriate response to treason, blasphemer!" He twitched the barrel of the pistol to one side and pulled the trigger twice more with the sights centered on the imam's forehead.

Ra'd bin Mazin merely blinked, his lids covering and uncovering his sightless, motionless eyes.

Faruq dropped the gun and leapt for the window. There was no balcony or roof beneath it, not even a ledge. What he expected to accomplish by reaching it was a mystery. But he never got that far. Fihr, charging like the footballer he'd been as a teenager, brought him down before he could touch the sill. He produced a pair of handcuffs from the back pocket of his jeans and snapped them on to the struggling spy.

"How are you still alive?" Faruq shouted, his face flushed and his legs striking out everywhere until Fihr sat on them. "I shot you both! I couldn't have missed!"

"You wouldn't have if your gun had been loaded with real bullets," Junayd said, picking the weapon up and bagging it so as to preserve its fingerprints. "I switched them with dummies that disintegrated on exiting the barrel. No harm done, and you didn't find out till it was too late."

"But you--" Faruq's eyes fixed themselves on the imam with a hateful stare. "You knew. You knew this would happen!"

"Asim came to me yesterday morning when he was first suspicious. Then we knew that you were a spy of the ministry, yes. You told me the same story of having been expelled from their ranks when you first arrived here. But Asim had found out that you were still in their employ. So he attracted your attention deliberately, then drew you out until you contradicted yourself again, then allowed you to apparently bully him into working for you."

"And then he let me betray myself?" Faruq laghed nastily. "Very clever. Now what? You can't kill me, and you can't keep me here. Eh?"

"You do present a problem," the imam mused aloud. "As you say, I cannot kill you. And I cannot take an oath from you and be sure you would keep it, because your devotion to idolaters causes me to be uncertain about whether you are a true believer or not. So I will show you mercy, but until we are safe, you must accept some discomfort as recompense for your own lack of honesty."

He held out his arm to Asim for guidance and moved towards the door. "Tie him up," he instructed Fihr, "and place him where he cannot hear or see. We are leaving."

7

      Steven Powers fidgeted in his seat. He wasn't sure why he had wanted to come to this meeting in the first place. Well, apart from trying to get a better look at that cute lance corporal who had just transferred into his unit. And he'd been curious. After much hemming and hawing and half a dozen policy studies, the Marine Corps had allowed the formation of an unofficial LGBT support group at Quantico. The base commander had taken great pains to distance himself from the proceedings to avoid the appearance of official support, but the absence of an endorsement from on high was more than made up for by the enthusiasm of the group's founders. They went out of their way to get noticed, writing editorials, being profiled in regional papers, hanging out with the new crop of congressmen who were struggling to force through the Equal Marriage Act over the president's veto. Powers thought it was all a bit overdone.

      And this much-advertised inspirational speaker of theirs was beginning to get on his nerves. So what if Ray Hasegawa had chained himself to the White House gates to protest his discharge under the Don't Ask, Don't Tell policy? It sounded like something from a Disney movie, passive aggression covered in sugar candy to make it seem more palatable. It hadn't really achieved anything. It hadn't even been very embarrassing for the government.

The question-and-answer session edged away from personal comments and queries to issues of policy. Almost at once, someone threw the current hot topic into the ring. "What about the ban on transgender service? Do you think that will come up for review soon?"

"Unfortunately, no. The Secretary has said outright that he won't consider it. We probably won't have a chance to change that until after the next election, given the current administration's hostility towards the LGBT community. So unless Congress gets involved, the policy will continue to stand."

Powers stood up. "That's a good thing in some ways, though, isn't it?"

The room went silent. Hasegawa cleared his throat. "How do you mean that?"

"Well, if the policy were changed, the Army would have to make concessions in its treatment of Chelsea Manning, wouldn't it?"

Hasegawa flushed.

"I hope not," he retorted angrily. "Manning is a traitor. *He* handed over secret military information to our enemies. *He* gave away national secrets. There's nothing to discuss there!"

"Except your unwillingness to grant her the same respect you would another transgender individual out of spite, and the fact that she's an American citizen."

The former army captain tried to pass the attack off with a disdainful laugh, but it was more like a baring of fangs. "I'm not even going to respond to that insinuation. As for him being an American citizen, that's also what makes him guilty."

"As an American citizen she has a right to free speech."

"Those of us who serve agree not to exercise certain rights during the term of our service to maintain good order and discipline. It's one of the sacrifices we're called upon to make," Hasegawa pontificated.

Powers shook his head. "It's a pretty shitty system that doesn't allow the defenders of freedom to exercise the freedoms they're fighting for."

The lieutenant who was one of the group's organizers looked as if he was about to strangle either himself or the offending corporal. He started to stand up, but Hasegawa waved him back down.

"Whether you think it's a bad situation or not doesn't matter," Hasegawa said. "You agreed to play by those rules. If you have a problem, you shouldn't be here. Manning knew that too, and he broke them. He put himself and his own personal views before those of his leaders. And we shouldn't be praising him or defending him for that. We--the LGBT community--should show that we're supportive of his conviction. Because we're as committed to our country and its institutions as much as anyone else, and we don't expect special treatment for one of our own."

"So we should be nice to the people who called us sick and tried to keep us from serving our country in the first place?"

"We should stop trying to offend the people who are trying to help us."

"The only people who are trying to help us are the ones we're putting in prison!"

"Like Manning, I suppose?" Hasegawa jeered. "How do you come to that conclusion?"

"Because it's freedom in general that matters, not gay rights!" Powers shouted. "If we can get married now but we aren't allowed to speak our minds anymore, where's there a net gain? It's the same freedom allotted differently, not more freedom and fewer rules overall!"

No one spoke for a minute. The lieutenant jumped up again, and this time Hasegawa didn't stop him. "Lance Corporal, I don't think your presence here is bringing anything substantial to the discussion."

Powers gave a barely noticeable shrug and walked out of the room.

*****

He was replaying the events of the meeting over and over in his mind when the long green hood of the Jaguar slid up beside the curb, eight cylinders ticking away beneath it. The officer in the driver's seat pulled his sunglasses down for a better look.

"Lance Corporal Powers?"

"Yes, sir."

"Gunnery Sergeant Mamoulian said you might want to talk to me. You're off duty this afternoon?"

"Yes, sir."

"Still interested?"

"Yes, sir." Powers opened the car door and climbed in. Major Martin spun it around in a tight half-circle and shot out of the gate under the admiring looks of the guards. Modern Jaguars, glorified Fords that they were, didn't have the same elegance as the last models of the twentieth century. He stepped on the gas pedal and headed west into the Virginia countryside.

The convertible top locked into place and the Major took his glasses off for good.

"So," he said. "The gunny told me that you were counseled for speaking your mind at that silly support group meeting the other day. Did you bring up the issue of Hasegawa's five-figure speaking fees, or was there more to it than that?"

Powers took his eyes off the screen of his phone and gave the Major a sideways look. "With all due respect, sir, are you setting me up?"

The Major was surprised enough that he almost stepped on the brake. "No, never crossed my mind." He read the suspicion and hesitation in the other man's face. "If this will make you feel any better…" He fished around inside his jacket and pulled out a letter, which he handed to the corporal.

"Read that and I think you'll realize that I don't have any reason to entrap you. Quite the reverse, actually."

Powers read it. "Holy shit--I mean, sir. You too?"

"It would appear that standing up for one's principles is becoming less and less fashionable these days, even among one's own," the Major said, his voice laden with irony. "You've met Colonel Lamoreaux?"

"No, sir. I've only seen him at a distance. Isn't he supposed to be some sort of poster boy for the open-mindedness of the Corps?"

"Supposed to be. As you can see by what he wrote, he isn't."

"But all you said was that people who are being attacked should protect themselves. Isn't that our job? Isn't that what we train to do?"

"Ah, but it's our job, corporal, not theirs. Deep down, his reaction is based in part on the idea that only certain organizations are capable of handling the problem of violence, and that anyone who tries to handle it on their own, without calling for help, is in the wrong."

"And the other part, sir?"

"The other part is that he has what my friend Dr. Goldstein calls an inferiority complex. He wants the acceptance of his peers. And as a gay man, he's only going to get that if his sexuality is seen as normal, ordinary, and non-threatening, both physically and intellectually. Hence his anger when I said that we should fight for our differences instead of suppressing them."

"But our sexuality is non-threatening, isn't it?"

"If it was, why do we still risk getting attacked for it? That's the obvious, practical argument. The abstract argument is that as long as it remains a minority viewpoint, or minority characteristic, whichever you prefer, it will be different. And human societies often view a minority group with different behaviors as an automatic threat. Particularly this society. Did you ever read an essay called 'The Paranoid Style in American Politics'?"

"No, sir."

"For some reason we are one of the most sensitive peoples in the world to differences of opinion. We strive to either destroy those who hold opposing views, or convert or assimilate them."

"What's wrong with becoming a part of society, though?" Powers demanded. "With being accepted?"

"You're still trying to work that one out, aren't you? To figure out if it's a valid question?"

"Yes, sir."

"Well, I can't tell you why in an objective sense. My own thoughts on the subject, for what they're worth, is that every time a minority group assimilates with a larger one, and gives up its most distinctive characteristics, two things happen. The amount of diversity overall in a society or an area is reduced, and the larger group is strengthened so that it becomes more difficult for other small groups to compete against it in the future. It's a sign that convenience is being prized over individuality, and it's my belief that individuality must be preserved regardless of the interests of the majority. Do you read fantasy at all?"

"Some of it," Powers admitted.

"Oh? The ones with the well-muscled men on the covers?" The Major shot him an appraising look, then laughed out loud when Powers hesitated. "It's all right. Anyway, the father of the fantasy genre, Lord Dunsany, wrote this once: 'In every country there are about a hundred individualists, varying to perhaps half a hundred in poor ages. They go their hundred ways, or their half-dozen ways, and there is a hundred and first way, or a seventh way, which is the way that is cut for the rest. And if some of the rest catch one of the hundred, or one of the six, they naturally hang him, if they have a rope, and if hanging is the custom of the country, for different countries use different methods.' That about sums it up."

He noticed that Powers's attention was divided between him and his phone. "Even in the classroom I can't hold them sometimes," the Major lamented aloud. "Anything going on in the world?"

"Oh? Yes, sir. Well--sort of. Some football player called his gay teammate a faggot and there's a whole fuss on Facebook about it."

"Hardly news," the Major observed. "Has he been suspended yet?"

"I think so."

"They always do that."

"There was some guy on Twitter who was really calling him out about it. Saying that he had no right to say those things and that he was a bigot and deserved whatever he got. And everyone agreed." Powers held up the phone so that the Major could look at it.

"Him?" the Major shouted abruptly. "How dare he? He's married to a porn star and has a boyfriend on the side--in two different countries, no less--and he has the nerve to criticize someone else for making a controversial statement? To demand that someone else's unconventional view be suppressed?"

"It was hate speech, after all," Powers ventured.

"From what I was told, you defended speech that could have harmed an entire country on principle. Are you going to adopt a double standard for speech that could hurt just a few individuals?"

"No, sir."

The Major sighed. "Once upon a time it was being gay that was deviant. Now it's saying that being gay is unnatural, or insulting the gays, that's deviant. The words have changed, the positions have changed, but the concept of deviance, and the moral outrage that accompanies it, is still out there. The oppression is still the same, except that the oppressed have become the oppressors. I despise these people who talk about equality when all they really mean is a different form of discrimination."

He threw the car violently into an exit and they drove on for a while.

"Sir, if you don't mind my asking," Powers said, "why did you bring me out here?"

"We're going to see someone. Do you have any leave available?"

"Yes, sir."

"Can you take it?"

"I think so, sir."

"How would you like to go to Iran?"

"Iran?"

"There's a gay couple there younger than you are who are going to die next week because they loved each other. I'm going to get them out, since the lawyers and the bureaucrats and the activists are useless pieces of dirt. I need a few men to help me. Would you like to be part of the team?"

"Sir, is this approved by the Corps? Or at any level of the chain of command?"

"Not a one. They don't so much as know it's going to happen. Do you think they have the courage to sanction an operation like that, for no apparent military objective?"

"That would be blatantly illegal."

"I know," the Major said. "And I'll probably be court-martialed for it when I get back. But at the end of the day, there are going to be two boys who are alive who would have died otherwise. And that's all there is to think about."

Five minutes passed.

"I'll help you, sir," Powers said, looking back at the Major.

"Thank you." Major Martin slowed the car.

"Who are we going to see?"

"Someone else who said things the Corps didn't want to hear."

* * * * *

A Cessna buzzed overhead as the Major parked the Jaguar. He led the way through the FBO office and across the tarmac towards the hangars, making his way around the idle aircraft with the air of one used to circumventing heavy machinery. Down at the end of the long row of steel buildings, one of the tall, forty-foot doors stood open, admitting the light and warmth of the afternoon to the interior. Someone in a blue flight suit was bent over a sleek, silver-skinned aircraft that rested just inside the line of shadow cast by the roof.

"Did you get the seal fixed yet?" the Major called.

"Last night." The pilot, a young woman with rich brown hair drawn back in a ponytail, turned to face him. "Major Martin?"

"Surprised?"

"When you said you wanted to talk to me I didn't think it was important enough for you to come all the way out here." She wiped her hands on a rag and stepped out into the sunlight.

"It was."

"So I assume you're not primarily interested in the progress I'm making on the Hispanio."

"You should get an F-86 to represent the period."

Amanda Price gave a disparaging laugh. "I'll gladly get an F-86--when and if I can find one priced much below a round million. It's your fault, you know. Perhaps you could talk to your friends in the Air Force and get them to unbelt. They have all those lovely airplanes sitting out in the middle of the desert going to waste, or parked in front of VFW posts where they can get rained on."

"I have no friends in the Air Force," the Major said.

"Occupational hazard, is it? Who's your friend in the stripes?"

"This is Lance Corporal Powers. He's working on a special project with me."

"Ma'am," Powers said politely. Price looked him over and switched her attention back to the Major.

"You brought reinforcements? You must think it's serious."

"You don't seem to agree."

"One, you haven't told me what it is you're up to, so I can't agree or disagree. Two, I still don't trust you all the way yet." The Major remembered that she had an abrupt, busy attitude more typical of the New England horsey social set than of a professional pilot.

He also remembered bumping into her, in the most literal sense of the word, outside a JAG courtroom at the Washington Navy Yard two years ago. He had been giving testimony in a pretrial hearing, a waste of time in his opinion. She and her lawyers had been waiting to meet with a panel of Navy lawyers to discuss her suit. The lawyers had hovered uncomfortably in the background the whole time, but their nerves had only set her own poise off to greater effect.

He'd recognized her immediately, of course. The youngest flight instructor in the country, the news reports had called her, although they were probably exaggerating. From a family of aviators, with thousands of hours already in her logbook, and now a freshman at George Washington University. And an aspiring Marine Corps pilot--except that her application for a pilot slot had been denied.

The previous summer, the Aircraft Owners and Pilot's Association had staged a demonstration outside the

Department of Homeland Security to protest the increasing number of pilots who were being arrested without warrants on landing because the department had tagged them as potential drug smugglers. It hadn't been a large protest by Washington standards. Fewer than three hundred pilots had turned up. But the Vice President had been inside the building for a briefing at the time, and the Secret Service, invoking the Trespass Act, had designated the premises a restricted area and arrested every one of the protestors. All of them ended up with felony convictions on their records, including Amanda Price, and the Marine Corps does not give pilot slots to people with felony convictions.

    She could have applied for a waiver, given the circumstances. She might have even gotten it. Instead, she decided to sue the Corps, arguing that its blanket ban on applicants with felony convictions constituted cruel and unusual punishment, as it allowed them to impose additional penalties on those applicants, who had already paid their fines and done their community service. She was trying, in fact, to reopen the felony disenfranchisement debate from the human rights angle.

    "I rather admire your tactics," the Major had said to her at the time. "Your reasoning is sound. But do you think you stand a chance of convincing them"--he jerked his head in the direction of the legal conference rooms--"of that?"

    "Not really, no," she had said. "But it sets a precedent. It starts a discussion."

    "Is a discussion worth the trouble?"

    Then she had leaned in close to him until she could whisper in his ear without her lawyers objecting. "Why do you think I applied for the pilot slot in the first place?" she had asked him, her eyes dancing.

    And the Major had smiled back at her.

He blinked. It was surprising how warm the sun was this late in the day. "You trusted me enough to give away your whole strategy the first time we met," he observed.

"You struck me as the innovative, unconventional type," Price replied. "And I'd overheard you speaking with the prosecutor. You were more concerned with why people did things than whether or not they did them."

"There's a principle at stake here, too."

"There always is when you come around. What is it this time?"

"I'm going to Iran. I want to pull out those two boys who they're going to kill before the government can get them to the gallows."

"Is this a community project?"

"An extremely unofficial community project. Neither of the two major communities I represent would approve of what I'm planning to do. If they knew about it."

"You're flying solo."

"Not quite. I'm putting together a team. Powers is part of it. I need a pilot--a real pilot, not some jet jockey or Airbus driver who lives and dies by his checklist. You're the best and most unrestrained pilot I know."

Price stared at him. "Audacious of you. But I'm not queer."

"Oh, yes you are. You put principles above convenience and quiet and conformity. And that makes you as queer as I am."

She snickered. "Words are so flexible, aren't they? Let's say I did agree to go along with this venture--it doesn't seem to involve the commission of a crime on American soil, so I should be safe there. What do you need me for? Your escape route, waiting with a battered old Ilyushin in the desert to whisk the infantry to safety?"

"Actually I was hoping you'd be the decoy," the Major said.

"The what?"

"The decoy. You know, like in duck hunting. You stick your neck out and say quack, and all the men in fancy dress with guns come running after you."

"I have four brothers. I'm familiar with the general idea. But what do I get out of it in return for taking fire for you? Aside from sharing in the credit and so on."

"You get a chance to show up the Corps and its superstitions, for one thing." The Major took a picture out of his attache case and handed it to her. "And you get to fly this."

* * * * *

Adam Randall looked up from his desk in the Cannon Building.

"Yes, Angie, what is it?"

His senior secretary, who was nearly old enough to be his grandmother, and who had in fact been a childhood friend of his grandmother, pursed her lips in disapproval. "Sir, Congressman Elliott is here and insists on seeing you. I told him you were busy this afternoon, but he won't leave."

"Elliott? Elliott of New York? I have no idea what he could possibly want over here. Can't he come back tomorrow?"

"I tried that, sir. He refuses to consider it. He says he must see you tonight. He promised it wouldn't take long, but--" Her silence expressed better than words the degree of trust she reposed in Congressman Elliott's promises.

Randall shook his head. "Okay, fine. But I have plans this afternoon. Make sure he knows that he can have five--five--minutes and no more. Go ahead and send him in."

Ten seconds later the two representatives were shaking hands and Randall was waving his guest to a chair. He offered drinks. Elliott declined. He was the younger of the two by several years, with lightweight good looks instead of Randall's rugged charm. This was only his second term in the House. A few years ago, his husband had gotten out of a tech startup with something in the low nine figures to his credit and had celebrated by buying himself a publishing company and his spouse an excruciatingly expensive seat in Congress. The incumbent, outspent by ten to one, had not contested the seat a second time, and so Elliott got to keep representing a district where he owned a home but spent little time.

"What can I do for you?" Randall wanted to know.

Elliott was carrying a manila envelope, which he presented to his counterpart. "I just had these sent over from Kyle's office. I thought it was important that you see them right away."

Randall opened it, then flinched. Without looking up, he forced himself to keep leafing through the contents.

A picture of him next to one of his staffers in a bar. A picture of him with the same staffer, lip to lip. A picture of him caressing his friend's rear. A picture of them leaving, hand in hand. A picture of them kissing inside his car.

He looked up to see that Elliott was already rising to leave.

"By the way," Elliott said, "I was glad to hear you'll be supporting the Equal Marriage Act when it comes up for a vote to override the President's veto."

"Did you also hear why I would be supporting it?" Randall inquired, letting his gaze drift down to the pictures and then back to Elliott again.

The other congressman smiled maliciously. "Yes, you said that after one imperial presidency, another would be excessive, and that laws which have been duly passed by Congress represent the will of the people and have a right to go into effect even if a president blocks them out of a righteous but misplaced set of priorities. One man cannot hold the rest of the country hostage." Then he was gone.

Randall went through the photos again. There were more. The photographer had tailed them all the way back to his Washington apartment. None of the shots were explicit, all were more than suggestive enough to make a nice cover story for *Democracy Today* any time it felt like embarrassing him and getting him ejected from the ranks of his own party. He put them back in the envelope, locked them in a secure drawer of his desk, and sat back to think.

The Equal Marriage Act had passed both houses by a fair margin, thanks to the Democratic majority in both after the last election. The President had vetoed it immediately, and the majority whips were fighting tooth and nail to get the veto overridden. Their majority didn't extend quite that far. Through some astonishing sleight of hand, they had pulled together a coalition in the Senate to get the necessary votes. But they were still missing two in the House.

Now they only needed one, thanks to Elliott's gift for spying.

Randall noticed that the building was getting quiet. He remembered his appointment, and reluctantly stood up. This one at least he couldn't miss. It wouldn't be fair.

Halfway across the outer office, he came to an abrupt halt. The long-suffering Angie looked up at him, but he ignored her. He bolted back into his private office, took the photos out of the drawer, and slipped them into a backpack.

"Maybe…" he whispered to himself, no longer feeling quite so trapped.

8

Asim carried the box of routers down the steps and placed it in the rear of the Land Rover. Behind him came Junayd with the wireless modems and jailbroken tablets that had enabled the flow of information between an abandoned turn-of-the-century tenement and the rest of the planet. Apart from their private phones and tablets, the core members of the Bahraini underground were now entirely offline. The computers were in another vehicle, an American import, fifty yards away under a rotting lean-to that sagged away from the mud-brick walls of the adjacent structure. There were no boxes of cords or cables. The links between the machines had all been insubstantial.

"Is that all?" he asked.

"Except for the rest of us. We'll leave the leftover lamb and rice for the next occupants. They'll appreciate it. I'll wait here if you go tell him it's time."

Asim nodded and went back up the steps. The rooms of the complex were deserted, except for one. Most of the hackers had left that morning, walking or taking a bus across the causeway to Manama, where they would disappear again into that city's still more expansive slums. Fihr had called in a favor and borrowed a rusting Ford pickup into which he had loaded Shadi. He had friends on the other side who would care for the wounded man while the underground found temporary quarters.

In the single room that had not been stripped yet, the imam knelt on his prayer rug, facing Mecca. His lips moved in the recitation of the basmala. Two of the remaining hackers knelt beside him. In a corner, Faruq al-Uthman strained against the gag that kept him from denouncing them, as he strove to put into body language what he couldn't express in words. Asim waited, but did not join them.

The imam turned his head and opened his eyes. "You are ready?"

"Yes, everything that we need has been removed. There's nothing left here that would tell the police more than they already know."

"Good. You will go with Shihab. He knows the location of our new refuge, and he is experienced in evading pursuit." He nodded in the direction of one of the men who had been praying with him.

"And our resident spy?" Asim wanted to know.

Ra'd bin Mazin walked across the room, sensing instinctively where Faruq had been left. He didn't look in his direction, but tilted his head instead, listening instead of seeing. "You were poorly named," he said. "But the name of your house is appropriate. When we are safe, I will tell your friends that they can find you here. If you suffer in the meantime, reflect that you would have killed two of us and delivered the rest to slow torture, and you would have thought it to be a virtuous act." He beckoned to his fellow supplicant, who came forward and took his arm to guide him down the steps.

The aging station wagon idled in the midst of six lanes of stalled traffic, inconspicuous among the Volkswagens and Maseratis that represented the extremes of vehicle ownership in Bahrain. Shihab leaned back in his seat, relaxed, his fingers tapping the wheel in no apparent rhythm. Asim was more concerned. He was looking around for the police while trying to give the impression that he was staring straight ahead.

"We're not being followed," Shihab said, breaking in on his carefully-timed swivels.

"Can you be sure?"

"Not in this traffic. But if we were, it wouldn't matter at this stage. I have plenty of time left to lose them."

"What if they have a helicopter?"

"Then we run."

"That's reassuring."

"After we destroy the computers."

"Great." Asim gave up his peering from side to side and stared straight ahead. "Can I ask you something?"

"Go right ahead."

"You're Shia, aren't you?"

"Yes; did the imam tell you?"

"No, I just thought you might be. From your point of view--theologically speaking--how do you feel about the imam's arguments? How do they fit in with your beliefs? Sorry if I'm prying," he added.

Shihab looked thoughtful. "It's a fair question. Well. To begin, Ra'd bin Mazin has made the case, from a Sunni perspective, that the Prophet has no successor to his authority. However, as Shia, we of course hold that the Prophet did--and does--have divinely appointed successors. The twelve imams. Authority still rests with the Twelfth Imam, the Mahdi--but the Mahdi is in occultation and has not appointed a deputy. Therefore, there is no legitimate source of divine authority on earth, either in religion or government. A different argument, but the same conclusion, you see."

"And our imam is well aware of this alternate argument?"

"Naturally. He helped me prepare it for release in Iranian and Iraqi channels, as well as some of the local ones."

"What about the hadiths, though?"

"Shia traditions reject the hadiths enjoining obedience to authority that are found in Sunni collections, you know.

Beyond that, we have a different view of hadith. No hadith can be infallible. If a hadith contradicts the Word of God, it must be unreliable. It is clear from the Quran that authority rests only with God and those to whom he has specifically granted it. If a hadith says otherwise, that hadith is untrustworthy."

Asim thought about this for a moment. "Isn't that line of reasoning ijtihad?"

"Yes, I suppose it is."

"I thought the doors of ijtihad were closed."

This time it was Shihab's turn to think. "Maybe not," he admitted. "In any case, the hadiths do not uniformly favor human rulers. Do you remember the one that more or less forms one of the themes of this campaign?"

"'He replied, "The office of a chief is necessary, for people must have chiefs, but the chiefs will go to Hell."'"

"That's it. Not an endorsement, but an acknowledgment of reality and of the impossibility of any human authority substituting for God's." Shihab pulled his phone out of his pocket, feeling it tremble in his hand. The undertone of its buzzing became audible for an instant before fading back into the traffic noise.

"It's time."

Just then the driver behind them pressed angrily on his horn. The jam was breaking up and they were drawn forward into the city.

* * * * *

In a server farm at an unknown location, an electronic clock tripped a digital switch and the scripts the hackers had spent days writing were executed. The imam's essays were published and republished, hyperlinked across Facebook and Twitter and Instagram and a dozen other services. Notifications landed in the inboxes of students and scholars and workers and journalists. The messages were tailored to each region, posted on the sites most likely to be visited by locals, and translated into the local dialect or language. In ten minutes, the Islamic world was awash in a discussion of anarchism where no such conversation had existed before. Imams preparing evening sermons received the news at the same moment that rioters in the streets did.

* * * * *

"The states which rule us have declared that they are Islamic, yet this is impossible. A state considers itself, first and foremost, to be a real entity, not merely an idea that is held in common by many. It holds that it is superior to individual men, as it embodies the combined authority of all men within its rule. It is immortal, for it endures regardless of whether its rulers live or die. It establishes laws and sets standards of behavior, and punishes those who contravene them. It issues its commands through mortals who speak its wishes, not their own. In what way is the state not an idol? In what way is it not an object which is deferred to in ignorance? In what way is it not a partner with God? But we say, 'Praise be to God Who begets no son and has no partner in His dominion: nor needs He any to protect Him from humiliation.' Therefore it was revealed to the Prophet, 'Invent not similitudes for God: for God knoweth and ye know not.' 'Associate not any thing in worship with Me.' 'And the places of worship are for God alone: so invoke not anyone along with God.' If we implore the state for justice or aid or protection, we implore that which is not God, which is forbidden to us. 'Shall I take for my protector any other than God, the maker of the heavens and the earth?' If we take that which we ourselves have created to be our protector, we are indeed fools. 'Those ye call upon besides Him are unable to help you and indeed to help themselves.' 'And God will judge with justice and truth: but those whom men invoke besides Him will not be in a position to judge at all.' 'The deities they used to invoke aforetime will leave them in the lurch and they will perceive *that they have no way of escape.' 'Those on whom besides God ye call cannot create even a fly if they all met together for the purpose!' Can the state call back the dead from death? Can it reshape heaven and earth in its might? Can it recreate man from a drop of blood? Can it prove itself as mighty as God? It cannot. It is unworthy of our obedience, and we are unworthy of God if we obey it."*

* * * * *

"The state is not a partner with God," the Grand Imam of Al-Azhar declared from his minbar. "The state has never claimed to be a partner with God. It is an expression of the will of the community, organized to better our lot. If it is immortal, it is because the community of believers is immortal. It is strong because we are strong to protect each other, to benefit one another and build together that which we could not construct alone." A stirring in the congregation became apparent. With curfews in place and government troops roaming the streets of Cairo, the protective, beneficent nature of the state was not obvious to most worshipers, some of whom were bloodied and burned from the protests earlier that day. A new general had seated himself in the presidential palace and the mood of the country was surly.

"Moreover," the Grand Imam continued, "the Prophet enjoined obedience upon us. "'A Muslim has to listen to and obey the order of his ruler whether he likes it or not.'"

"'As long as his orders involve not one in disobedience to God!'" a voice shouted out from the back of the hall. The Grand Imam gasped. For an instant he tottered on his platform. It was unheard-of for the senior scholar of all Sunni Islam to be corrected publicly in his own mosque. The correction was all the more embarrassing because he had deliberately failed to quote the last portion of that hadith.

"The very nature of our faith," he went on, trying to shout down the audible murmurs of dissent in the crowd, "is submission. Submission to the will of God! How can we submit to God's will if our spirits are rebellious, if we seek every possible excuse to rise up against those who try to maintain order in our society so that we may live in peace? We are not living in submission to God if we demand that institutions which have served us well be destroyed altogether, that we might live without any to enforce the laws that He has ordained!"

All across the prayer hall, worshipers were holding up their Qurans and waving them. Waving them before his eyes to remind him that what he declared to be the truth was not in the Book.

* * * * *

"'Is it not to God that sincere devotion is due? But those who take for protectors other than God say: "We only serve them in order that they may bring us nearer to God." Truly God will judge between them in that wherein they differ!' There is no distinction between those who serve a false god, claiming it to be a servant of the true, and those who submit themselves to the self-constituted authority of a so-called Islamic state and its servants, claiming it to be ordained by God to bring them closer to Him. At times God has bestowed authority upon one of his servants, but not one of these men now sits at the head of any government which claims to be Islamic. And a man, who is mortal and the creation of God Himself, is a very different thing than a state, which has no term to its life and is the creation of man. 'Do they indeed ascribe to Him as partners things that can create nothing but are themselves created?' The state, it is argued, benefits man. It provides us with security, employment, direction. What are these benefits in comparison with the rewards

God will bestow upon true believers? Expediency is not a sufficient defense for submission to the state rather than to God."

* * * * *

In Mosul an execution squad of the Islamic State in Iraq and the Levant was spontaneously attacked by a crowd which had gathered to witness a beheading. The soldiers, taken by surprise, had no time to train their weapons on it. The mob, emboldened by its success, stormed a number of local government buildings, capturing several. Rioters tore down and burned the flags and other emblems of the ISIL shadow government, as well as those that had previously denoted the Kurdish regional administration. Propaganda posters and billboards were torn down or spray-painted over with large quotes from the Quran, and with the phrase that was rapidly becoming the slogan of the Arab Spring 2.0: "The chiefs will go to hell." Al Jazeera reported that civilian attacks on ISIL forces across Iraq had reached an all-time high. Several videos of such attacks surfaced on Youtube, with the protestors screaming "Blasphemers! Blasphemers!" at the soldiers. They were removed almost at once for showing violence and bloodshed, but half a dozen users immediately reposted them, and Google's engineers were drawn into a losing battle of their own to prevent the information from spreading.

* * * * *

A professor at the University of Bahrain looked up at a poster on the wall of his laboratory. It was a copy of an old Associated Press photo taken during the first Arab Spring. The photo showed an Egyptian army helicopter, rockets and missiles suspended from its belly, hovering above a lighted boulevard in Cairo. The night sky was dark in the background, the buildings dim in comparison with the golden lights that shone in the street. Here and there the gold was speckled with bright white where protestors held up reflective placards or were using their cameras. They were holding up other things, too. Threads of light, green and purple, joined the helicopter to the ground. Hundreds of them. A pyramid of spiderwebs. The crowd had trained laser pointers on the machine in an attempt to dazzle the pilots and force them away from the protest, but their improvised weapons were not strong enough to burn through its metal skin.

The professor turned away from the photo, back to his work, and slid his protective goggles down over his eyes.

* * * * *

"We have tried revolution before, and we failed. Perhaps it was best that we failed. We demanded neither faith nor obedience to God, but democracy. What good would democracy do us? How would it affect the workings of the perpetual, indifferent state if its nominal head was appointed by a vote rather than by an accident of descent? There is only one way in which it would have altered the situation. It would have made each of us who voted complicit in the promotion of idolatry and deceit, and we should have drawn down the anger of God upon those we appointed over us. 'Verily God loveth not any that is a traitor to faith or shows ingratitude.' 'God forgiveth not that partners should be set up with Him.' Therefore it was to our benefit that we should not be the ones to set up partners with God.

"Man is given free choice by God. God permits him to do well or sin as he chooses, and will reward or punish him accordingly. He forbids us to act on His behalf. 'And those who take as protectors others besides Him, God doth watch over them; and thou are not the disposer of their affairs.' 'If any turn away from God, it will be the task of God to call them to account.' He enjoins us instead to be faithful to that which we know as individuals. 'Therefore expound openly what thou art commanded and turn away from those who join

false gods with God.' We are not to support unbelievers, nor are we to fight them out of a conviction of our own righteousness. We are not to support the state, nor are we to fight it out of a conviction of our own righteousness. We are to turn away from it and go our own way, the way that God has commanded us to go, without reference to its desires or demands, for it is false and powerless."

* * * * *

The pattern of violence in the streets of Bahrain shifted. At first the changes were subtle. Then they were too striking to ignore. The protestors, who had come out by the tens of thousands, were no longer throwing stones, overturning cars, hurling Molotov cocktails or torching shops. Instead, they stood and watched the armored soldiers encircle them. They did not move. They waited, contempt in their eyes. If they chose to cross a street, they did so en masse. If they chose to advance, they walked forward, and the weight of their bodies against the shields forced the police back. Even when they were beaten, even when they were gassed, they ignored it and kept moving. On previous occasions, they had fenced with the police. Their actions had shown respect for an equal adversary with whom balance had to be maintained. Now that respect was gone. They no longer fenced, they pushed on as if the weapon in their adversary's hand had no power to harm them. They spread their rugs in the streets and the squares and prayed facing Mecca, while the police danced in agony on the sidelines, trapped between their outrage at being defied and their sure knowledge that attacking protestors at prayer would damn them as unjust brutes forever in the sight of every good Muslim around the world.

They killed where they could, but they could not kill all of Bahrain. They could beat the migrant workers who were ceasing to work, but they could not force them to their tools again, or stop the networks that had suddenly sprung up to feed the workers when the companies for whom they slaved had tried to starve them into submission.

* * * * *

Men in khaki uniforms and blue uniforms left the conference room in the Al-Qudaibiya Palace. The Prime Minister, His Majesty's uncle, remained behind, but the King waved him out of the room. He waited, considering the opinions of his cabinet, his soldiers, the foreign soldiers whose wishes he would be wise to consult--and his own inclinations. But, he realized, he had already decided. To say yes was an easier course than to say no, and would stand a better chance of success.

He nodded to an aide hovering at the far door, then passed out of the larger room into a private office. Seating himself, he looked down at the telephone and waited for his call across the desert to go through.

9

Inside the fuselage of the C-160, the sound of the propellers diminished sharply and the aircraft's nose pitched down. The Major put away the latest Dirk Pitt novel and looked up at his team. The three Marines were nodding against each other, their jackets zipped up all the way, trying to stay awake but having little reason to in the chill and noisy atmosphere of the cargo hold. By contrast, Amanda Price was sitting bolt upright with one ungloved hand resting on the side of the hull. She was frowning. It was clear from the expression on her face that she did not trust the pilots to put the airplane on the ground correctly, and that she would much rather be flying it herself. That she could have done so the Major didn't doubt. But the pilots were supposed to be ignoring the team's existence, and that would become difficult if one of its members walked into the cockpit and demanded the controls. He caught her eye and shook his head at her. She frowned, but stayed in her seat. When the nose-down angle didn't change and the nosewheel hit the runway before the main gear, she gave him a disparaging look.

"Welcome to Herat," the Major said.

The process of getting that far had been long and tedious, although not difficult. From Washington the five of them had flown to London, then from London to Istanbul, then from Istanbul to Dubai. While they waited in the gleaming modern terminal with their carryons, the Major had plunged into a coffee shop with a bald-headed, plainly dressed man who had former special forces written all over him. The consultation over, he had shepherded them out to the curb, where a black SUV was now waiting for them.

"A little conspicuous, isn't it?" Price had remarked.

"It's expected in this line of work," the Major said, climbing into the front seat next to the driver. "To not use it might expose us to comment on the platform. Are we all in? Good."

The SUV had driven an hour south into the desert and slipped through a back gate, also guarded by contractors in civilian garb, into Al Dhafra Air Base. A considerable expansion of the base's facilities was under way on the American side. The few remaining French airmen that they passed looked sulky. Then the vehicle stopped in front of an unmarked shed and the Major hurried them into the building.

"Sir, are we allowed to be here?" Sergeant Carl Brassey wanted to know.

"Technically, no," the Major said, making himself comfortable in a beaten-up chair and taking his book out again. "If any of you have friends in the Air Force, I recommend a good disguise in the strongest possible terms." The closer they got to Iran, the more facetious he became. "But all of this part of the base is controlled by a private firm, some of whose members I trained and know well. They're highly paid to ignore everything that goes on around them, lest they see something that's actionable back home. That means they won't see us, and any favors I call in will go unnoticed except by the grantees."

"He means there's honor among thieves," Price said cynically.

It was late afternoon when the same bald man who had met them at the airport popped his head through the door and nodded at the Major. They had grabbed their packs and followed him between the rows of plastic huts to a spot where a forklift loaded with pallets of bottled water was waiting on the tarmac. A Transall C-160, obtained from a bankrupt Indonesian airline, was warming up its engines not far away.

"Match your pace to that of the forklift," the Major instructed them. "If anyone does notice you, they probably won't think anything of it, but with that thing in the way, they can't be sure, either."

He led them up the loading ramp and into the forward section of the plane. It was already loaded and the pallets had been secured. The Major strapped them all into some very uncomfortable folding seats with no leg room. No stewardess came through to check his work; no pilot announced their departure over the cabin intercom. The aircraft merely revved up its turbines and pointed its nose skyward and came down six hours later in Herat, diving in at a steep angle to reduce the chances of a surface-to-air missile attack.

The pilots shut down the engines. The Marines could hear them chatting in the cockpit. One of them came down and opened the forward door, letting in a new rush of cold air. He exchanged words with someone on the ground, then called up to his counterpart, who clattered down the ladder to join him. They both left the aircraft. The sound of their boots scuffing the tarmac died away.

"That was easy," the Major said.

"Major Martin?" He turned in the direction of the voice. A man in a leather jacket that bulged under both arms was leaning in through the door of the aircraft.

"Present."

"I'm Jennings. This way, please, and don't waste time."

"You heard the man. Time to move," the Major ordered. The Marines unstrapped themselves, stretched, and heaved themselves down out of the aircraft onto the ground.

"So this is Afghanistan," Price observed, looking around.

"Been here before," Lance Corporal Ramirez said.

"Never been here. It looks boring."

"Where are we, anyway?"

"Herat International. Unless they decided to divert to Shindand at the last minute."

"No, this is Herat. Look at the signs."

"Get in here!" the man who had ushered them off the airplane barked. He was clearly irritated. Next to him, the Major stood framed in the lighted doorway of a concrete building.

"Pick out a uniform to fit you," the Major instructed. He wasn't at all ruffled by the hostility of their reception. In fact, he was quite cheerful. "Then add it to your gear and choose your weapons from that rack over there. Consistency in your choice of rifles, please."

All four members of the team knew what was coming, but the piles of worn, odd-looking uniforms laid out on two tables in the middle of the building intimidated them anyway. They made their selections with a minimum of joking.

"Sir, what should we be carrying to go with these?" Sergeant Brassey asked from in front of the rifle rack.

The Major turned away from what appeared to be a heated discussion with Jennings. "Use the Heckler & Koch ones."

"But they look beat to hell, sir!"

"Don't worry, they work fine. No more ammunition than each of you can easily carry for your own weapons."

"Do I need a rifle?" Price wanted to know.

"Yes, for now you'd better take one. You can ditch it later."

Jennings stomped off in a huff.

"Is he a risk, sir?" Powers asked.

"No, he understands my motives. But he thinks I'm a fool anyway." Major Martin shrugged. "Not his concern. He's done his part and we'll be gone in five minutes. Pad the weapons and put them in a separate bag. Each of you take one of these water bottles."

It was still dark outside when they left the building by a door at the far end. It opened outside the secure perimeter of the airfield and sealed itself electronically as it closed. Behind them, an Air Force KC-135 came thundering down into Herat. Operational tempos in Afghanistan had been stepped up a great deal in the past year or so. But the parking lot was deserted except for a dusty Toyota not far off. A dim figure leaned against the hood, the ember of a cigarette glowing where its mouth might have been.

The Major stepped forward and addressed it. The cigarette blinked out.

"This is Javed," the Major said in a low voice to his team. "He will be our guide into Iran."

Javed was a middle-aged man whose expression was both sad and peaceful, as if he had sorrowed and come to terms with it. He held open the doors for them and assisted them in loading their bags into the trunk.

"A larger vehicle would have been conspicuous?" Price needled the Major.

"A larger vehicle would have been conspicuous," the Major agreed.

"What are we supposed to be, anyway?"

"Just another border taxi. You'll find dozens of them plying this route until the Masshad-Herat rail line is completed. If it's ever completed now."

The sun came up in the rear window of the taxi as it made its way out of Herat, casting a faint light over the city. In the morning, it didn't look so plain. The few patches of green were darker. The minute differences between one shade of brown and another were more apparent. New buildings thrown up out of bricks and concrete harmonized with ancient ruins of stone and mortar, none of them tall, all of them scattered widely over the flat plains. In a sparsely-used graveyard, a tiny mosque of white stone and blue glass sparkled like an ornament fallen from a satrap's hand.

Brassey, who was seated on the extreme left inside the car, twisted his broad shoulders and leaned forward to speak to the driver. "Excuse me, sir, but where does this road take us?" Beside him, Ramirez was trying to unfold a map without putting an elbow through the face of one of his fellow passengers.

"To Islam Qala," Javed replied. "In Afghanistan it is called Islam Qala. When the border is crossed, it is called Taybad."

"It lies on both sides of the border? Are we going to try to cross through the middle of a town?"

"Not even close," the Major put in. "We'll be crossing a long way north of there. Don't look for the exact location on that map, you won't find it and I couldn't tell you what it's called, I don't know myself." He chuckled. A very small smile touched Javed's lips in response.

Four hours later, a sign declared that they were approaching Islam Qala and the border checkpoints. Javed spun the wheel to the right and took a side road, one which was in much poorer condition than the highway he'd been following.

"Trade from Iran does not come along this route," he explained. "The government in Tehran has no reason to maintain the road, and the government in Kabul has no incentive to improve it."

Ahead of them, to the north, a range of low mountains was visible, a slightly more defined form of haze in a hazy sky. It stretched away sporadically on either hand.

"The mountains are our highway," the Major said.

"Are we back in mountain warfare school, sir?" Powers asked. The Major chuckled again. He was in excellent spirits.

The taxi passed through the village of Kohsan, where Javed paused to refuel it, as well as to refill their water bottles, which they had half emptied on the trip from Herat.

"Drink sparingly," the Major advised them. "You'll need that water this afternoon."

A few paces away, Javed was talking to a heavily bearded, scowling headman, who was gesticulating with energy and determination. He calmed the man down to some extent and came back over to the vehicle.

"We are being blackmailed," he said quietly to the Major. All four pairs of ears in the rear seat pricked up. "Ali Patik suspects my motives and the neatness of your personal appearance." The Major sniffed at that. "He threatens to report us to the Afghani military outpost at Islam Qala."

"And if he did?" the Major wanted to know. "Could they do anything about us?"

"It is possible," Javed admitted. "They have helicopters there. Old Russian machines, and they are starved even for Iranian copies of spare parts, but if only one got airborne…"

"It could still trace us," the Major said. "There are a limited number of roads here that we could take. How much does he want?"

"He asks for five hundred dollars."

The Major produced a fold of bills from his sleeve. "Give him a thousand."

Javed conveyed the money to Ali Patik, who thereupon became effusive in his protestations of friendship and offers of assistance.

"But sir--" Sergeant Brassey protested. "What if he turns around and sells us out anyway?"

"He won't," the Major said. "You've deployed to Afghanistan before. You know what hard currency is worth in this country. I agree that he'd sell us out if he thought there was a profit in it, but there isn't one. The army wouldn't pay him a reward for informing them on the movements of

American military personnel, and they might go so far as to confiscate his bribe. He could only lose by talking. Hence he'll keep his mouth shut."

"Is a thousand enough?" Price asked.

"Plenty."

"I still think Javed should arrange for him to be shot," Brassey said.

"Who can tell me what was the first American weapon to land in this country when the war began?" the Major inquired.

"A Tomahawk missile," Brassey suggested.

"A Paveway bomb," Powers offered.

"Wrong. It was a flight of KC-135 tankers out of Grand Forks Air Force Base loaded to the gills with extra fuel and pallets of cash. That's what revitalized the Northern Alliance forces before any of our advisors parachuted in."

Javed slid back into the driver's seat.

"He loves you like a brother," he said to the Major, "and calls down the blessings of God upon you and your companions."

"Sufficient to the day is the evil thereof," the Major answered. "Ready?"

The road began to climb. The Marines in the back took turns twisting around to see the dusty plains of Herat sliding away behind them. The mountains, visible in the distance, jumped closer. As near as the Major could tell, the route they were taking was trending away from the Iranian border and back into the wilder parts of Afghanistan.

"These mountains. Do they have a name?" Price said, leaning forward in her seat. Her voice broke the relative silence that had enveloped the occupants of the car.

"They are called the Selseleh-ye Safid Kuh," Javed replied. "They are one branch of the Hindu Kush range, the largest in this part of the country."

The scattering of fields around Kohsan had disappeared long before. Except for the unpaved road beneath the Toyota's wheels, and an occasional house perched on a slope, the little expedition was alone as Alexander's legions had been. One much-abused Soviet-era truck squeezed past them, and a little farther on they had to make way for two donkeys and a herdsman. Then the track was empty again.

"This isn't how I pictured it," Price remarked. Her conversational abilities, like the Major's good humor, were emerging in proximity to isolation and danger, which tended to rub the Marines the wrong way. They had been trained to be quiet when threatened. "No militants waving plundered rifles, no land mines, no roadside bombs, no Erik Prince speeding along in an armored car. I feel more insecure every time I go into Washington."

"Yeah, well, this part of the country doesn't have anyone in it," Ramirez said.

"Herat had plenty of people in it, and that looked just fine to me too."

"The State Department exaggerates," the Major said. "As do the journalists employed by *Esquire* and the *New York Times*. Afghanistan is far from being the zone of constant danger it's portrayed as--provided you apply common sense."

"And Herat is a quiet province," Javed added. He waved his hand, taking in the barren surroundings. "You cannot live here easily, you cannot grow poppies here, and the terrain is so severe that the smugglers prefer to operate in the south of the country, where there are deserts less difficult to traverse than these mountains." A second later, he applied the brakes and worked the complaining car around a two-hundred-and-eighty-degree turn, underlining the point.

"It's flattening out again, though," Price noted.

"We've come out the other side, onto the declining northern slope of the Safid Kuh." The Major looked at Javed for confirmation, receiving a nod in response. "But we're going back into them soon."

"By going through them?"

"These roads were laid out by villagers for their convenience, not by engineers to aid in cross-border transactions of a dubious nature."

"And there's another village up ahead."

"Khvab Gani," Javed said. "Many of the roads come together here." Roads, and it was apparent from their higher elevation that a twisted, dried-up stream had also passed through the village at some remote historical point.

"We've been longer in getting here from Kohsan than it took us to come from Herat to the border."

"We still have some distance to go," the Major said. "Enjoy the rest while you can."

On the other side of Khvab Gani the villages became more frequent, collecting in little valleys or along the course of a half-hidden source of water. Narrow strips of field lined both slopes of the regular folds in the earth, tended by farmers in little houses standing apart from each other in their own grounds. Once they crossed a ditch that might have been a substantial river in the spring. Green trees, brilliant against the unrelieved tan of the background, clustered in the surrounding gullies and the tortuous bends of the streambed. Then the houses and fields grew fewer again, and the road, which had been leading away from the mountains, swung about. Now it was running parallel to them, and another spur of the Safid Kuh could be seen licking down across their path. The car climbed again as an outcrop of weathered hills rose on their right. The hills must have been able to trap rare moisture, because there was a scattering of houses at their base and a scattering of trees along their sides.

"Siah Kamarak." Javed was becoming increasingly wary as they advanced. The Major assumed it was because they were nearing their destination.

At the next village he swung the Toyota sharply to the left, into the heart of the hills. The road squiggled and curved along the banks of another dessicated stream. Then it began to jackknife every half a mile or so. Javed eased the car through the turns and pushed it on as quickly as he could in the straighter sections. There were no more villages here, only farmhouses and huts standing alone. The earth was dry and the sun was hot, and the Marines started to wonder if this expedition was really a good idea.

They were still thinking about it when the road ended and Javed steered the car off the track and behind a clump of twisted shrubs that would shield it from the view of any nearby farmer.

"We have arrived," the Major said.

"When the road ends, the journey begins," Price responded. The Marines were looking confused, but they piled out of the vehicle anyway, swearing as the cramps in their limbs began to wear off. "Where are we?"

"As close as I can tell, in the vicinity of a place called Nang Adad. Go on, pull your packs out of the trunk. We have a nine-mile hike ahead of us as the crow flies."

"Nine miles? Sir, that's nothing!" Brassey declared. He looked happy for the first time since leaving Herat.

"I said as the crow flies, Sergeant. No one knows how long it will be as the scorpion crawls on its belly."

* * * * *

If God has a sick sense of humor, as certain scholars have suggested, He was certainly exercising it when He made the westernmost corner of Afghanistan. Every geographic and geologic feature of the place screamed that it had once been wet. Very wet. So wet that the earth itself had softened and rippled and flowed together and retained the ripples after it hardened again. These ripples had later been divided into chains of hills by sudden additional rushes of water that had carved elaborate drainage patterns and deltas through them, patterns resembling the flowery branches of tropical corals. There were reminders of water's existence, and evidence of its previous abundance, on every side. The only thing that was missing was the water.

The rescue party might have found some if they had gone along the south face of the ridge, but Javed quashed that idea. There were too many tiny villages to the south where someone might spot them or try to stop them. Instead, he led them to the north again, where the hills were a trifle lower and altogether unpopulated due to the lack of any watercourse, seasonal or otherwise. That also meant the trails they followed were less well-defined and that there was no convenient water-worn valley pointing west. They scrambled up the hills on all fours and slid down them on the heels of their boots, fighting the olive drab duffel bags the whole way and sipping their water cautiously. As if that were not difficult enough, the Major had also made each of them throw a light robe over their clothes, to make them less noticeable among any shepherds who might be roaming the Safid Kuh.

He had said nine miles. Any of them could have walked that distance on level ground in less than four hours, probably in less than three. By the time the sun went down, they had covered a little more than five of those miles. Distance measurements on the Northwest Frontier never were reliable.

"Rest," the Major ordered. "It will be harder work traveling by night in these hills. And we have to be across the river long before first light."

"River?" Powers whispered to Ramirez. "What river?"

* * * * *

Amanda Price looked up at the stars. Her eyes had adjusted fully to the darkness in the past two hours. She could trace the moving speck of a satellite across the blue-black background as it sparkled with reflected light and occluded other, vaster, objects at a greater distance. It wasn't the satellite she needed, which was invisible at a range three times the diameter of the earth, but it was reassuring to know that there were other metal shells up there, ready to be called on if needed. Although that one was so low that it was probably an American or Russian reconnaissance bird. And that was pointless and less reassuring.

She pulled an Iridium phone out of her pocket and extended the antenna, which locked on to the phone's parent satellite at once. Calls from central Asia presented no problem to a network which had been expanding its coverage of the area in anticipation of an upcoming surge in Pentagon and State Department contracts. Covering the dim glow of the screen with one hand, as much to protect her own vision as to hide it from the sight of her teammates, Price began typing on the phone's keypad. She paused several times, choosing her letters carefully for the sake of brevity. When she was done, she tucked the phone away under her robe for the moment.

Five minutes later, it vibrated against her side. She pulled it out and read the reply from halfway around the world. It was satisfactory.

* * * * *

"Keep moving," the Major said, pulling Lance Corporal Ramirez out of a ditch. The land had begun to change again. The rippled slabs of sandstone and sediment, a throwback to an earlier, more Hyperborean age, had given way to low hills and stretches of plain cut through with branching gullies. Water had been at work in the cold desert, and it must have still lurked somewhere beneath the surface. The Marines were stumbling across more plants. The hills they were crawling through actually bore vegetation of a sort. It was stunted, and it was inedible and useless, but it spoke to the presence of moisture.

"A mile and a half to go." The Major's own breath was ragged and came out in a cloud against the shadows. He drank from his water bottle and sloshed the remaining contents around in it. Not much left.

More level, or at least gently sloping, ground. More streambeds, dry, barren, and twisted like the path a worm or a virus might take. The complaint of a goat farther off. Javed's whispered words to the effect that there were still one or two small crofts in the area and they must continue to be cautious.

Then the land dropped away into a mighty gorge and below them, in the moonlight, they could see water flowing at last between the walls of stone.

"The Harirud," the Major said. Javed made no remark. For several minutes he leaned forward, peering at the opposite bank of the river, looking for any trace of light or movement. At last he drew a sigh.

"It seems safe," he replied. "We will chance it."

"Keep your weapons close," the Major warned his team. "Sidearms only, but be ready to fight if challenged."

They slid down the walls of the gorge. Just south of where they had come out, the drop was sheer and unscaleable, but Javed had brought them out at a point where a flood or floods had washed them a clear path in previous decades or centuries or millennia.

"It's empty," Powers said, his voice low. The water ran muddy over the usual bed of rounded stones, except that broad stretches of the bed were uncovered and dusty on either side of the actual stream.

"It goes north and loses itself in the Karakum Desert," the Major said. "Not twenty years ago it dried up completely. Keep your weapons above the water." Javed, who was hauling the rifles, was already halfway across the diminished river. At no point did it flow above his waist.

They stumbled exposed across acres of smooth, polished rocks on the opposite side of the stream. It made the Marines very uncomfortable to have no cover. Price, on the other hand, nearly swaggered across, giving the appearance of being in no hurry at all, and the Major ran lightly up the banks before turning and reaching down to help his men. They dug the toes of their boots into soil that crumbled and ran out in rivulets beneath them, scrambling to gain two feet for each foot they lost, clinging to handfuls of dirt and dried roots. At the top, Javed waited for them, looking back with a plaintive expression.

"Welcome to Iran," the Major said.

"Just like that?" Sergeant Brassey's tone expressed surprise.

"You expected there to be a party of Revolutionary Guards waiting for us?" Price was being sarcastic again.

"Well given that they have hostile neighbors and all--"

"You expected better border security?" The Major shook his head. "You couldn't bring an armored force or a convoy through here, and that's what the Iranians would expect from the US Army. The occasional smuggler or shepherd who crosses over to run a pound of explosives or see a family member isn't a concern of theirs. They've no reason to secure this part of their borders, not when the area around Zaranj is getting worse on a weekly basis."

"How much farther do we have to go, sir?" Ramirez asked.

"Less than a mile. The more distance we put between ourselves and the border, the safer we are. Let's move."

Javed rose without a word and headed off into the darkness again. They followed. He took a route between the hills, along yet another runoff channel. Brassey stole a look at his pocket compass. Now they were heading southwest, albeit in a roundabout fashion, following the curves of the land. But it did make for easier going. Once they crossed a stream that was actually moist, where the banks were covered in trees and shrubs. Fresh greenery, not dried stuff. They slid out of it covered in mud. One more rank of hills, then another tortuous climb up a contorted gully.

The Major signaled them to stop. He held a whispered conversation with Javed in the vanguard. Their guide slipped away and ran ahead. Two minutes later, the Marines heard him calling to them.

They scrambled up the last stretch of dirt and found themselves on the edge of a paved road. Javed was standing next to another man who looked like his brother beside an old but well-maintained van.

"Quickly!" Javed urged them, holding open the rear doors. "Inside!"

Ten seconds later he shut them in and ran around to the passenger side of the cab. His compatriot was already at the wheel and starting the engine, having closed the hood and thrown away the dirty rags he had been tinkering with to give the appearance of an accident. The van swung out of the narrow curve on which it had been parked. Its nose pointed south. The road twisted and doubled at first, but then it turned west and became a narrow track laid out perfectly straight for mile after mile. The driver gunned the engine.

Half an hour later there were lights ahead.

"Torbat Jam," the Major clarified. "We'll be in Masshad before morning. From here on, as long as we use common sense, we'll be safe until we make the rescue. So enjoy the peace and quiet while you can."

* * * * *

Summer is a season of pilgrimage in Masshad. The city is home to the tombs of two of Iran's greatest poets, as well as to that of the Eighth Imam, Ali al-Ridha, famed for his medical knowledge and his rivalry with Haroun al-Rashid, Caliph of Baghdad. His mausoleum rests beneath a golden dome at the center of the largest mosque in the world, visited daily by tens of thousands of worshipers and tourists. The five Americans disappeared in the crowds. It would take Javed a couple of days, the Major said, to make the rest of the arrangements for their journey. So they went sightseeing.

In one of the newer parts of the city, Price was surprised to see Javed himself standing on a sidewalk and staring across the street at a new building that was under construction. A school, she gathered from the signs posted in front of the site and a glance at her phrasebook. Nothing odd about that. Then why was Javed staring at it so intently?

On impulse, she crossed the street and asked him straight out, keeping her voice down to avoid attracting attention.

The guide stared back at her. His face was wet, she realized. He'd been crying.

"I apologize," she said. "Perhaps I shouldn't have--"

"No." He stopped her attempt to withdraw. "It is not an improper question, though I must be more careful. You have reminded me of what I forgot, and I am grateful to you. And since we will be traveling together later, the two of us alone, it is perhaps wise that you should know." He sighed. "The land that building sits on was, until a few years ago, a cemetery."

"That's a very odd use for it. Especially given how much the Iranian government supports religious facilities."

"Ah, but this school will be a religious facility when completed. And the one it replaced was one that the government hates. It was the cemetery of my people. I am a Bahai."

"I must apologize again. I assumed you were Muslim."

"No, I am not. Since the founding of our faith, the government of Iran has persecuted us, under the shahs as under the ayatollahs. We acknowledge that there is no God but God. We acknowledge that Mohammad is the messenger of God. But we also testify that no messenger of God is His final messenger, or bears His final word. In each era there is a messenger who brings the revelation of God as most fitted for the people of that time to understand. For this reason, the orthodox scholars have hated us, and the state has found us to be convenient scapegoats, a ready distraction to divert the public mind from more serious issues."

"And that's why you're helping Major Martin."

"To retaliate against the nation that has persecuted me and my brothers and sisters? Yes--and no. It is forbidden for us to do violence to another. But it is not an act of retaliation I undertake. It is one of mercy. The Major does not wish to hurt or kill; he wishes to prevent killing. In this manner I help him to show that oppression may be countered with freedom, and murder with life."

"That's a better way of getting your point across than digging up people's grandparents."

"My grandparents." Javed blinked once more. "First in Shiraz and Yazd, now here. This is the third cemetery to be destroyed with official sanction in recent years. But I will not claim dry bones from them. Instead I will save lives they would take. It is so easy to kill and destroy, so difficult to give life."

There was genuine sympathy in his face as he looked at her.

10

     A chauffeured Mercedes pulled away from the villa of the Minister of Foreign Affairs. A police chase car followed it. None of the cars' occupants took note of a dirty, dark-skinned man running a lawnmower over the grass at the far end of the lawn, its blades ruthlessly slicing away the grass that absorbed so much of the small nation's precious water supply, the most expensive in the world.

     The noise made by the spinning blades was the only consistent sound inside the villa as the Minister's maid moved from room to room. She was as silent as she was efficient. The fading bruises on her face and arms, courtesy of the Minister's wife and children, were all too typical of a domestic servant in Bahrain to have attracted notice if she had walked out into the street. So were her dreams of the Ganges Delta, as green and lush as the Prophet had described Paradise. So was her despair. Her passport lay in a safe at the offices of the agency that had hired her, and the agency had yet to pay her a single dinar. Again, she was like every other servant in Bahrain: a foreigner imported to do the dirty work and legalistically trapped there on arrival. The Minister and the government paid for her; that is to say, they transferred to the employment agency a portion of the taxes they forced out of the rest of the population, which the agents salted away in Switzerland with the connivance of the officials, to whom they were closely related. But it never would have occurred to anyone to pay her, and if the subject had been raised, they would have become very angry.

She looked around the corner into the Minister's office. The door stood wide open. The Al Khalifa were confident of their domestic security and of the submission of all those who surrounded them. Now she was going to destroy that security. She uttered a prayer under her breath and stepped boldly into the room.

The office could have housed any politician from anywhere in the world without making him feel lost or disoriented. Rich carpets on the floor, a massive polished desk in the center, armchairs for distinguished visitors, paintings on the walls--the usual fittings of a fish tank for the elite. The maid was used to polishing the wood and dusting the imported limited edition bronzes by third-rate Western artists, and went straight past them all to an elaborate calligraphic work that hung just to the right of the desk. It was not heavy. As she lifted it down from the wall, she couldn't help but notice the telltale smoothness of the surface, its uniform glossiness. It was a reproduction, not an original. Behind the simple frame, the canvas was stretched tight over wooden spreaders an inch deep. More than enough room, she decided.

From one of the pockets of her apron she produced a short, thick wire with a little cylinder about an inch in diameter attached to one end. The face of the cylinder was pierced with holes, and was attached on one side to an adhesive mount. The maid tore off the plastic wrapper protecting the cylinder and mount, held the canvas from the front, and pressed the mount against it from the rear. After a few seconds, she let go. The cylinder and wire hung down inside the painting, invisible and not touching it anywhere except at the insulated mounting point. When she replaced the painting, it lay perfectly flush with the wall. There was no sign it had been tampered with.

Popularly called a "Thing", the correct name for the device was "passive cavity resonator." One had been presented to the American ambassador to the Soviet Union by the Young Pioneers in 1945, and for several years thereafter, the Soviets had enjoyed top-level access to some of the most sensitive American foreign policy secrets. The Thing was a listening device, a bug with one feature that placed it above all its peers: it never ran out of power or needed to be recharged, because it was energized by a radio transmitter outside the building.

The maid had no idea how it worked, but she knew that it would allow someone hostile to the Minister to hear his conversations, and she was satisfied.

Next, she crossed over to his desk and pulled out the narrow drawer beneath the center where the wireless keyboard for his computer rested. Crawling underneath the desk, she took out another set of wires, thin and black and attached to a small card-shaped object, and taped them securely to the underside of the desktop. When the drawer was closed, the net of wires would be positioned over the keyboard, and if the keyboard was taken out and placed on top of the desk, the wires would be exactly underneath it. Even if the keyboard was used with the drawer withdrawn, they would be close enough to it to pick up the electronic signals generated by each keystroke, and to transmit those signals to a nearby receiver.

There was a screech of tires in the driveway outside. The Minister's son had returned home in his Ferrari. Composing herself, the maid slipped away into another part of the house, leaving the office a trap for the Minister to fall into without suspecting it.

* * * * *

"We have the Minister of Foreign Affairs coming online," Fihr announced.

"That was fast. How many ministers do we have bugged now?"

"Sixteen, including two deputy prime ministers. And that's not counting other department heads. It's stupid to mistreat an impoverished minority, then grant members of that minority unrestrained access to your homes. Are you getting the character stream?"

"It looks perfect," Asim said. "Not that we know what it means yet."

"But it will probably have usernames and passwords in it. It's not hard to construe."

"It would be better if we could use Van Eck phreaking to read his screen."

"That requires equipment too bulky to hide in a maid's pocket, and it might look easier, but it would leave out the most crucial information. There isn't a website on earth that displays passwords in plaintext. As I read it"--Fihr leaned over to look at the screen--"the Minister just typed in the password for his user settings. Now we know that, which may or may not be useful." He was scribbling the information down on a piece of paper as he spoke. "There's a pause, that means he's probably opening a browser. Now we have a group of three letters, 'r-e-t'. And then he pressed the enter key. So he did open a browser and started to type the name of a website into the address bar, and it completed the address for him."

"Yes--but what address starts with the letters 'r-e-t'? It could be anything."

"Not necessarily. That's where knowing and remembering past patterns of behavior comes in handy." Fihr flicked open a new tab and typed a line of text into the address bar.

"The National Bank of Bahrain?"

"Their login page for online banking. He's not the only official to bank with them, I've seen the address before. Obviously the next set of letters followed by the tab key is his username, and the set after that is his password. Then enter, yes, and now anything that follows is likely to be the answers to his security questions."

"In other words, we were just given access to the Minister's personal bank account."

"Of course. We'll check it later, after he's logged out, and see what kind of a balance he maintains close to home. Keep an eye on the keystream. Hopefully he'll check his email next, and that will be interesting."

"I have something here from Defense that you should see," Shihab called from the other side of the room.

"I think we just got a better present than a minister's bank balance," Fihr said ten minutes later.

"Recognition codes for the army command and control system?" Asim asked, his eyes scanning the incoming sequences of letters and numbers on his screen.

"That's handled at a lower level. This--this is political dynamite. Where's Junayd?"

"Downstairs, I think."

"But he's in the building?"

"Yes."

"Text him."

In thirty seconds Junayd popped through the door. "What's going on?"

"Get the imam in here. He needs to hear this too."

Ra'd bin Mazin was in a room down the hall composing a sermon. Junayd was back with him almost immediately.

"As you may recall," Shihab began, "the government has spent the past few years trying to decide if it's going to buy new fighter jets from the Americans or the British."

"New fighter jets we don't need," Asim put in.

"That's beside the point. The Air Force wants the airplanes. And Crown Prince Salman in particular wants them. Well, it appears the cabinet has finally decided on the Eurofighters."

"That's not unreasonable," Junayd said. He knew more about defense procurement than anyone else present. "They are half the price of the American Joint Strike Fighters, after all."

"It's not that simple. Going through the Minister of Defense's emails to several of his subordinates, and to the Crown Prince, I found a chain of messages extending back over the past several months. There's been two sets of negotiations going on the entire time. One was the official round of talks handled through the diplomatic corps. The other was being conducted by the ministers directly with the BAE representatives."

"Kickbacks?"

"Yes, but again, it's not that simple. BAE originally proposed that the Air Force order twenty-four Eurofighters, enough to replace all of the old F-5 aircraft still in service while boosting the Air Force's capacity in a chaotic region. At least that's what the documentation said. The general staff allowed themselves to be persuaded that they needed twenty-four airplanes to replace sixteen. BAE suggested a package price of one point six billion dollars for the whole deal. But that was in informal talks at the beginning of negotiations, before the Air Force was sold on the Eurofighter and was willing to go on fact-finding missions with the Americans and Swedes."

"How explicit are these emails?" the imam asked. "Do they explain the bidding process clearly enough for the public to follow it?"

"Yes. Of course there's a lot that isn't in the emails, the things that were discussed in person and not minuted. But there are lots of hints, and when you take the messages together with the government's press releases, the picture that emerges is clear enough."

"I understand. Please go on."

"Anyway, BAE offered the jets at a certain price, but that was two years ago. When the deal is announced, in a couple more weeks, it will have gone up to one point eight billion dollars."

"That's a lot of inflation, even taking the weakened state of the dollar into account," Junayd remarked.

"It's not inflation. This is where BAE got creative. Everyone knows that a few years back, they were prosecuted by their own government for taking bribes from the Saudis--in pursuit of the same goal, no less. Eurofighter sales. The email exchanges all but say flat out that the British could have still delivered the package today at one point six billion, or possibly a little more."

"They raised it to hike up their own profits and the government went ahead with the deal regardless in order to save time and avoid losing face? Or to avoid being blackmailed by BAE for accepting bribes?"

"No! Not at all! That's the catch! The price increase did not come from BAE. It was requested by Bahraini negotiators through informal discussions!"

"That's ridiculous! The Ministry of Defense *asked* to pay more when it could have had them for less?"

"Yes."

"I don't believe it."

"I believe it," the imam said, his face as placid as ever. "And I also believe that I see where this information is leading."

"The extra cost of the contract is to be split between the two parties," Shihab announced. "A hundred million dollars will go back to BAE Systems, and will be written down as pure profit for a company whose total profits from all its sales last year were less than twice that. The rest is to be divided among the Minister of Defense, the Minister of Foreign Affairs, Crown Prince Salman, who didn't participate in negotiating the deal but agreed to overlook the irregularities in it, and sundry other officials."

The hackers sat there in silence. The audacity of the ministers and the size of the theft stunned them.

"The Khalifa dynasty feels that its position at home is weakening," the imam said, breaking in on their thoughts. "And so its members prepare for retirement or exile with a greater round of plunder than usual."

"A hundred million--"

"Has the money been paid yet?"

"Asim! We have the Minister's bank account information right there. Pull up his balance and see if there have been any seven-figure deposits lately!"

"Don't waste your typing," Shihab said. "The payments haven't gone through yet. But they're due next week. Besides, the bribes are only half the story."

"There's more?"

"Political pressure and state inertia. BAE's asking price for the Eurofighters was about sixty-five million per plane. Gripens are a little less expensive, Rafales a little more. Joint Strike Fighters, unsubsidized by the Americans, are twice as much, as Junayd pointed out. Well, there was a small American company that submitted a bid to the Ministry of Defense as well. It argued that Bahrain's air defense needs could be handled by its existing F-16 fleet for the foreseeable future, and handled better than by the larger, heavier proposed replacements. This company, Caravel Air Services, offered the Air Force *one hundred planes* at a price of two million dollars each."

"How could they deliver at that price when every major firm wants so much more?"

"Because the company wasn't selling multirole fighter jets. It was selling small, fast, nimble ground attack aircraft powered by engines of its own design. They proposed that Bahrain replace its jets with these rugged little planes, capable of saturating a battlefield and operating out of forward posts where it would be impossible to get conventional jet fighters.

There was nothing radical about the design. It was a further refinement of the American close air support aircraft project of the 1960s, which was corrupted into the much less capable OV-10. But the cabinet wasn't interested in so much as seeing the plane fly."

"So if it's that good and cheap, why did the government--aside from the bribe issue--turn down the offer?"

"I can answer that one," Junayd said.

"Without even looking at the emails?"

"It's always the same reason, isn't it? Small, simple aircraft have no appeal to generals who like their equipment big and new and full of computers. They also have no appeal to bureaucrats who would rather dispose of a large budget inefficiently than a small one efficiently. And then Shihab mentioned political pressure as well."

"No less a person than General John Campbell, who is head of United States Central Command, visited the Minister of Defense and the Crown Prince to personally advise against a Bahraini purchase of such an incapable aircraft. Or, reading between the lines, to convey that the American government would be very displeased if Bahrain bought a defense product from an American company that the Pentagon disliked."

"Did the American military ever test the aircraft themselves and reject it?"

"No."

"Did the company need an export license but fail to obtain one?"

"No."

"So it was sheer spite."

"It always is," Junayd remarked. "Such an aircraft doesn't fit into the high-technology world the American armed forces envision themselves fighting in. And when someone goes ahead and builds one without regard for their official doctrine, it makes them feel threatened."

"Let's review," Asim said from his computer. "The government had a chance to buy a cheap airplane that would have expanded the Air Force's fighting abilities while saving the country over a billion dollars. It chose not to under foreign pressure. It then chose to buy a far more expensive aircraft, and asked for the price to be increased in order that the ministers would have a larger sum to divide as bribes."

"That's what it comes to," Shihab agreed.

"Are these emails that you have read and analyzed in chronological order?" the imam asked.

"No, they're more or less in reverse chronological order, but the sequence isn't exact."

"Sort them into the proper order," the imam instructed. "Then package them as a single file. I believe you can do that?"

"Oh, yes."

"In addition, write down everything you have just explained to me as an essay on the subject. Attach the file to the essay, and schedule it to post across all our sites--"

"The ones that are still up, that is."

"Yes, those that the government has not yet shut down or complained about. Have it posted on the same day the bribes are scheduled to be paid into the ministers' accounts."

"But we have all their information here," Asim objected. "Are we just going to let them take the bribes and protest about it? We could get into their accounts, change the settings, prevent the deposits from being made--"

"I have an alternative solution," the imam replied. "In the meantime, let the student leaders know that a document release is imminent, and arrange with them to schedule additional protests for that date."

"Big ones?"

"Yes. Have them throw in all their reserve strength. Anyone they were waiting to call in anticipation of a major political event that would demand high turnout in order to make the greatest impact."

"But will this be enough to warrant that turnout?"
"Not yet," the imam said. "But it will be by that time."

11

It began as a short article halfway down the homepage of the *Democracy Today* website. It wasn't much of an article at all, really. More of a tip that hadn't been acted on yet or a sketch that required fleshing out. Four short paragraphs containing two typographic errors. The paragraphs--not the errors--stated that Major Matthew Martin of the United States Marine Corps had gone to Iran to liberate the two teenagers sentenced to death, that he was a prominent academic within the Marine Corps who had made a recent controversial speech, and that neither the Major nor the Marine Corps University had responded to requests for comment. Simple. Innocuous, apart from the content.

Within the editorial offices of the magazine, there was a sharp and violent squabble over who had been responsible for posting the item in the first place. It was supposed to have been fact-checked first, but had accidentally been shifted into the publication queue without proper authorization from the appropriate editor. At least, that particular editor denied having given the authorization. His superior insisted that he must have done so, otherwise it wouldn't have been sent out to the editing team. Then word came down from the editor-in-chief and owner that it didn't matter who had made the mistake, as it had turned out to be newsworthy.

Kyle Scott Bradley had his own reasons for letting the report stand as well, and his employees didn't care to speculate about those. Or if some of the more free-thinking ones did, they kept their conclusions to themselves.

An hour later, the article was accumulating a thousand visitors per minute and had become the most-retweeted piece on the entire site. The office phones were deluged with calls from activists, rival journalists, and members of the public wanting to know if it was true, where the information had come from, what progress the Major was making--and most of all, what the magazine's editorial stance would be. The staff tried to ignore them, and turned their efforts, on Bradley's orders, to digging up corroboration of the report.

By lunchtime the Office of the Commandant of the Marine Corps had bowed to journalistic pressure and released a statement. "Major Matthew Martin is currently relieved of duty pending the outcome of an investigation into his remarks during a speaking engagement at Eastern High School. He is not engaged in performing any assignment on behalf of the Corps or any other Department of Defense agency. The USMC does not have any operation under way to interfere in the internal judicial affairs of the Islamic Republic of Iran, nor has any member of Major Martin's chain of command authorized an incursion into a foreign nation for the protection or rescue of non-U.S. citizens."

The Secretary of the Navy elaborated on that statement during a press conference at two in the afternoon. "On checking with the Immigration and Naturalization Service, we found that Major Martin has in fact left the country. He departed from Dulles Airport and arrived at Heathrow in London the following morning. We have not yet been able to discover if he is still in the UK, or if he has gone on from there, but we are continuing to work closely with British border control authorities in order to determine his current location."

"If you find him, will he be arrested?" one reporter wanted to know. Well, all of them wanted to know it, but someone had to get to the question first.

The Secretary hesitated. "He will be detained for questioning," he said cautiously. "Given that he made certain public statements supportive of violent action, that he left the country immediately thereafter, and that he is reported to be attempting to interfere in a judicial proceeding in a foreign nation, we will ask the appropriate authorities in Britain or elsewhere to hold him until this matter is cleared up."

"What if he turns out to be in Iran?"

"We have no evidence that he has applied for or received an Iranian visa, so if he attempts to enter Iran, he will be turned back at the border."

"But what if he enters the country illegally?"

"Then it is likely that the Iranian authorities will deport him, unless he is caught committing a crime on Iranian soil, in which case they will no doubt try him themselves."

"He's a career infantryman and a specialist in asymmetric warfare. What are the chances that Iranian authorities can actually catch him if he goes after those two boys?"

"Good," the Secretary said, with a bit too much conviction. "Iranian police are very thorough and used to conducting internal checks on transients, while Major Martin neither speaks Farsi nor has Iranian identity documents."

"Isn't that speculation?"

"It's unlikely that he would escape detection himself, let alone be able to aid in anyone else's escape," the Secretary glowered.

"Suppose he does manage to get them out of Iran. Would they be offered asylum here?"

"I'm not in charge of reviewing asylum petitions."

"What's your reaction to the Iranian Supreme Court's verdict in the case?"

"The United States government does not approve of the use of the death penalty as a punishment for consensual sexual activity."

"Has the government taken any steps to prevent the execution of Kadivar and Jan?"

"You'll have to ask the Secretary of State that question."

"Would the Department of Defense ever consider military intervention in order to protect foreign nationals unjustly convicted of a crime in their own country?"

"No. Next question."

"Does the US government consider protecting friendly regimes in the Middle East to be more worthwhile than protecting the people of those countries from human rights offenses?"

"I'm sorry, that's all the time we have today," the Secretary's press secretary said, interposing himself between the crowd of reporters and his perspiring boss.

Meanwhile messages were flashing between the State Department and the Foreign Interests Section of the Swiss Embassy in Tehran, from whence they were relayed to Iranian diplomats. The tenor of these messages was that the United States government was not attempting to interfere in Iran's internal affairs, and that Major Martin was a loose cannon whom, if he turned up there, they were welcome to deal with as they saw fit.

And closer to home, the blogs and the newsfeeds and the pundits and the commentators ground away, denouncing the Major and his actions. Completely inappropriate, the gay community said. A reaction far out of proportion to the problem. Iran's laws and government were reprehensible, of course, but that was no reason to retaliate with violence, much less for a private individual to act on his own. He couldn't succeed. He would only make things worse and stiffen the Iranian government's resolve. They were outraged that he had thrown away their strategy of slow social change. They were outraged that he had upstaged them. Really, what it came down to was outrage that he should undermine the entire system they had worked hard to become a part of, by acting in such a way--again!--as to throw the values of that system into doubt. The Human Rights Campaign, GLAAD, the ACLU, and their sister organizations had demanded that sexual identity be protected by the government, and they had almost gotten their demands. For that same government to be portrayed as incapable of protecting gays, to the point where a single man had to step in and substitute for it, would threaten the validity of all their arguments. And they didn't want to admit that possibility. So they smeared the Major, called him psychotic, and quietly hoped he would fail.

* * * * *

In a dirty conference room redolent of the usual cigarette smoke and coffee fumes that characterize police headquarters the world over, senior Iranian military and security officials stared at a map and looked worried.

"We don't even know if this is a real threat or not!" one of them protested in exasperation.

"Would you like to be the one to tell the mullahs that if it does turn out to be real in a few hours?"

"So we act on the assumption it's not a hoax or a false report?"

"Our troops can use the extra training. We'll call it security drills."

"What do you propose?"

"Roadblocks around Tabriz, in three layers. Additional street patrols. Strong guard forces placed at every entrance to the stadium. Visitors searched for weapons before entrance."

"Suppose this American got close enough to suborn one of the crane operators?"

"We replace them with military drivers in plainclothes at the last minute, without announcing the change."

"And the prison guards?"

"They have all been changed already and will continue to be at irregular intervals until the execution takes place."

"We are not thinking this through. We will not catch him this way."

"Explain."

"We are thinking in terms of trying to comb a crowd of tens of thousands for a single man, possibly a few men. They have the advantage there. They can hide in the mass. Even if we can stop them almost at once when they reveal themselves, they may still accomplish their mission or humiliate us first."

"We can only prepare within the limits of our abilities."

"Do you have an alternative suggestion?"

"Two. First, consider this. Can an American, who does not speak our language and is not familiar with Iranian culture, blend in with an Iranian crowd or recruit supporters in Tabriz without being detected? No. It would be implausible for him to do so. If he expects to effect a rescue, he must already have resources here to draw upon. Local dissidents or Western sympathizers."

"You say he has a power base in the city?"

"And he is doubtless in Tabriz himself by now, making preparations. If he does rescue the prisoners, where will he take them? How will they travel? Will they be disguised? Will there be a diversion? He cannot bring a jet with him to whisk them out of the country; he must have made arrangements with locals."

"So we sweep the city. House to house searches. Call in neighborhood leaders to see if they have suspicious activity to report."

"That is a beginning, but it does not guarantee that we will capture the American or prevent his interference."

"What does, then?"

"We have the Tabriz authorities transfer the prisoners to Evin and replace them with doubles for the time being. The execution will be canceled at the last minute and carried out here in Tehran instead. It will be too late then for this Marine, however flexible he may be, to adjust his plans, and we will catch him when he tries to get away himself."

*****

Two roads run southeast out of Tabriz. For all practical purposes, they are the same road, since they follow the same course, apart from a single stretch from Bostan Abad to Rajeyin where the lesser road diverges from the Zanjan-Tabriz Freeway and slinks north through the foothills of the Elburz Mountains. A double lane of well-maintained blacktop follows the course of earlier railway tracks for much of its journey. Due to the lack of any large towns along its course, the number of sharp curves it contains, and its proximity to the wider, faster freeway, the road sees little use. After traversing the center of a chain of hills, it cuts through the industrial town of Miyaneh and abruptly turns south at the junction of the Shaharchay and Qezel Ozan rivers. From there it plunges back into a series of water-cut canyons hemmed in by shale embankments.

The prison guard driving the unmarked van sighed as he braked for another curve. The pleasing greenery of the farmland around Miyaneh had dried up and his surroundings were depressing again. This early in the day, the road was deserted and the only risk with which he had to contend was driving off it altogether, which would be regrettable. For choice, he would have taken the freeway like everyone else, but the orders from Tehran had been specific. The van was to stay off the freeway for as long as possible. Iran has fast roads and fast drivers, and a correspondingly high accident rate. The Ministry of Justice wanted its prisoners to arrive without being dismembered, it having reserved the job of dismemberment for itself. Also, the officials had considered that a traffic jam on the freeway would delay the transport and give the American more time in which to realize that he'd been outmaneuvered.

None of this had been explained in detail to the sergeant at the wheel, so he tried to puzzle it out while driving. Inquiries directed at the lieutenant seated next to him had been a failure. The officer was quite open about not having been told anything beyond that the prisoners' friends might make an attempt to rescue them. He finished denying any inside knowledge and stuffed himself back into a thermos of coffee. He'd been on duty all night by the time he was pulled off the job and ordered to convey the prisoners scheduled for execution to the capital. The coffee was necessary.

The van slowed almost to a stop as it rounded the sharp bend. The sergeant prepared to accelerate again, then hesitated. Just ahead there were men in army uniforms blocking the road. They had even erected an emergency gate across it for good measure. And they were heavily armed. The driver nudged his lieutenant back to full consciousness. The lieutenant frowned and felt in his pocket for their orders.

As the van pulled up at the gate, a bundle of rags that had been lying off to one side scrambled to its feet and came hurrying over to the passenger door. It turned out to be a woman in a very dirty black chador. "Water? Water?" she whined in a nasal tone, holding up plastic bottles and a battered canteen and shaking them. The lieutenant ordered her away and turned his attention back to the approaching officer, a captain with an NCO following him. He handed his documents to the driver, who leaned closer to the window in order to pass them along.

The army captain, though he had a rifle slung over his shoulder, was fumbling with a thick folder of papers. He nodded in response to the sergeant's greeting, then shot him in the neck with a taser that somehow emerged from between the paperwork. The police lieutenant barely had time to notice it happening before his entire body convulsed as the water-seller gave him the same treatment.

"What's going on?" one of the guards in the rear of the vehicle called out. He began to stand up to see for himself, but was startled when a metal canister hit him in the chest and tumbled to the floor. He looked down at it. It burst into a cloud of smoke and he doubled over, howling in pain and sucking more of the poisonous gas into his lungs with every squeal.

The two soldiers who had remained behind to man the gate came pelting up, rifles unslung. The NCO who had been trotting along behind the captain was already setting a small explosive charge on the van's rear doors. He stepped back and fired it. The doors flapped like laundry on a breezy day, and the soldiers grabbed them and ripped them open. A mixture of smoke and tear gas rolled out of the vehicle, condensing near the ground. The captain, his face obscured with a mask the water-seller had passed him, reached inside the van and pulled out the first body he could reach. It was one of the guards, weeping and struggling to aim a pistol. The soldiers promptly butt-stroked him with their rifles. Next came one of the prisoners, in handcuffs. He was half lifted out by the water-seller, who had climbed into the van and was feeling around in the murk. She stumbled and fell to the floor. An instant later she lashed out with her legs. A shrill scream was the result. The captain leapt up to help her and tossed her unfortunate victim, the other guard, out onto the pavement. The final occupant, a large man restrained with a full set of shackles, had to be carried out by both of them. He was apparently less affected by the gas than the others and kept glaring around at them between coughs.

"Thirty-eight seconds," the Major said, consulting his watch. "Textbook." His Marines had already secured the wrists and legs of the two guards with plastic ties. Now they were dragging the driver and the officer out of the cab and doing the same to them. Tears streamed down their faces, but they were trained to cope with those.

Price took off her mask. "That's awful stuff."

"It had to be, to act fast enough to keep the guards from killing them."

"Do you think they would have?"

"I'm not sure, but it was best not to take the chance."

The larger of the two prisoners started talking. He didn't look happy about it. From his tone, he was insulting them, or even sneering at them.

"This might be the hardest part of the whole trip," the Major reflected aloud. He turned to the man and rattled off a sentence in Arabic. No response, apart from a deeper look of suspicion. "If he speaks a second language, it's most likely Azeri. And I don't know enough Azeri to ask my way to the head."

A softer voice joined the conversation, an inquiring one. The other prisoner was speaking now. The Major's face brightened.

"That's more like it!" He knelt down and offered the young man some water to clear his throat. The exchange between them was brief and punctuated by wheezes and gasps, but it served its purpose. The Major got to his feet again.

"This is Arash Kadivar," he said, indicating the man he'd just spoken with, "and this is Feroze Jan." The Marines nodded in acknowledgment. "Fortunately Kadivar speaks Arabic better than I do. Find the keys to their shackles. Check the officer's pocket first."

Sergeant Brassey flipped over the Iranian guard, who was beginning to struggle against his bonds, and went through his pockets with the air of a man who was used to searching people. As a military policeman, he probably was. "Right here, sir," he announced.

"Get them unlocked and give them masks. Powers, see what you can do to cover that hole on the van's door. Ramirez, Price, take the second emergency barrier and run it up the road to where we can get it when we leave." The Major himself began stripping the prison guards of their radios, phones, and weapons, flinging them all into the canyon below, where they would be lost in the Qezel Ozan. He came back from the edge of the gully and saw Feroze Jan standing erect now, watching. The expression he wore was not one of joy, but one of triumph instead. The world that had attempted to destroy him had been smashed around him and he had survived, and he gloried in that fact. He picked up the last remaining pistol from the ground and tucked it into his belt. It was clear he would use it to protect himself and his lover if he felt threatened.

"Once upon a time, there were human beings," Major Martin said to himself.

"Sir?" Powers asked, bent over the van's rear door, which he was covering with a mud-colored putty to disguise the damage.

"Yes, Lance Corporal?"

"How did you know they'd take this road?"

"There's only one other road, and this one is the less traveled and therefore less risky of the two."

"Not that, sir. I know we had a couple of Javed's friends stationed up ahead to tell us which route they'd take. Why did they move the prisoners in the first place?"

"Because I leaked the story about our little trip to the press back home," the Major said.

Powers stood up in shock. "You blew the mission!"

"Of course."

"I don't understand, sir."

"Tabriz is not a particularly secure city. If the Iranian government thought a rescue attempt would be made, they would deem it more sensible to move Kadivar and Jan to Tehran immediately before the execution was scheduled, in order to throw off the timing of any such attempt. They decided to trade numbers for mobility--four guards on the van as opposed to dozens at the prison, but those four harder to locate. That's not a bad tactic, and it would have worked if I hadn't been the one prompting them to do it in the first place. I acted, they oriented themselves in response to my action, and since my decision cycle was working faster than theirs, I knew where to put us so we'd be waiting for them. The trick of warfare, Lance Corporal, is not getting in position to cut your enemy's throat. The trick is persuading him to stick out his neck so you can do it without having to strain yourself."

He turned and exchanged a few more words with Kadivar, who translated for his lover. The two Iranians climbed back into the van, now mostly clear of the poisonous gas. For good measure, the Major handed them the masks he and Price had used. Powers finished with the door and climbed in after them. Brassey was already at the wheel. The Major settled into the passenger seat and nodded to him.

The van wobbled into reverse, made a tight U-turn, and eased back around the curve, heading north, the way it had come. A little farther down the road, Price and Ramirez swung the temporary barrier across the road and climbed aboard, letting Powers wire the rear doors shut behind them. The two roadblocks would keep out the curious for the time being, until some disgruntled driver complained to the local police station about them and officers came out to investigate. As for the guards, exposure to fresh air wouldn't hurt them, not after being gassed. Brassey had very thoughtfully set up a shelter for them to keep them out of the afternoon sun.

*****

"Do you have a death wish or something?"

Randall halted and twisted his head around to see who was shouting. Congressman Elliott was hurrying down the Capitol steps towards him. His hair was as neat and his perfect teeth as level as ever, but he wasn't wearing his usual thin-lipped smile. Randall thought about ignoring him, but dismissed the idea. It was better to have it out here and now.

There were a few other people around, but no one close enough to overhear the conversation. Apart from that initial threat, which was all to the good.

"I feel like a drink. Is alcohol poisonous all of a sudden?"

Elliott came to a stop less than two feet from him. "How dare you fuck this up for us," he hissed. "Are you oblivious to what we talked about the other day?"

"I must be, because I don't recall us talking about much of anything."

"You were committed to voting to overturn the veto."

"You're committed to that. I'm not. And if you think I'm going to abandon my convictions and vote for whatever piece of crap you shove in front of me, forget it."

"Your convictions? That's rich, coming from someone who's as far back in the closet as you are."

"And if I were as far out of it as you were, I'd still vote the other way. I vote my constituent's interests, not my own."

"In seventy-two hours your constituents are going to be demanding your resignation."

"Thanks, but I've been winning elections since I was a teenager. I don't need advice on how to manage voters from a spoiled little parvenu who had to marry someone who could afford to buy him a seat."

"I'd sue you for slander, but it's going to be more fun destroying your career this other way."

"Well, you know, I never went to law school, but I've heard that one of the things you've forgotten since you were there was the principle that slander's a public act. I don't see anyone else close enough to hear what I'm saying, do you? So your slander suit wouldn't work any better than whatever else you're planning."

"Oh, it'll work and you'll know it soon enough."

"You must really be needing a shoulder to cry on right now. Your precious co-sponsored bill's not going to get another chance till next year, the Majority Leader's lost confidence in you now that you failed to deliver the votes you promised, and by that time you may not have a majority anymore. Good luck with being a single-issue candidate in that environment."

"It's better than being a liar and a hypocrite."

"I think you'd be surprised. Wait, you wouldn't be. You're one already."

"I'm the hypocrite here? How do you figure that?"

"Well, I'm not the one who set up a bunch of super-PACs to push for campaign finance reform while my boyfriend dumped wads of cash into my own campaign. And I'm sure as hell not the one who pushes for open government while blackmailing my congressional colleagues."

"Enjoy prodding me while you can." Elliott finally cracked a smile, though his pale, handsome face was still paler than normal. "Enjoy all your congressional privileges while you can. Because your career here is done. I offered you a chance to play nice. You had a simple choice. We can live without you joining us, there's plenty of better men than you in Washington. But if you wanted us to leave you alone, you should have gotten out of our way and stopped obstructing us. And you were stupid and you didn't do it. So now we're going to destroy you for good. We are the future, and we are going to make the most of it. And it looks like you're just another deserving casualty in the fight for equality." He almost spit out the last words before turning away, his body shaking with anger.

Behind his back, Mark Randall's fingers drifted up to the breast pocket of his jacket.

12

Asim sat back on his heels and wiped the sweat off his forehead. An hour before noon, and the thermometers were already pressing against their stops. Bahrain was in the grip of one of the fiercest early summers in years. Children's voices drifted up from downstairs, sounding limp and listless in the heat. The imam's deeper tones were an almost inaudible murmur. None of them took much pleasure in their faith, it seemed. It was another of the constant contrasts to Ra'd bin Mazin's activity and vivacity.

He leaned over the box again. The wood was old and dry, and in spite of the lack of moisture, the metal components were corroding anyway from exposure to the salt air of the Gulf. It was necessary for him to scrape a couple of wires clean of rust before he could attach them to the new circuit board. The gleaming emerald surface of the silicon was completely out of place among the decades-old audio components, but it could be hidden underneath part of the wiring and no one would ever notice. As long as he got the connections right, that is. If he screwed them up, or screwed a part in wrong, then the local imam might call in a technician to fix the mosque's public address system, and that would have consequences. The parts could be traced. Apart from that, any good repairman would wonder why a public address system that was never used for anything but issuing the call to prayer had a wireless receiver wired into it.

The little light on the board blinked on, a pale jewel in the dark interior of the case. Asim nodded in satisfaction. He finished splicing the last two wires. Now the system could receive pre-recorded messages from outside, store them on a buffer chip, and play them back at a preset time. All without any involvement from the mosque's imam or anyone else. The board and its coding also included an override that bypassed the system's power switch, so that it remained powered up twenty-four hours a day without showing any indicator lights except when the switch was pressed. A perfect disguise.

Asim resealed the plastic case with a few twists of his screwdriver and closed the doors of the wooden cabinet. A simple steel pick relocked them. He stood up cautiously and looked around. The little room adjoining the minaret was still empty; there were no unusual shadows in the hall. It was very easy to slip out of the mosque through the service room and a back door. In his opinion, that was the least tricky part of the job. This was his fourth mosque refitting of the morning. As a rule, they were trying to finish the installations early in the day, before the muezzins began calling the afternoon prayers.

The back streets of Manama were mostly quiet. A taxi blew its horn from time to time, or one of the new energy-efficient cars the government had persuaded the Saudis to subsidize trickled past, its tires making more noise than its engine. In the distance, there was a low hum. Asim remembered the sound from the first Arab Spring--or the beta version, as members of the underground were inclined to call it. He had been too young to be part of the street protests then, and he hadn't cared much. He didn't understand the goals of a revolution. But he did recall being fascinated at the time by the youth of the other protestors. Students just a few years ahead of him in school, neighbors who lived across the street from his family--real people, fighting the king? He'd thought it was epic, in a sense. Perhaps that was why he had grown up skeptical of authority. He had seen too early how easily it could be challenged and defied.

And now he had come from being part of that process to being behind the process, to managing it. To feeding the thousands of would-be revolutionaries the ideas that kept them in motion. They went into the streets and the squares and the parks and the noise of their voices covered the kingdom--and he was one of the small band who had sent them there.

In his pocket, his phone vibrated against his hip. He tensed for a moment. There was always the chance that a message over a burner phone meant that their operation had been discovered again. He checked it, and relaxed as quickly as he'd frozen. It was no threat. Only a request to pick up a box full of parts for another of Fihr's ideas. As he thought about it, he smiled. The smile turned into an outright laugh, earning him a curious look or two from his fellow pedestrians, which disappeared when they saw the phone in his hand and assumed he was reading a joke.

So this is what it meant to be a master of the revolution, he thought. To be a messenger boy!

* * * * *

"You got my text? Good."

Asim set the box down. "Yes, and whatever you wanted is bulky. What's in here?"

"More burner phones."

"I thought we had all of those we needed for the time being."

"This is for a different project."

"Which one?"

"Jamming."

"You're building jamming devices using cell phones?"

"No, the cell phones are the jamming devices."

"I don't get it."

"You will. Think about it for a minute. In the meantime, come help me with this."

"What's this?"

"We're hacking the school system."

"The whole thing?"

"Just the secondary and intermediate schools."

"Let me guess. The imam wants access to their internal communications networks so he can use those networks to mobilize students against the wishes of the administrators?"

"If we did it that way they'd figure it out pretty fast and shut their internal email networks off. Depending on how bad things get, the government may order the schools to shut down the systems before any new protests break out, to prevent them from being planned. Or the Ministry of the Interior will be reading all the traffic in order to anticipate any demonstrations."

"So we go after the private email addresses listed in the student records instead."

"Right. The ministry can't shut down service providers on a large scale without crippling the entire country."

"It can block the traffic, though."

"There are workarounds."

Asim shrugged. "Well, we knew how to use proxies at fourteen, but is the current generation as computer literate as we were? They're used to punching bright shiny buttons. They don't know how to code."

"As the saying goes, 'There's an app for that.'"

"No there isn't."

"There will be in a few days. Shihab is building one. One touch and it automatically routes all your traffic through a proxy server. Easy for even the most brain-dead iOS users to activate."

"There's another catch. Most of the emails listed in student records may be for the parents rather than the students themselves."

"True. But there will be separate phone numbers listed for the students and parents, because the school may need to send class or campus-specific updates to the former. Those are more useful anyway, since we can send updates to the protestors on the go and not have to wait for them to look at their email."

"All right. How far are you into it?"

"Not very. But we should be able to finish it up by tomorrow at the latest and get back to work on that other code."

"Where should I start?"

"I'm doing the Al Raja School at the moment. You might as well try the Al Noor School. I have a list here with student login information for it that we got from friends of friends who are still attending. Once you put that in it'll make hacking the databases easier."

The room went silent except for the sound of typing and an occasional comment as the two of them cut through the firewalls that protected the personal information of thousands of students from the outside world. The walls weren't very strong. In spite of the Bahraini government's expressed wish that the country should become a leading player in the digital economy, Bahraini computer technicians were still not among the world's best. Computers meant circulation of information, and circulation of information was felt to be dangerous to an organized society. The preference among Bahraini companies was to subcontract such work out to an Indian firm, thereby eliminating the possibility that they or their employees could come under suspicion for subversion or inciting disorder. And the state smiled on this attitude, even subsidizing it to a certain extent. The result was few computer specialists in Bahrain who were willing to turn their talents to domestic employment and a generally poor build quality for domestic websites and information management systems. True, the actual database software was often purchased from a large international firm, but when it was grafted onto a local frontend, gaps and loopholes were created. Lots of them. A good hacker could slip right into the underlying system using only a small amount of information.

Asim realized with a start that Ra'd bin Mazin had been sitting off to one side of the room watching them, presumably for some time. He considered starting a conversation, but decided against it. The imam seemed content to listen and observe.

"I can almost understand what you are typing at times," the imam said eventually.

"From the sound of our typing patterns, you mean?"

"That, and each key produces a distinctive sound when struck. If you count the number of times each key is heard in a given period, you can work out which sound belongs to which letter. I cannot process the information that quickly, but at times I feel that I can discern the content of your words because certain keystroke sequences are familiar, or accord with the beats of a spoken word."

"You can use that technique to spy on a target's communications," Fihr suggested.

"Our 'things' aren't powerful enough to do that, though."

"No. But they can record the words of the ministers, and that will be far more useful than knowing their bank balances or the contents of their emails."

"You do intend to distribute the recordings, then."

"'Secret counsels are only inspired by the Evil One in order that he may cause grief to the Believers.'"

"No concept of national security in Islam, either."

"No," the imam said. "God provides security. Telling lies and plotting to hurt others does not."

"We're plotting," Asim observed.

"That is true. But we do not intend to harm our fellow men. Also, we have every intention of bringing our actions out into the light of day. We have already done so to some extent. Is that plotting, or is it preparation?"

"I don't know, so I'm going to meet your question with another question. Who pays for it all?"

The imam smiled. "The computers we use? The phones? The bandwidth?"

"Yes. And don't say that charity is the duty of every Muslim and leave it at that."

"But charity is your answer. There are many wealthy and successful Muslims outside the Arab world. And it costs so little to run computers. Much less than it costs to buy bullets or fund a nonprofit organization.

"Those of us who have lived all our lives here in Bahrain are among the most insular of all Muslims. In Saudi Arabia, it is possible for Sunnis to look across the Gulf and see Shias in Iran. In Iran, it is possible for Shias to look across the Gulf and see Sunnis in Saudi Arabia. In both cases, there is an awareness of difference. Here, where our population is split between the two, we look abroad for no such difference. We see the two divisions of our faith, and we assume, from constant exposure to both, that those are all that exist. We lack a constant sense that there are alternatives.

"And from this limited viewpoint of ours we forget that the majority of the world's believers consider themselves to be neither Shia nor Sunni, but merely Muslim. Many freely interpret the Book for themselves, rather than relying on the ulama. Views that are considered radical and heretical by our scholars are seen as reasonable and normal by many believers abroad."

"Meaning that some foreign Muslims see even anarchism as more Islamic than supreme rule by a group of selfish men."

"And they are the ones who fund our campaign, yes."

"Suppose it doesn't work?"

"How do you determine whether it has succeeded or not?"

"Well--if we get rid of the government for good, we've succeeded. If we don't, it hasn't."

Ra'd bin Mazin considered this. "That is only a fair definition of success in the most immediate sense. Even if we fail to immediately supplant the state, we will still have established a new line of thought in Islam that will be studied and debated and preserved, perhaps to take effect when we are long dead. What are you copying out there?"

"The phone numbers of secondary school students."

"Who will participate in demonstrations driven by the concept of Islamic anarchism. And that will linger in their thoughts for the better part of a century. It will influence their actions, drawing them towards it or driving them away from it. They will write about it and speak about it, publicly and privately, giving it time to spread and be elaborated on by successive generations of scholars and activists. In the long term, it is immaterial whether the Al Khalifa dynasty collapses next week or a century from now. Reaching the students is of far greater importance. They are the single most important group in any society. They alone possess the combination of energy, dissatisfaction, familiarity with new ideas, leisure, and future time necessary to ignite a permanent revolution."

"Which is why all revolutions traditionally begin with students?"

"Exactly."

* * * * *

Junayd snapped the ethernet cables into their sockets one by one. It was turning out to be a task that required a fair amount of walking. Down from the router to each machine, then back to the router, then from the router over to the next cluster, and so on.

He was surrounded by hundreds of computers. None of them were new. Most of them were old. They belonged to a dozen different brands and almost as many different years of manufacture. Their plastic cases were scuffed and dirty and covered in a startling array of stickers displaying everything from institutional barcodes to Pokemon characters. It didn't look anything like the nerve center for a major information campaign.

It didn't look much like a server farm, either. A few dim bulbs burned high up in the rafters of the warehouse, and a nest of rats, the same variety once accused of spreading the Black Plague all the way from China to Ireland, slumbered in a remote corner behind a packing crate. As a side effect of such intensive competition from higher-level scavengers, there were no mice. Or keyboards, or displays, or monitors, or desks, or chairs, or a water cooler or a coffee machine. It was a computer graveyard where the corpses rested undisturbed. Apart from the enthusiastic young man who was running around sticking blue cables into all of them.

13

The 79th Infantry Division poured out of its barracks in Tabriz. The luckier units were sent west towards Maku and Khvoy and Orumiyeh, or east to Ardabil. The unlucky ones had to leave the main roads and take up positions to the north along the Aras River. By along the river, the commanders at First Army Headquarters in Tehran had made clear, they meant on the banks of the river itself with the soldiers looking across into Azerbaijan. Overhead, venerable Sea Cobra helicopters hovered, their short wings hung with pods of rockets and whatever sensors the maintenance teams had been able to scrape up on short notice. Infrared cameras were most in demand, although with the summer getting warmer, and the number of soldiers scattered along the border growing every hour, their utility was turning out to be limited. The army belatedly realized it was jamming its own sensors, but decided to keep using them, just in case they happened to spot the fugitives. The pilots struggled to cope with the added workload of constantly identifying their own personnel on the ground and cursed their indifferent superiors, as pilots always do.

A few of them had more cause to fret than others. They were close enough to the river to look over and see an occasional helicopter racing back and forth on the Azerbaijani side of the border. Azerbaijan's army wasn't large by Iranian standards, but if someone on the Iranian side pressed a button by mistake, it was large enough to shell the living daylights out of all the Iranian soldiers standing exposed along the course of the river. Whose stupid idea was that, anyway? they asked themselves and each other.

They weren't underestimating the dangers of the situation. Iran's explanation as to why it was massing an entire division along the border had not been received well by the Azerbaijani government. The Foreign Minister had expressed polite, albeit guarded, incredulity when told that thousands of soldiers were racing in the direction of his country in order to prevent two escaped prisoners from crossing the border. He suggested, without saying so outright, that if Tehran was telling the truth, it was overreacting to a ridiculous extent. But his tone and expression made it clear that he was not convinced that Tehran was telling the truth. His phrasing conveyed to the Iranian diplomats a sense that an outsider viewed their panic as implausible. As for the Iranian diplomats, they had not troubled to be especially pleasant when they arrived to inform the Minister, and that worked against them. It was the Iranian position that Iran had a perfect right to prevent Iranians who had been convicted of a crime from leaving the country. If that required the deployment of the army along a border, it was still an internal matter, and if the adjoining nation objected, it was unfairly interfering in Iran's internal affairs. The meeting ended badly, and the Azerbaijani government decided to send a few light infantry and artillery units south, just to make sure the Iranians were aware of their position. That is how wars start.

The Tabriz police, along with special units deployed from the capital, were turning Iran's three northernmost provinces inside out. However, the police themselves viewed it as a waste of time. The American Marine and his party had been seen heading north by the prison guards. It was logical for them, with the start of twelve hours that they had accumulated, to keep heading for the border instead of holing up in Tabriz or another large city. The journey was short, and it would be easy to hide out near the river or cross the dividing line immediately. The terrain was mountainous and in places heavily wooded. If the fugitives were not across it already, they were doubtless nearby, and the army would make the capture, not the police.

And if they did get across? There were little-publicized American air bases scattered all over Turkey, and as for the prisoners, the Turkish government had been softening its stance in recent years on asylum seekers from Iran. Azerbaijan was perhaps even more promising as a final destination. While the Azerbaijani government played its neutrality for everything it was worth, and would be unwilling to offend its larger neighbor by offering convicted Iranian nationals asylum, it had also been unwilling to offend the Americans when a new administration came calling armed with wads of cash, oil drills, and small pilotless aircraft. The country was packed with American military observers keeping watch on the slow, brutal progress of the Russian-Ukrainian war. Referendums in the former eastern provinces of the Ukraine had come out in favor of union with Russia, but the irregular troops who enforced the results of those referendums had never quite been able to topple the government in Kiev. Vladimir Vladimirovich, playing a close hand as usual, had refused to mobilize the Russian armed forces to finish the job. If the eastern Ukrainians and Russian volunteers did it themselves, it would be easier to pass it off as a movement of national liberation. So they fought, and Turkey refused to get involved, and the United States fell in love with Azerbaijan as a new forward operating base where they already had a foot in the door via the oil industry. The Iranians, who didn't fully believe Washington's denunciation of Major Martin, were confident he would be heading for his military friends in one of the two neighboring countries. Hence their urgent desire to close their borders before he could get close enough to call for backup.

* * * * *

The Major hummed to himself, making a low buzzing sound. He was trying to substitute for the Buick's lack of a radio with his own rendition of popular Arab music. To his own surprise and pleasure, he was moderately successful. In the passenger seat, Sergeant Brassey turned mournful eyes on him every so often but was otherwise silent. The occupants of the rear seat were also unappreciative. Jan and Kadivar, in the middle, had very little to say to anyone, even each other. On either side of them, Powers and Ramirez stared out the windows, their nerves on edge. Crossing the Afghani border and attacking the prison van had been as dangerous as driving through Iran, but those experiences hadn't felt as dangerous. They were over with quickly, and they'd demanded action. Sitting in a car all day, in the middle of enemy territory, was more wearing than fighting, because it ate away at the stagnant mind. The Marines were beginning to miss the spacious rear and tear gas stink of the van, which the Major had disposed of, along with their uniforms, in Miyaneh.

"Oh, bother," the Major said, stopping his buzzing. "Make sure your weapons are out of sight."

Ramirez tried to leap out of his seat and bashed his head on the car's roof. "Shit! Police, sir?"

"I believe so," the Major said, without turning his head to look. "I do hope Javed didn't get us a car with an expired license. That would be inconvenient to explain away for the next few thousand miles." Jan became aware of their predicament and uttered a low growl, digging in his pocket for his gun. The Major barked a command in Arabic and Kadivar managed to calm him. Behind them, the police car swept up between wings of dust, its lights flashing. The Major obligingly pulled over.

A single policeman climbed out of the car and trudged towards them. Not an elite officer, by any means. He looked tired and displayed no particular enthusiasm for this stop. The Major noted that in a split-second glance at the rearview mirror and was reassured. He cranked down the window.

"License, please," the officer said in a bored voice.

"Sorry, can't oblige you with that," the Major replied in English.

The policeman frowned in puzzlement. Then his eyebrows shot up almost far enough to touch his bushy hair. In a practiced move, the Major flipped out a can of mace from inside his sleeve and shot him in the face from eighteen inches away. He went over on his back, choking and retching.

"Stay in the car," the Major ordered, and opened the door.

The policeman was flailing on the ground in a blend of suffocation and fury. He had practically inhaled the entire contents of the can in one breath and had thrown up all over the road. The Major rolled him over, pulled a rag out of the back pocket of his grubby trousers, and wiped his face clean. Then he grabbed the policeman under the arms and lifted him up, helping him to stand against the car. It was difficult. The Iranian was striking out all over the place, making noises that would have been as unintelligible to a speaker of Farsi as they were to a speaker of English.

"Gently, now," the Major admonished him. "Breathe through it." His right hand was hidden from the view of anyone else on the road by its position. From inside the car, though, Powers could see him produce an injector--how does he do that? the Marine wondered--and stab it deeply into the policeman's shoulder muscles. The Iranian spat out another clump of curses and spittle all over the front of his uniform.

A third car pulled up beside them, its emergency flashers on. A well-dressed man, in a business suit but no tie-- ties are considered an imperial affectation in Iran--got out and hurried over to the Major. "Can I be of any assistance?" he asked.

"Crap," the three Marines thought.

"Yes--yes--please--" The Major seemed to realize that his Farsi was mangled and impossible, and abandoned the attempt. "Do you speak Arabic?"

Understanding filled the businessman's face. "Yes, certainly. What's wrong?"

"We were on our way to Khorramabad and this officer stopped to help us with some engine trouble." The Major gestured at the hood of the Buick, which he had popped open before stepping out of the car. In the excitement, no one had noticed it. "Then he suddenly became sick and vomited. He can't stand, and now he seems to be having a hallucination. I think we need to get him to a hospital." The policeman was swaying unsteadily and ululating in a way that made the Marines' flesh creep.

"Your car is broken? Here, help me get him into mine." The newcomer took one of the policeman's arms and the Major took the other. They managed to ease him into the back of the vehicle, where he lay uncomplainingly on the upholstery. His eyes spun around the interior but never rested on anything for more than a second at a time.

"I'll send another officer back to help you as soon as I get him to a hospital," the businessman promised.

"We'd appreciate that. Thank you!"

The luxury sedan pulled away in a hurry. The Major walked back to the dusty Buick, shoved the hood back into place with a thrust of his hand, and climbed in. "Problem solved," he said. "We'll give our rescuer a chance to get a head start. And I'll drive slower from now on so that doesn't happen again."

"Sir, what was in that injection you gave him?" Powers asked.

"A very large dose of GHB."

"You gave him a date rape drug?"

"The problem with most psychotics is that they don't last long. GHB does--and it produces drowsiness and forgetfulness as well. By the time he's able to report us, he won't be able to tell his bosses anything more than I want them to hear."

"More than you want them to?" Brassey wanted to know, his voice suddenly suspicious. "Sir--were you speeding on purpose?"

The Major grinned. "If you act before your enemy can, Sergeant, it speeds up your decision cycle and slows theirs down, and it results in their having to act on less information, meaning their reaction is not well considered. Remember the OODA loop!" He switched the ignition on again and drove off.

"What if we hadn't been stopped by a passerby who could speak Arabic?" Powers demanded.

"Kadivar could have translated. A group of monolingual Arabs traveling in Iran is not exactly suspicious in and of itself. 'Tis the season for pilgrimage, after all."

"Well, now they know we're here," Sergeant Brassey observed. "What next, Major?"

"What do we usually do?" the Major replied. "What they don't expect."

The road forked ahead. The Major turned east, away from Khorramabad.

*****

"How many of them were there?" the colonel demanded.

The patrolman struggled to sit upright in his hospital bed. "Five--no, six--I think. The back of the car was full…" His voice trailed off and his eyes wavered in the direction of the nightstand.

"And how many attacked you? One? Two? More?"

"Just…just one. He sprayed me…" The officer mumbled something under his breath. "And then my shoulder…" He attempted to rub it, but forgot and gave up halfway. He was still disoriented. The colonel shrugged in despair. "Which direction were you heading when you stopped them?"

"Ahead?" the policeman asked. His face lit up with a smile and he dissolved into a fit of giggles. The colonel left the room, suppressing an urge to chew off his own beard.

Out in the waiting area, the businessman who had brought the policeman in proved to be more informative. "No, I'm afraid I didn't notice the make of the car. It was a large one, though. Four-door sedan, a light gray, I believe. The driver said they had engine trouble."

"Did you count the occupants?"

"No, but I could see that there was someone in the passenger seat, and the rear seat was occupied as well."

"Where were they heading?"

"Along the highway sound to Khorramabad. The driver corroborated that."

"Did he speak Farsi?"

"He tried at first. He was an Arab."

"An Arab? Can you be sure?"

"If he wasn't, he has a better grasp of the language than most of our countrymen. I've spent time in every Gulf state. His accent was definitely Saudi."

"Did you check the engine of the car yourself to see if he was telling the truth?"

"No. It never crossed my mind."

"What did you think about the condition of the patrol officer when you brought him here?"

"I thought he was more feverish than hallucinating. Also I noticed a chemical smell on his clothes, but I assumed that was from helping the Arabs with their car."

The colonel excused himself and crossed the corridor to a vacant office where he could make a call in private.

"Yes, it's the men we're looking for," he said to his superior in Tehran. "They didn't head north. They expected us to look there and went south instead! Our troops are three hundred miles away from where they should be looking. My guess is this American is making for the sea. No, we couldn't positively confirm that the prisoners were with him. No one has been able to identify them." He paused. "Then send us his photo and I'll check it with our one reliable witness." Another pause. "How can I be sure? The witness said he spoke with a Saudi accent. Which is the same description given by the lieutenant who was escorting the prisoners!" He nodded in response to an invisible command. "Yes, I'll circulate the description immediately, but one nondescript car in the middle of summer…One other thing. The officer who stopped them isn't very reliable at the moment, he's been drugged, but he thought there were only six people in the car. But five attacked the prison van, so one of the Americans must be missing. Which means we can't take our forces off the northern border, either."

* * * * *

Second Army Headquarters in Isfahan threw the 40th and 64th Infantry Divisions into action. They spread out, beating the countryside, looking for fugitives and turning up dozens of low-level drug and arms smugglers, but no Americans escorting escaped homosexuals. In and around Isfahan itself, the 84th Mechanized Division established checkpoints on every major road, as well as conducting random patrols of the less-frequented tracks. Soldiers dropped by the dozen from heat exhaustion, even at night. Airborne sensors became exponentially less useful. An experimental drone crashed and had to be covered up, for the sake of morale, with shovels and earth. A nest of ISIS guerrillas took advantage of the distraction and slipped across the border to attack the Iranian divisions in the rear. More chaos followed while Second Army straightened out the mess. The generals were becoming paranoid enough to wonder if the American had not only sneaked past their picket lines, but also turned around and counterattacked.

In Tehran, the members of the Assembly of Experts were well aware that they were making a spectacle of themselves. But their honor was at stake. They could not accept defeat on their own soil.

* * * * *

In Washington, the rescue operation and the backlash it had provoked were shoved off the front page and relegated to a few inches of small print in the back of the paper. The cover of *Democracy Today* was filled with a grainy photograph instead, showing two men kissing outside the door of an upscale apartment building. Underneath, the headline stated very simply, "Congressman finally steps out."

The article inside was no less smug. "Mark Randall," it began, "has consistently been one of the strongest opponents of equality in the House. More than that, he was *the* single member of Congress whose support could have guaranteed that the Equal Marriage Act became law--and he failed to cast his vote in favor of it. He has argued that voters in his district would not support the bill. Will they support him dating a male staffer working for the Republican National Committee?"

Most of the piece went on in the same tone of borderline sarcasm. Randall's previous behavior was reviewed in exhaustive detail. His media appearances, his shirtless tweets, his long conversations with interviewers about shoes, the pink shirt and tight pants he'd worn to a campaign event, the rumors that he'd been seen frequenting gay clubs in his home state, the story that he'd been caught in the shower with another man--all innuendo and no proof, repeated in order to lay a juicy foundation for the unveiling of proof at last. Then came the photos, in chronological order, accompanied by the testimony of a private investigator who admitted to tailing Randall for weeks in the hope of getting a compromising shot. "I knew he must have a private life," he was quoted as saying. "I just had to wait until I caught a glimpse of it." The article failed to specify who was paying his expenses during this time.

According to his tale, Randall had met the staffer, identified as one Adrian Meyers, for a quick drink at Nellie's. They were shown sitting together at a table on the roof, both laughing at a joke that the camera didn't catch. A closeup revealed Randall's hand resting on Meyers's knee. From there, it was off to the Tabard Inn for an early dinner. Again they chose the patio, which the photographer confessed had been a relief to him. They had lingered over their cocktails, browsed leisurely through the appetizers, and stayed for dessert and several rounds of coffee. The caffeine didn't help much and they were noticeably tipsy when they walked around the corner to the congressman's convertible. The photographer had parked his own car nearby and, in walking to it, had been able to capture a perfect shot of them embracing. The photo was crisp enough to show Meyers gently tugging at Randall's lower lip with his own mouth while Randall caressed the back of his head.

The rest, the would-be paparazzo said, had been easy. He'd followed them back to Randall's apartment, watched them walk hand in hand to the door, leaning against each other for support, and then, while the congressman had fumbled for his keys, Meyers had reached over and undone his belt. The editors gave that shot, taken seconds after the cover image, a full page of its own. The expression on Randall's face left no doubt that he was enjoying himself.

The article added, with an air that said "I told you so," that Randall, Meyers, and the RNC had all been contacted for comment but had not been heard from as of press time.

It didn't help matters any when the first wave of calls for comment from other papers to hit the congressman's office rebounded from his secretary's austere statement that he was at his gym.

When Randall did emerge, he walked right by the reporters without so much as making eye contact with any of them. It was a performance that far surpassed his previous standards of showing mere disdain for the fourth estate. He stepped into a waiting car and was at his office twenty minutes later. Journalists hovered in the halls, expecting him to call a press conference at any time. Others staked out the Minority Leader's office and hounded his departing visitors to see if he'd let fall any hints about the fate of an errant party member. They were disappointed. Some of the reporters went out and bought lunch for the others--wisely, as it turned out. At five o'clock that evening they were no wiser than they had been all day. As for Adrian Meyers, he'd been invisible since the story broke. Two of the committee members made personal statements disparaging his behavior, but nothing official was forthcoming.

Democracy Today had contented itself with painting the congressman as a hypocrite on gay rights without directly calling for his resignation. They left that task to the *Washington Blade*, which took it up with glee. The *Blade*'s columnists leapt on the story and by nightfall had explained in detail how the Republican Party would have no choice but to discipline Randall for his actions, which ran counter to party policy, how if they didn't the voters in his district would surely demand that he step down, how he would never be able to hold political office again, how much he deserved such treatment, and how happy it made them. Any voices raised to protest the principle of forcible outing were drowned out by the repeated assertions that in the case of an anti-gay gay politician, outing was not only justified but necessary.

Randall finally came out of his office, laughing to himself. Not smirking to cover a grimace of embarrassment. Laughing, as if he were enjoying being outed to an audience of several hundred millions. That confused the reporters. They surged forward, cameras and phones out, but the Capitol Police made a lane for the Congressman, and as far as anyone could tell, he made it all the way home without ever uttering a word.

*****

The Major bit into a hot and spicy kebab and sighed in appreciation. He sipped at his glass of ice water, ignoring the bottle of Zam Zam Cola with which the street vendor had insisted on burdening him. The land that had invented refrigeration, and they had to go and corrupt their beverages with sticky syrup. Down the street, a poet was reciting ghazals to the accompaniment of a guitar and the appreciative whispers of his listeners. The Major felt his satellite phone vibrate inside his shirt. He glanced at the screen, nodded, and shut it off, then went back to his dinner.

14

Strings of numbers unspooled on the screen in front of Shihab. Each line never contained more than twelve digits and three periods, except for those that contained no more than thirty-two digits, seven colons, and the first six letters of the Latin alphabet. Most of the strings were of the shorter variety. The transition from IPv4 to IPv6 numbering was far from being completed, and as a result the internal workings of the internet seemed even more chaotic than usual when stripped down.

The strings of letters typed into the address bar of a web browser or displayed in a hyperlink may carry some meaning to a human operator, but they are meaningless as far as the computer is concerned. They are not binary code, nor are they hexadecimal code that can be translated into binary. The computer cannot, by itself, do anything with them. So when it is fed an address and told to do something with it, it goes running for help. The computer version of a human-language-to-machine-language translator is a domain name system, or DNS, server. Over four hundred of these live in various secure buildings around the world. Their job is to keep track of a collective index of the entire internet. In their databases are maintained copies of every human-entered internet address, called the uniform resource locator in tech-speak, together with the equivalents of those addresses in computer-speak, the internet protocol addresses. When a DNS server is asked for a translation, it provides the requesting machine with the internet protocol address of the destination machine and the routing chain needed to reach it, allowing the two to then connect directly.

The use of the DNS system is necessitated by the fact that not all internet protocol addresses are permanent. Many are reassigned on a continuous basis. There is also another factor involved. Even prior to the exhaustion of the IPv4 numbering system, there were slightly over four billion possible addresses. Machines running scripts that do not require human recognition can interact using IP addresses alone. These connections run beneath the visible surface of the internet, without fancy dotcoms attached to them, carrying out a range of mundane--or not so mundane--tasks.

It was these connections, and the IP addresses that they used, that Shihab was scanning. He knew the address that redirected to the National Bank of Bahrain's homepage. He knew the one that sent the visitor to the login page for online banking. But what about the numbers used by the bank's servers to talk to the servers of the ABC Islamic Bank, or the Gulf Finance House, or the Khaleeji Commercial Bank, or the SWIFT network? Those had no obvious human-language addresses, but they existed all the same. Each one formed a viable path of communication in and out of the bank apart from the main page. And he needed the ability to access all those paths if the imam's plan was to work properly.

Across the room, Junayd frowned.

"The prime minister just sent a message to the Minister of Justice," he said aloud. He was reading the live feed of the Minister's email traffic before it reached the Minister himself.

"He does that every day. Sometimes he does it more than once a day. Don't they argue about Prince Salman enough in person?"

"It looks like he wants the Minister wearing his Islamic Affairs hat for this one. Uh-oh."

"What have they cooked up between them now?"

"Between them? Nothing. That's the problem." Junayd ruffled his hair. "Apparently it was the king who thought this one up. His uncle suggested it, but the king never told him he was going ahead with it. And now the prime minister has found out, and he's springing it on our dear friend the Minister for Justice and Islamic Affairs, who should like it in theory, but is going to be very unhappy about it in practice."

"Is the king going to make a concession? Or is his response to the increasing noise around his palace going to be to order the streets swept thrice daily with water cannons?"

"Neither. It's more subtle than that. He's called in the Haia."

"Wait--the Haia, as in the Saudi traditionalist thugs?"

"The very same." The Haia, officially the Committee for the Promotion of Virtue and the Prevention of Vice, were Saudi Arabia's religious police, or mutaween. A collection of street brawlers with government insignia and sponsorship, they roamed the streets of Riyadh and Jeddah and Mecca itself, beating up anyone they thought was behaving in an un-Islamic fashion. Conservative and liberal Muslims alike tended to view them with disdain. The Haia were so extreme in their views that lower-ranking members had engineered the removal of their own local directors on at least two occasions on the grounds of unorthodoxy.

"Last time he called for the Saudi army to come and protect him. But the Haia?"

"He doesn't live in contact with them, or have to deal with them on a daily basis, so he probably doesn't see them as a threat to himself, either."

"I'd rather have Saudi soldiers."

"So would the rest of Bahrain."

"I suppose it never occurred to the king that his little arrangement with our neighbors will backfire the second the population finds out about it."

"From the context of the email, it appears he's hoping the Haia will be able to hunt down and kill--yes, kill or damage, it says--the leaders of the pro-reform movement before anyone realizes they're here. Then they can slip back across the border while the local opposition implodes without leadership."

"Obviously the king hasn't figured out yet that someone is reading his ministers' mail."

"Speaking of which--it could always be a ruse."

"How do you figure that?"

"Maybe the cabinet has traced our sedition back at least part of the way and is trying to use an outrageous proposal like this to draw us out. Wait for us to make the announcement, then deny it while the Ministry follows the electronic trail back underground."

Shihab shrugged. "We'll see. In the meantime, we don't act on it and wait till anyone who is unmistakeably a member of the Haia turns up in Manama. That should be easy to notice."

"And we hole up until it's time for the final campaign."

"That would be harder, but we could manage it."

"Let's get the imam down here and see what he thinks."

"Don't get up," Shihab said, stopping Junayd halfway. "He went out with Asim."

Junayd settled back onto his heels in shock. For the first time in months, he actually looked worried.

"A wanted man and an anarchist scholar out on the same streets as that pack of Saudi bullies," he said under his breath. "I don't like it."

* * * * *

"Will you accept," Ra'd bin Mazin asked, "for the purposes of our discussion, that man has a soul?"

He moved with a surprising lack of hesitation for a blind man. A touch now and then to indicate direction, an arm to lean on going up or down steps, was all he required from Asim. Passersby, noticing the cane in his hand and the fixed stare of his eyes, moved respectfully to one side to let them through. The sun was hot, but he soaked it up with a benevolent expression and without complaint, enjoying the change from the cool, dark rooms where he spent most of his days.

"For the purpose of argument, yes," Asim said. He remained cautious.

"I can hear that you are still hedging your words in your mind. But no matter. Would you also agree that the soul is not the body?"

"That's pretty well established, isn't it? The definition of a soul is that it's immortal. It can't be the same thing as the body, then, because the body is most definitely not immortal. Also the body has a physical existence, whereas no one has ever demonstrated the physical existence of the soul."

"Well reasoned. The two concepts are separate. Now, the body possesses the attribute of gender, does it not? A body is either male or female. But the soul is not the body, so which gender does it possess?"

"Can it possess either?"

"That is the answer to your question."

"But the Quran speaks continually of the differences between man and woman."

"Which gender is a human being?"

"Either male or female."

"Then humanity is a result of the possession of a mortal, physical body, not an immortal, incorporeal soul?"

Asim said nothing.

"You see the problem," the imam went on. "If humanity, and consequently our treatment of one another, consists of the possession of a physical body, then the abstract concept of humanity must take on the attributes of the body as well, including gender and mortality. But if humanity consists of the possession of a soul, then it acquires none of those attributes from the body if the soul does not have them in the beginning."

"Which brings us back to your so-called answer. Do you always reason in circles?"

"Only to emphasize that the circle itself may be the only answer we can find."

"You should have been an ascetic philosopher in the age of a past caliph."

"I enjoy the blessings of life too much to have ever been an ascetic. Are those fresh oranges that I smell?"

Asim looked around him. "Yes, over there. I don't smell them, though."

"You can see them. Let us have some and wait for Fihr. He will be joining us soon?"

"In about half an hour, he said when he called."

* * * * *

Fihr could see them out of the corner of his eye, but he didn't rush over to the rickety table where they were sitting. The imam was clearly enjoying his orange and there was no point in interrupting him. He didn't wave, either. It would be bad tradecraft. Granted, he didn't think that anyone was following him, or them, but it never hurt to keep public demonstrations to a minimum. Restraint bought you more time to identify a tail in a worst-case scenario.

He paused at a bookseller's stall and began flipping through the back issues of *Saudi Aramco World*, picking out one or two that he didn't already have. As a rule, when a city burned, the documents it contained burned up with it. The prevalence of cheap semiconductors, combined with the world's newfound paranoia over the hazards of asbestos, had quashed any large-scale production of fireproof paper for archival purposes. Information was being left in the same old fragile forms while human beings became more able and more inclined to destroy it. Perhaps, he reflected, Sima Qian had been right with his theory that dynasties began with rulers of skill and intelligence, then decayed over time until they became so indulgent and foolish that they were destroyed and replaced by new, fresh blood. Except it wasn't the rulers who mattered in the broader application of the theory. What if it was all mankind that decayed and had to be replaced or reinvigorated? It came back to him that Frank Herbert had said much the same thing two thousand years after the Chinese historian. Herbert had appropriated the word jihad from the Arabic to describe his galactic upheaval, too. An endeavor so deeply encoded in human genetics that no amount of social or political manipulation could prevent it.

He noticed a Robert Howard paperback buried at the bottom of a basket of random items, and bent to pick it up.

A thin wooden cane came down across his fingers as he wiggled it loose. He jumped back, startled, colliding with the long wooden table on which the bookseller had placed most of his stock and sending a cascade of books onto that unfortunate man's unprotected toes. His angry screeches were all but unnoticed by Fihr, who was staring at his assailant.

Who would have been an extremely handsome man once upon a time, until a blow had split open the entire left side of his cheek and embedded it with cordite or some other penetrating substance that lingered in the tissues and couldn't be removed. The permanent stain was noticeable even under the layers of dirt and grime caked on the man's face. His beard was poorly trimmed, and he wore his keffiyeh without an agal, a characteristic that struck a chord in the recesses of Fihr's mind.

"May I ask why you hit me?" Fihr inquired. His voice was the epitome of urbane politeness, barely touched with irony. He was a good six inches taller than the man who had attacked him.

"For touching trash." The man lashed out with his cane again, without warning, sending the book flying out of Fihr's hand. He stepped on it and ground it into the gravel. Fihr raised an eyebrow and examined the welt that was forming across the backs of his fingers. "That's an unacceptable reason."

"A good Muslim does not indulge in Western sexual perversions."

"A good Muslim does not attack a fellow believer in an attempt to alter his behavior in accordance with his own personal interpretation of his faith."

"We are commanded to chastise those who deviate from the path."

"Commanded by whom?"

"By the Book, by the Prophet, by our king and by your king."

"And who might your king be?"

"Salman bin Abdulaziz Al Saud."

"Oh, so you're the Haia, are you?" Behind his attacker, who had pushed up offensively close to him, Fihr could see three more men edging in his direction. They were all as unwashed as the first. "That was a foolish move on Hamad's part. Does he really think anyone in Bahrain will tolerate you foul little--"

The first of the mutaween lunged with his cane. Fihr was prepared for it this time. He blocked the blow with his forearm, gave his wrist a turn, and the fragile wood snapped in two, leaving the Saudi hanging onto a stump shorter than a drumstick. The three newcomers rocked forward on their toes, then hesitated.

"You foul little bullies?" Fihr finished, as if he'd never been interrupted. "You have no place here, or anywhere else on earth. It's a marvel that your countrymen haven't stamped you into the dirt yet. Go away."

"We have authorization from the Prime Minister's office--"

"There is no God but God, and Mohammed is the Messenger of God. The Prime Minister is neither God nor Messenger, and your authorization is worthless."

The four men gave a series of shouts in which the word "blasphemy" could clearly be distinguished and leaped at him. Fihr vaulted over the bookseller's table, placing a barrier between himself and the attackers for a brief moment.

* * * * *

"Do not stand up," the imam said, tightening his grip on Asim's wrist with a suddenness that made him flinch.

"But Fihr's being attacked by four men," Asim hissed, trying to keep his voice low.

"He can defend himself."

"And if he can't? I should--"

"Expose yourself to his attackers? What if they are police?"

"All the more reason to help him!"

"Noble, but impractical. He can beat them. Do not risk it. Tell me what is happening."

* * * * *

The mutaween barked their shins trying to scramble over the rough wooden table to get at Fihr before they realized he wasn't behind it anymore. He had slipped out through the curtain that formed a makeshift partition for the stall on one side. Their sandals skidding on the badly-maintained asphalt pavement, they spun around and took off in that direction. He was running ahead of them, not pushing himself, keeping them within a matter of yards by choice.

All at once he stopped, grabbed an unworked pole from a woodcarver's stall as he passed it, and turned to face them. The first man was still waving his broken-off cane and gibbering. Fihr held the staff in his right hand and pitched it like a javelin without letting go. The butt of it took his attacker in the sternum and dropped him like a stone on the spot where he stood, destroying his momentum. He flipped the staff up, took the end in both hands, and brought it down on the head of the second Saudi, who was also brandishing a thin cane more useful for beating old men than young ones. His assailant tried to dodge, but Fihr was too quick and too powerful. The blow he gave the man knocked him unconscious.

The third of the mutaween was more creative. He pulled a whip from underneath his clothes and advanced on Fihr with a vicious, toothless smile splitting his face. He tried to strike at the hacker's legs, to trip him up and get him on the ground where he would have the advantage of height. Fihr sidestepped the first few thrusts, but tired of the game. Raising his staff, he let the Saudi snare one of his legs. The man gave a cry of joy and threw his weight on the lash, only to overbalance and skin his knees on the pavement. Fihr hadn't budged under the force of his pull, and now casually shook off the lash and stepped away from it as if to give his attacker another chance. Enraged, the man struck out again, and this time Fihr caught the blow on his staff. He clapped one hand over the lash, which had twisted itself around the pole, and jerked it towards him. The handle of the whip flew out of the Saudi's hands so fast it left painful scorch marks behind. The man screamed and took a step back, his eyes afraid. He was too slow. Fihr lunged and spun. The end of his staff took the third man in the temple the way a capstan bar strikes an incautious sailor.

His lunge also carried him out of the way of the last of the group, who had been sidling towards him along the line of stalls the entire time, hoping to sneak up and take him from the rear. It was why the third man had tried to keep Fihr in play for so long. He was hoping his associate would do the deed from behind with a knife. The sight of the steel blade, already drawn, surprised Fihr. The Haia, by their own choice, never carried deadly weapons inside Saudi Arabia. They beat people with joy, but they avoided killing and maiming in order to give the courts more to do. Here, the courts would never sanction an arrest by non-credentialed foreign police--which meant that the sole limit on the behavior of the mutaween no longer existed. And King Hamad and the Prime Minister would have known that, which meant that they had intentionally called in the Haia for the purpose of terrorizing Bahrain's population. That kind of treachery irritated the community-minded Fihr. He spit in the fourth man's eye, distracting him for an instant. His hands moved in a blur, spinning the shaft, feinting. Then the wood struck the Saudi's wrists so hard that it broke both of them. Any protest the man might have made--a yell, a groan, a prayer or curse--was cut off as Fihr thrust his staff under the attacker's chin, shoving his jaw closed at the probable expense of his tongue, and threw him backwards. The force of the throw bounced his head off the cinderblock wall of a small store and he crumpled up like wet newsprint.

Fihr replaced the pole in the woodcarver's stall, to the carver's astonishment, and trotted off. He was out of sight among the crowd in the bazaar in a matter of seconds.

* * * * *

Asim sighed in relief.

"Yes, he can fight," the imam said. "He can fight as few men can."

"But that--that--" Asim checked his phone. "It didn't even take a minute! Every time he struck at them--"

"Now you understand why I told you to wait. He is safe, and they cannot identify us to the police as his friends."

"But I should have helped him anyway."

"'And why should ye not fight in the cause of God and the cause of those who, being weak, are ill-treated and oppressed?'"

"You're asking me to find an answer for the question I just asked you?"

"I was agreeing with you, as was the Prophet."

"But supposing he smashed their heads in? Suppose he killed them in defending himself?"

"He could not have. He would have to restrain his actions in accordance with his beliefs."

"You say that as if it couldn't happen."

"In a man of faith, it could not happen by intent, and intent is what matters."

"Intent is enough to stop a blow?"

"If intent is strong enough, the blow will never fall in the first place, because with the intent comes foresight that will prevent the blow from being struck."

"So how do we keep those blows from being struck at us?"

The imam was silent for a few minutes. His face was sad, Asim realized.

"We must go," he said eventually.

"Hiding isn't a permanent solution."

"But for the next few days, it is a sufficient one." The imam rose from the cane chair. "You watched the fight, but I listened to it. Tell me, what did you hear?"

"They argued with Fihr, and then they shouted at him, and then they attacked him."

"That is all?"

Asim shrugged. "That I noticed, yes."

"They were Saudis. From the words they chose, they were members of the Haia."

"Not possible. The Haia have no authority in Bahrain."

"Is it unheard of for King Hamad to invite his neighbors to solve his problems for him?" Asim remembered the photos of the soldiers marching across the bridge.

"The mutaween are among us," the imam said. "That means that the state has taken notice of our group in particular. Mere activism can be met with a police or military presence, but religious activism must be countered by a force noted for its strict religious orthodoxy. It may or may not prove effective, but it makes a statement. It is personal now. We have affronted the kingdom's official interpretation of Islam, and we must die for it to feel safe again."

15

Clarissa Montgomery leaned back in her chair. As a rule, furniture in a District of Columbia Starbucks is more comfortable than it is in similar outlets elsewhere in the country, and this store was no exception to that rule. With the air conditioning running at maximum capacity, the enveloping arms of the chair didn't feel oppressively hot, either. Outside, conditions were a little different. The second most prominent news story that morning had been the sudden deaths of three people on the street the previous day, including a retired senator, from heat exhaustion. Dozens more remained hospitalized from the heat wave, which had pushed local temperatures briefly into the triple digits.

The most prominent story, of course, taking precedence over weather trivia, was still Congressman Randall's outing. Two days in and neither Randall nor his alleged lover nor the Republican National Committee had commented yet. Montgomery admired their restraint, but found it irritating as well. With nothing new to report on, she was reduced to rehashing old facts and analysis to produce copy, and the *Washington Post*, in spite of the decline in journalistic standards, nevertheless continued to prefer new stories to old ones. Randall's silence also reminded her that her profession was threatened. The paper might have no news to publish, but it had to publish something, and so it turned to its bloggers and editorial writers to spawn dozens of pages of fresh content for its website. Commentary on the social aspects of the Congressman's outing, his future in the House, the speculations of forced resignation--these were opinion and published as such, and didn't have to be held to the same standards of verifiability as actual reporting. Which made them much easier to produce, and therefore more plentiful. Plentiful enough to force the work of professional journalists like herself into the background.

Her fingers skated over the glass screen of the iPad. It was largely unscratched, meaning it was new. A company computer. De rigueur for the modern reporter, because you could write with it and speak into it and take photos with it all at once, and there would be no lag time in getting the content back to the typesetters.

An earnest-looking, floppy-haired blonde stared up at her from the screen. She scowled and flicked him away. Kyle Scott Bradley had finally deigned to emerge from his editorial office to make a statement on the article his magazine had published. Behind his right shoulder, Congressman Elliott hovered, waiting his turn to speak. Montgomery had been at their press conference, and the photo brought back unpleasant memories. Their words had been gloating enough, under the veneer of bureaucratese, but there was more to it than that. She remembered looking at their faces in person. They both had been...jubilant. Not just pleased at having scored a coup over a man they considered their enemy, but delighted in a way that they felt they needed to hide. Mixed in with their pleasure was a trace of viciousness that she hadn't expected.

Her mother had been a professional fortune-teller who had taught her daughter to look for the little things, and the little things in this story disturbed her.

Who tipped the magazine off? she asked herself once more. Bradley hadn't bothered to comment on why the private investigator had been following Randall in the first place. His name had been printed in the *Democracy Today* article, and she and about twenty other reporters had checked out his background. He was a licensed, experienced detective all right, not a paparazzo chasing a story he happened to catch a glimpse of while out for a drink. Did the magazine have a detective permanently tailing Randall, waiting for him to slip up and embarrass himself? That would be expensive. But Bradley was a multimillionaire. He could afford a regiment of private investigators for years on end if he wanted them. Bradley. Why did her thoughts keep coming back to him?

He instigated this, Montgomery said to herself. This wasn't a sub-editor's decision, or a volunteer assignment that some reporter thought up. It came straight from the owner-editor's special projects drawer. He and his husband carried a grudge against Randall. That much was obvious from their words--hell, it was obvious from their eagerness to get involved in such a peripheral issue at all.

And if there was a grudge involved, the source of that grudge was easy enough to find. Elliott had lobbied harder for the Equal Marriage Act than any other member of the House, even twisting a few arms behind the scenes, if Capitol Hill gossip could be trusted. He hadn't been able to hide his fury after Congress proved unable to overturn the veto. A few days later, his husband's magazine published a lead article naming Randall as the person most responsible for that defeat at the same time that it outed him. Was the article their form of revenge? Had they just gotten lucky and caught him philandering right after he shot down their pet bill, or had they been sitting on the information for some time?

Montgomery realized immediately that blind luck was by far the less likely of the two alternatives. It was known that Elliott had confronted Randall on the Capitol steps after the final vote on the Act had been taken. Randall would have been aware that his actions would be scrutinized from then on, unless he was stupid--and he wasn't that stupid, she decided. He wouldn't have exposed himself right after pissing off two rich men with every incentive to humiliate him. She remembered also that the article in *Democracy Today* had not mentioned the date the photos were taken--or any date at all, for that matter.

Did Bradley have the photos long before the Act was voted on? she wondered. And if so--and her mouth watered as she thought about it--did he and Elliott try to use them to pressure Randall into voting their way?

Journalism is hunches, she reminded herself. Let's see where this one leads.

She tapped the screen and brought up a list of the *Democracy Today* staff. The editors were all familiar to her. A brief scan through their names and she dismissed them out of hand. Their politics were all much the same as Bradley's, differing in the details only. Neo-progressive thought with an underlying sense that gay rights were The Struggle of the present day, the battle that must be won before humanity could move on to anything else. None of them were likely to talk to her.

There were dozens of contributors whom she could have called, but it was hit and miss whether they would have talked to her where their boss was concerned. If she could see in Bradley's eyes that he would fire an intellectual dissident and pay whatever it cost him if sued, then the people who worked for him certainly could see that as well, and would keep quiet. That was another problem. Many of the contributors were freelance or part-time. They wouldn't be in the office on a regular basis, able to hear the gossip or find out what articles were in the pipeline.

On second thought, that was a partial answer. Montgomery chuckled to herself. She was working, and she wasn't anywhere near the *Post* building. Journalists in general were not in the offices of their paper much these days. They were out researching their stories, or at home or in a convenient coffee shop typing up copy and livestreaming it to the proofreaders and copyeditors via their tablets.

So that line of reasoning narrowed the field to regular employees, rather than creative ones, who still had access to planned future content, or were in a position to overhear it being discussed. And those were the ones who would be harder to talk to. Their contact information was not listed as it was for the journalists, and they were the ones who had the least incentive to tattle in a stagnant economy.

Then her eye drifted down to the bottom of the list and stopped at a single word.

Interns. Naturally. They were her best potential sources. They didn't expect to spend a career, or even the next few years, at the magazine, they were exposed to a wide range of content, and they were staff, meaning that they were in the offices all day long and able to pick up all the local gossip. Also, she thought, criticizing herself at a lower level for her cynicism, they're young and haven't grown used to keeping their mouths shut yet.

* * * * *

Montgomery considered starting an argument with the bouncer, but decided it wasn't worth wasting her breath. She handed over the cover charge, was given an appropriate wristband, and let the crowd suck her in under the green awning, taking the opportunity to check everyone's face against her trained memory.

JR's Bar and Grill was comfortably full without being crowded. The middle of the week was a slow time for heavy drinkers. One of the District's older gay clubs, it was also one of the more mellow. The moose on the wall looked doleful, but then it always had. The rest of the crowd was cheerful, enjoying the crooning of a local Broadway enthusiast while a glitter-covered Death Star shimmered up in the rafters. Montgomery checked her phone one last time. Nothing new.

Democracy Today listed ten interns as members of its staff. Four had not returned her calls. Two had rung back to decline to be interviewed. She had managed to net two others by buying them dinner. It was clear to her that the male intern thought that a joint interview would be a good excuse for spending his leisure time in the company of the female intern, but it was less certain whether the female intern agreed with him on that. Neither of them had contributed much, apart from nailing down that the Randall article had been Bradley's pet project, and that it had definitely been in the works for several weeks, not several days. The girl remembered seeing the private investigator talking to Bradley on two or three occasions--but she was positive that none of their meetings had taken place after the final failure of the Equal Marriage Act.

Montgomery tapped her nails impatiently on the bar. Speculation. All speculation. It would be irresistible to insinuate that Bradley had been blackmailing Randall, or trying to, and only published the photos when he found out that he couldn't extract anything from the congressman. And Elliott was his go-between for that. It explained his rage after such a double defeat, and his confrontation with Randall. But if she printed that, Bradley wouldn't hesitate to slap her and the *Post* both with a libel suit. She needed more information, and pulled out her phone to make a note. If Elliott was blackmailing Randall on behalf of his husband, he would have had to visit Randall. Randall's secretaries might be able to give her dates and times.

Then she looked up and spotted him. Dark, thoughtful, dressed in a tight tank-top and fitted jeans. His attention was fixed on the singer. He seemed to be having fun. Sorry, Montgomery mentally apologized to him as she crossed the room and tapped him on the shoulder.

"Jasper Holloway?" she asked.

The young man turned towards her, puzzled. "Yes?"

"I'm Clarissa Montgomery, with the *Post*. I understand you're an intern at *Democracy Today*. I'd like to talk to you about the Randall story."

Holloway was looking much less happy now. He stared back at her, not with hostility, but with deliberation.

"Why do you want to talk to an intern?" he finally asked, bending closer to her to make himself heard over the music.

"I want to find out why Bradley published the story when he did after sitting on it for a few weeks."

"So you know he was holding it back."

"Yes, and so do you, apparently."

* * * * *

"How did you find me?" Holloway wanted to know. "My contact information is not online." He was exploring the situation, feeling it out, and Montgomery let him. It was better to have him comfortable before he started talking.

"Your Instagram feed. You posted a few pictures of singers from earlier this evening, and they were geotagged as JR's Bar and Grill."

"That's cyberstalking."

"Or journalism."

Holloway sipped at the iced latte and examined her again. They were back at her favorite Starbucks, which was almost deserted at this hour except for a group of nervy venture capitalists at the far end. Would-be green energy executives, or some such thing.

"Clarissa is an unusual name," he said, going off on another tangent.

Montgomery shrugged. "My parents were fans of the Aubrey-Maturin novels."

"So they named you after a transported convict?"

"The way they saw it, that was the middle ground between an expensive prostitute and a dimwitted member of the landed gentry. Besides"--she smiled to herself as she said it--"they're not exactly conventional themselves."

Holloway nodded. "How many of my fellow interns have you talked to so far?"

"Only two. Two others refused to be interviewed. Four I haven't heard back from."

"That narrows your field of inquiry."

"I still have two possible leads left, and that's enough."

"What are you trying to find out?"

Montgomery leaned forward. "I want to know how long Bradley had those photos of Randall for before he decided to publish the story."

"At least three weeks, possibly more."

"And when did he give the final go-ahead for it?"

"The day of the vote."

"How can you be certain?"

"He was in the newsroom when we found out that the House had failed to overturn the veto. Someone shouted it out. He cursed and pulled out his phone to make sure. Then he went storming into his office and closed the door. I walked past it and heard him talking to someone--I assumed it was Congressman Elliott. He stayed in there for the rest of the afternoon. Elliott joined him shortly thereafter. Then Bradley came out of the office with a thumb drive and handed it to the editor on-duty. He ordered him to pull the lead story for the next issue and have it replaced with one that he'd prepared. The editor complained about the time factor, but he did it."

"So Randall's outing followed his defeat of the Equal Marriage Act by a few hours."

"Is your story about malice?"

"That looks like malice to me. Punishing him for his vote by trying to ruin his political career."

Holloway said nothing.

"Or wasn't it an attempt at ending his career?" Montgomery pressed him. "Were Bradley and Elliott willing to let him keep his career--for a price?"

"You mean were they blackmailing him."

Montgomery waited.

Holloway reached for his phone. The screen glowed at his touch, the gleaming buttons scrolling past in a surge of light and color. It blinked to the white of a folder, showing a list of some kind. Montgomery couldn't read it. Holloway tapped one of the lines and placed the device on the table between them.

"…it's not as easy as just going on Rentboy," Kyle Scott Bradley said out of the phone's speaker. "We have to find someone reliable."

"Well, the more expensive escorts are discreet, that's why they're expensive," his husband replied.

"So discreet they're not findable."

"I could ask one of my Congressional colleagues," Elliott joked.

"Very funny. Especially in these circumstances. No, the high-priced ones aren't any more trustworthy. Look at Calvin Klein's last boytoy. Look at Brent Corrigan. I could name others. They're all trying to write tell-alls cashing in on the names of their clients. We have to find someone who won't talk. Ever."

"You have a bunch of interns here. Offer them a permanent position, a bonus, a long-term contract."

"And if in ten years that staffer screws up and has to be fired and decides to revenge himself on us by exposing this? It's too dangerous."

"The idea is dangerous to begin with."

"Look, I know that. But how are we going to get at Randall without something drastic? His constituents love him. He gets reelected with sixty or seventy percent of the vote every time. He's got the best social media profile of any member of Congress. And he keeps quiet on the hot-button issues to the point where we don't have anything to accuse him of except being in the closet. And that hasn't worked out so well."

"Yeah, yeah." There was a pause and a crackle on the recording. "We don't have much time to pull it off. We won't be able to get the votes next year. Such is the nature of the seesaw."

"All the more reason that it needs to be something spectacular. Otherwise he'll just brush it off like the shower story."

"Maybe that's it."

"What's it?"

"Do we have to actually frame him for it to work?"

"Go on…"

"The shower story. Think about it. He's a health nut in his early thirties who's a bit of a showoff but has to take his pleasures on the sly given his public position. Would the rumors have started if he wasn't taking them at all? Why don't we just sit back and wait for him to go to bed with some trick he picked up at a bathhouse?"

"You think he'll do it in the next month or so?"

"I think the chances of that happening are better than us finding a trustworthy escort to toss across his path."

"But if we use an escort we can catch them in the act."

"We don't have to. All we need is a shot of him making out with another guy in a private setting. He can't get around that."

"But how do we get it? That's why an escort would be better. We could control the situation that way. Burglarizing his apartment is way more risky than setting him up for a photo op in the first place."

"That makes it tougher but not impossible. We'd just have to have a photographer on his tail every second he's outside the Capitol."

"Half a dozen photographers, probably."

"Yeah, but they'd all look like tourists with superzoom cameras. They'd blend in. And if they didn't catch him in the act they'd still probably come up with information we could use."

Another break in the conversation. "Okay," Bradley said. "That makes sense. And we can start doing it right away, so we have more time. But I'm still going to look for an escort in case we don't catch him with one of his regular playmates."

"Eh, I don't think you'll find one, but fire away."

"This is too important to miss any chance, even a small one. If we lose…"

"…then we may not get the opportunity again till we're old."

"Well, older, anyway."

"So we get the photos and I take them to him, and he votes for the EMA, and for any other piece of gay rights legislation we want him to support for as long as he stays in the House."

"Unless he wants to be the first Republican member of Congress to try to win reelection as an out gay man."

"You think he could?" Elliott sounded unsure.

"Not a chance. The party's core already thinks he's too moderate. They'd force him out and hope that the people who'd been voting for him since he was a teenager would switch their loyalties to his replacement in the blink of an eye."

"And we'd stand a better chance of winning the district in the confusion, especially if Randall fought the RNC and split the vote three ways."

"Yep. There's no way this doesn't work out better for us in the end."

"Okay. That takes care of all but one vote, and I think I know how to get us that last one. Remember that trust you set up--"

There was a burst of static, and the recording came to an end.

"My supervisor walked by, and I had to move on," Holloway said apologetically.

"Holy crap," Montgomery muttered under her breath. "They set him up. They really did set him up!" She sank back in her chair. "Why didn't you make this public earlier?"

"I wasn't sure how to," Holloway said. "And besides, it doesn't really change things, does it?"

"Excuse me?"

"Randall's still been outed, after all."

"Oh, bull! That's not the real story here! The real story is one congressman blackmailing another to get a pet bill passed. And the victim having the guts to stand up to his blackmailer at the cost of his own career. That's what counts!" A thought crossed her mind. "Would you be willing to let me borrow your phone for a few hours? I'd like to take it over to our tech lab and make sure there's nothing amiss with the timestamp, nothing that Bradley and Elliott could challenge in court. We could go over there right now and you could wait."

"I'm not sure I want to be involved in this," the intern said, hesitating.

"I won't name you if you don't want me to. Even so, if you're looking for a job in journalism or publishing, I'll give you the best reference ever written for helping me out here. This is a national story. Having it on record that you were part of it, that you blew it wide open, could only help you get a start."

Holloway finished the rest of his drink and crunched the ice cubes in the bottom of the cup up with his straw. He sat and stared at them for a couple of minutes.

"All right. You can take a copy of the recording, and I'll answer whatever questions you have left."

* * * * *

At six o'clock the following morning, early readers of the *Post* picked it up from their front steps, or at a newsstand in the Washington Metro, and were greeted with a reproduction of the photo of Elliott and Bradley that Montgomery disliked so much.

"Congressman, journalist conspire to entrap, blackmail Randall," the headline above the photo read.

Montgomery had taken her cues from Bradley's original article. She kept her comments to a minimum and let the evidence speak for itself, adding little beyond an introduction which stated that the conversation she was about to describe had been recorded by a *Democracy Today* staff member outside a conference room over a month prior to Randall's outing. As for the rest of the story, the *Post* printed the transcript of Holloway's recording in full.

"Mr. Bradley's motives were never unclear," she wrote in her conclusion. "He wanted to punish Congressman Randall for being, in his own assessment, the prime mover behind the demise of the Equal Marriage Act, which his husband has spent the past year fighting to get through Congress. However, it now appears that spite was not his only motivation. Outing Randall was a secondary substitute for not being able to manipulate him into supporting the EMA. Bradley took it upon himself to be the arbiter of justice for the gay community, to make sure they got what they wanted even at the expense of the democratic process.

"We don't know what Randall's understanding of his own sexuality is like. We were never given the opportunity to form that judgment, because Kyle Scott Bradley gave him no choice in the matter. Either Randall would conform to the Bradley/Elliott plan for the political legitimization of gay marriage, or he would be shoved out of the closet, regardless of his own wishes, to live a life he didn't want. He was not treated with the respect or the equality that Bradley and Elliott have constantly demanded in print and in public. They have broken the law, breached every ethical principle of good journalism and good activism--and those actions pale into insignificance next to their real offense: bullying a fellow gay man to force him to prevent them from being bullied."

By the time Bradley woke up that morning, in response to a frantic call from his night editor, the *Post* article had been read half a million times. By the time he and Elliott managed to issue a joint statement flatly denying that they had ever had such a conversation and promising legal action, that figure had increased by an order of magnitude.

The gay press found themselves with little to write about, the *Blade* in particular. Their two great heroes had been exposed as hypocrites beyond the possibility of recall. Under the circumstances, the best they could do was remind their readers that Randall had still been outed. However, outing proved to be much less of a draw than conspiracy and blackmail. One daring columnist pointed out that what Bradley had done was the same kind of direct action that the still-missing Major Martin was taking in Iran. He was promptly shouted down on Twitter.

* * * * *

"So," Congressman Randall said, letting his overstuffed leather chair rotate beneath him on silent bearings.

Clarissa Montgomery didn't say anything. She waited for him to continue the conversation. In the meantime, she found it very enjoyable to think of her fellow journalists slavering outside the glass door of the front office. None of them had been invited to interview the Congressman or hear the first words he'd spoken to a reporter since the story broke.

"Thanks for the vindication--of a sort."

"It was a fair, unbiased assessment."

"More courageous to fight than play ball with a blackmailer?"

"I always thought Elliott was a slug," Montgomery said frankly. That earned her a chuckle from Randall. "So you confirm that he was blackmailing you, then."

"Are you recording this?"

"No."

"I would be if I were you."

"You want to go on the record?"

"I didn't ask you to come in here to play word hockey."

"Okay." The *Post* reporter opened the cover of her tablet and tapped the screen. A green line flashed across it, trembling as the vibrations of their voices were converted into a visible pattern while simultaneously being stored away in the computer's flash memory. "I'll ask the question again--for the record. Were Congressman Elliott and Mr. Bradley blackmailing you?"

"Yes."

"When did they let you know that they had the photos?"

"A few days before the vote on the EMA. Elliott came here. You can check the exact time with my secretary."

"Did he threaten you?"

"Not then. His choice of words was much more subtle. He said he was glad that I'd be supporting their attempt to overturn the veto, right after he handed me copies of the photos. I asked him how I was supposed to explain my change of heart to my constituents. He smirked and threw the last administration in my face. Said the President couldn't be allowed to get away with overriding the will of the people as expressed by Congress."

"You say he didn't threaten you at that time. Meaning that he did later?"

"Oh, yes."

"Publicly or privately?"

"On the steps of the Capitol as I was leaving after the vote. You noted it in your report."

"Yes, but no one who witnessed the confrontation heard what you were saying."

"I can remedy that." Randall reached into his desk drawer and tossed her a small, flat silver iPod. "I thought he might try running me down right away."

"You recorded the encounter?"

Randall clicked a button on his laptop.

"Do you have a death wish or something?" the absent Elliott asked them again from the speakers.

The recording ran its course without comment from Montgomery, down to the Democratic congressman's promise to make Randall a "deserving casualty."

"He must have been really pissed off at you," she finally said, shaking her head. "He doesn't seem to have showed much restraint at any point during this business."

Randall waved that aside. "He's committed to his ideas. I can understand that. But I don't like being threatened."

"So you needled him about Bradley buying him the seat."

"Of course. Come on, everyone who's the slightest bit in touch with politics on the east coast knows damn well the only reason he won his seat in the first place was because his husband outspent the competition by ten to one at least. And with all that spending he still barely squeaked in. That's not a fair fight."

"No, I admit it's not. Did you see him again after that?"

"Only on the news."

"He didn't deign to revisit the scene of the crime?"

"I guess I wasn't worth the trouble. I deserved to be a casualty, after all." Randall grinned a dry grin tinged with mock sorrow.

"Well, you've had the chance to defend your actions now and prove that you won't give in to career pressure. What's next for you, Congressman?"

"Telling you the rest of the story."

Montgomery had already been reaching for her iPad when he said that. She paused. "There's more to this?"

And Randall laughed. "Hell yeah. What actually happened."

"I'm not sure I follow you."

"What do you think of Jasper Holloway?"

"Nice kid. Polite, self-effacing--wait. Hold on a second. I didn't name Holloway in my story. How do you know about him?"

"Because, as you just said, he's one of the good guys. You weren't the first person to hear that recording of Bradley and Elliott planning to set me up. You were the second. I was the first."

"He brought it to you."

"About a month ago. He said we might differ in our politics but he didn't think I deserved to be set up by a pair of self-righteous, self-interested rich dilettantes. He's got a very strong sense of fair play. I thanked him for the warning and told him I'd be on the lookout for anything Bradley might try to pull, and asked him to keep quiet about what he'd overheard while I figured out what to do about it. He agreed. Then I went out and called an old friend of mine. Adrian Meyers."

"You set Bradley up?"

"I set Bradley up." Randall's face radiated pure delight. "I thought it would be better to head him off than to wait for him to come up with an escort or another compromising situation on his own. I took his words about controlling the situation to heart. So Adrian and I deliberately gave him something to use against me."

"Did your party leadership know about this?"

"Nope. I couldn't have trusted them not to screw it up. I had to call in every favor I've accumulated in five terms and rack up a few of my own to keep them from making a statement or demanding one from me, but it was worth it. They still don't know. They won't until you go to press."

Montgomery shook her head in astonishment. "Wow. I'm still struggling to wrap my head around this, honestly. A conspiracy that actually worked and didn't go off half-cocked?"

"That's what it sounds like."

"When were you going to blow the whistle?"

"I thought I'd give Bradley and Elliott plenty of time to commit themselves to attacking me from an assumed position of moral rectitude. Say a few more days, maybe a week overall. But you got to Holloway first."

"And your date with Adrian Meyers was all part of the plan."

"A performance from start to finish."

"So you're not seeing him romantically."

"Sorry to disappoint you."

"In all fairness, it makes a better story that way," Montgomery admitted.

"I thought you might say that. Journalists just aren't sensitive."

"And politicians are?"

"To opinion polls--certainly!"

* * * * *

The English-speaking world laughed its head off. In those countries where cricket was traditional, jokes about Congressman Randall being "not out" acquired a sudden and disastrous popularity. Where Randall had been admired for refusing to cave in to blackmail, he was now applauded for having turned the tables on his enemies so neatly. Even moderate Democrats across the aisle admitted that he'd been well within his rights in allowing Bradley and Elliott enough room to betray themselves. It was their idea in the first place, after all. As for the general public, they just loved the trick. It was the cleverest thing anyone in Washington had done in decades, and the best bit of showmanship, too.

An internal investigation at *Democracy Today* turned up Holloway as the source of the leak within a matter of hours through a process of elimination. Which interns had talked to Montgomery, which ones hadn't, where they'd been the night before the *Post* story was printed, what their politics were. It simplified the process that when asked, Holloway admitted talking to a rival journalist straightaway. Bradley personally fired him, right after calling him a liar and a traitor to their cause. The senior senator from New York took him on as a staffer exactly three minutes before a job offer arrived from the *Post*. Fair play was suddenly a desirable commodity in Washington.

Subscriptions to *Democracy Today*, which had spiked in the aftermath of the original Randall story, dropped by fifteen percent. Bradley was informed that the National Press Club wanted to hold an inquiry into his magazine's reporting techniques and policies. Elliott was informed that the House Ethics Committee would be trying him for his activities. Early reports suggested that he would not merely be censured, but expelled from Congress altogether.

16

"God is the greatest, God is the greatest! I bear witness that there is no god but God, I bear witness that Mohammed is the Messenger of God! Hasten to worship! Hasten to success! Prayer is better than sleep! God is the greatest, there is no god but God!"

A Reuters photographer captured that moment. Thousands of Bahrainis, kneeling on the prayer rugs they had carefully brought with them to Al Farooq Junction, facing towards Mecca and the Kaaba, bowing themselves in submission to the divine. Around them, more imposing in the dim light, stood rank upon rank of soldiers and police. Soldiers belonging to the same faith, who by rights should have been kneeling and praying with their coreligionists, but who had set themselves above their fellow men so that prayer and obedience were no longer required of them. Their shadows fell across the suppliants like those of colossi. At that moment, it did not require much stretching of the imagination to agree that they had made themselves as gods.

The junction, which had never operated as a traffic feature at all, could not have been opened now if the government had wanted to make use of it. There were too many Bahrainis who had stood in the middle of it all night long. Now they were performing their devotions in it. They moved only to make way for new arrivals. The pavement was completely blocked with flesh and blood instead of plastic and steel, as were all the surrounding streets. The police could hem them in, but without a tank or a bulldozer, they couldn't break the mass, and they knew it would be suicidal to try.

The sun rose. The delicate blue of the morning sky faded away, and Manama stood out harsh and tan and dirty against it again. Almost at once, the older of the protestors began to weaken, but within the crowd were embedded physicians and nurses who had left deserted offices to do their duty where it was needed most. Bottles of water were passed from hand to hand. When the police arrested a dozen vendors selling along the edges of the crowd, and the drivers of trucks hired by the organizers to distribute it for free, new arrivals scaled the buildings overlooking the streets and pitched the bottles gleefully to their counterparts over the heads of the officers. Sweetmeats followed.

And the crowd grew. It grew until more than one policeman had the breath crushed out of him, his face to the mass of humanity, his back to a palm tree or armored car. It grew until the concrete blocks which had barred the streets to traffic began to shift and grind against the pavement, pushed out of position by the combined weight of the revolutionaries.

King Hamad and his government had miscalculated badly. By demolishing the Pearl Roundabout and building the junction over the location where it had once stood, they had believed they were eradicating a symbol of revolution. It had occurred to them too late that the place, not the monument, had symbolic value as well. So they sealed the junction to traffic, hoping that would solve the problem. But human beings can pass obstacles that stop machines, and when protestors had suddenly flooded the junction at night, the government had hesitated. There were too many of them for the security forces on duty at the scene to repel. The troops were ordered to wait for reinforcements, and by the time those arrived, the crowd had been reinforced as well. And ever since then they had stood in solid formation within the junction, immovable without butchery. The cabinet now had to face the humiliating realization that with the monument gone, and the area cleared, there was far more room for protestors than there had been prior to the demolition.

This protest had a different character from those that had preceded it. In the past, the red-and-white flag of Bahrain had dominated the scene. It was the way in which the participants asserted loyalty to their country, if not to its corrupt government. But now the flags were fewer in number. White and green were the dominant colors, banners emblazoned with quotes from the Quran, repudiating rather than upholding Bahraini national identity.

The banners told the government as plainly as if it were written on them, "You made a mistake."

* * * * *

"Are we there yet?" Ra'd bin Mazin asked.

"It's so hard to tell," Shihab said in exasperation. "We can count the number of protestors in a known area and then multiply that by the total area of the protests, but that may or may not be accurate. And the counts we're getting from the protestors themselves are almost sure to be too high. They're trying to make themselves look stronger than they really are."

"The police must have some metric they use."

"The Minister of the Interior just got an update," Fihr put in. "The police estimate fifty thousand on the streets right now, to double by noon."

"Those are February 22nd levels?"

"At least. Possibly higher, given that it's so early in the day."

"That is good enough. Release the documents."

* * * * *

All over Bahrain, messages and alerts began popping up on screens, ringing phones, setting off buzzers. The same links were instantly cross-posted on dozens of Facebook pages and inserted into hundreds of Twitter feeds. And then there were the text messages. Pupils and students in every school in the country felt their mobiles tremble as school emergency alert networks were appropriated by the underground. A few incisive words and a web link, that was all, but in a matter of minutes it provoked whispers and commotion in the classrooms.

A side effect of the wide distribution net cast by the underground was that teachers received the texts as well as their students. And they were outraged. The government paid their salaries, after all, gave them jobs from which they could be fired only with tremendous difficulty. Why should they cavail if that generous government overspent on fighter jets, which didn't matter to them at all? The obvious support among their pupils for the uprising disturbed and infuriated them; the audacity of the underground in sending disclosures of government abuse into their own secure little worlds made them afraid. Some teachers resigned themselves to the pressure of current events and dismissed their classes. Others, older and more rigid, attempted to confiscate students' phones and went into shock when many students refused to comply. They spluttered and shouted, but could do very little to prevent wholesale walkouts. Thousands of teenagers joined the crowds in the streets. Some produced banners declaring that the same logic which enjoined them to refuse the government their obedience also dictated that they refuse it to instructors who wished them to listen to lies.

They joined the ranks of protests that were springing up spontaneously throughout the capital. Instead of marching to Al Farooq Junction, activists unfurled a flag and gathered in the middle of the nearest street, summoning their friends to join them there. The new tactic of dispersed rather than centralized demonstrations drove the Bahraini police wild at first, before it rendered them incapable of driving at all. With every major street and traffic artery blocked by protestors who linked arms and refused to make way for vehicles, the armored policemen were unable to reach the demonstrations in many cases, let alone travel from place to place quickly enough to disperse or prevent them. Drivers whose vehicles were stopped often recognized the futility of trying to break through the crowd, shrugged, turned off the ignition, and threw their support behind their fellow Bahrainis.

Five blogs in five different languages told the story of how the members of the cabinet had asked that the country pay more for something it didn't need in order for them to line their own pockets. The confidential contracts and negotiation documents which revealed the story, combined with the ministers' own private emails, were available for anyone to inspect. The Ministry of Defense, rather than deny the allegations, ordered the Bahraini ambassador to the United States to phone Mountain View and put pressure on Google to take the items down. Google, as it was not quite a government itself yet, was forced to bend. It was a pointless exercise. The only result of the Bahraini "copyright claim" was to make the collection of documents relating to the Eurofighter purchase the most downloaded torrent on The Pirate Bay. Bahrainis kept reading them anyway, even after the king issued an emergency decree criminalizing the possession of government papers without proper authorization. And having read them, they took to the streets, angrier than ever.

*****

"That must have been the quickest the cabinet's ever taken action on anything," Junayd said, watching the Minister of Interior make a live statement on Al Jazeera about the new law.

"The amazing thing about it," the imam said, "is that they are perfectly serious. If they can demonstrate that five hundred thousand Bahrainis have read those emails, they are determined to fine or jail all five hundred thousand of them. They have the resolution. They have become so imbued with the sense that their power is righteous and unchallengeable that they are willing to paralyze their country in order that the abstract ideal of the law might be upheld. Have any of the ministers moved to halt the payments yet?"

"Not a single one of them. Although several of them are just sitting there, watching their account balances and hitting refresh every so often."

"And BAE has not stopped the transfers either?"

"They won't do anything until the British government forces them to act. Their lead negotiator said as much in one of his emails. Which means the payments will go through and when someone from the civil service calls round next week to protest, they'll solemnly deny that they ever had illicit dealings with members of the Bahraini government."

"How much time do we have left?"

"Four minutes."

"That is close enough. Carry out the attack."

Asim typed a command into his terminal and pressed enter.

* * * * *

In the musty warehouse two miles away, the hundreds of computers Junayd had spent days hooking up received the command and went to work.

Each machine was running a single program on top of the barest, most stripped-down operating system possible. The program, called Fikri, took all the available resources of each machine and used them to spawn an entire series of virtual machines. A virtual machine has no hardware of its own, but thinks it does and can simulate that hardware when necessary. Fikri placed no extraordinary demands for simulation on the newly-created virtual machines. All it required was that each of them register a distinct IP address--not a network subaddress--for connecting to the internet. That way, when each virtual machine went online, it would look like a separate system to the rest of the network and its requests would be processed as such. Since the only piece of hardware the virtual machines had to account for was a network card, they didn't use many resources and the program could create them by the thousand. Thousands of separate computers where there had been only hundreds moments before.

Then, all at once, these simulated machines began asking to connect to the IP addresses that Shihab had extracted from the databases of Bahrain's banks.

The sudden influx of requests, and the frequency with which they were being repeated, created a level of traffic that the National Bank of Bahrain and the ABC Islamic Bank and the Khaleeji Commercial Bank had never anticipated. Their servers couldn't keep up with the pressure of nearly a hundred thousand page requests per second. So the servers did the only thing they could do under those circumstances: they crashed.

They didn't all go down at once, of course. Fikri was targeting dozens of IP addresses in its sweep. If one became unresponsive, it reallocated the pattern of its attacks to put additional stress on those that were still resisting. If an address started working again, it shifted some of its page requests back to that address. By demanding the constant attention of the banks' servers, it prevented anyone else from connecting to them. The process was known as a denial of service attack. One set of computers, through persistence, could block all access to the targeted servers until and unless the operators of those servers brought additional capacity online to meet the demand. No computer server in the world, including every one of the precious DNS servers, was immune to a denial of service attack. And some servers, like those belonging to Bahrain's banks, were far less prepared to cope with such an attack than others.

* * * * *

Screens across Bahrain lit up again, with a new link this time. This one directed the viewer to a Facebook page for the Bahraini underground. That in itself was startling. The underground had never declared its existence before. The content of the first and only message it had posted was even more provocative.

"As the members of the cabinet who were involved in the Eurofighter scam have refused to admit their guilt," the post read, "and as several of them have denied receiving any kickbacks for their role in negotiating a higher price for the contract, we have decided to make sure they are telling the truth. Effective immediately, we have shut down the websites of all banks at which the involved ministers are account holders. This includes the private communications networks of those banks as well as their public sites, and will prevent any bribes from being deposited into accounts owned by members of the government. We invite our fellow Bahrainis to join us in supporting this venture by attempting to access the websites of these banks as often as possible, thereby denying the ministers the opportunity to receive their alleged kickbacks, which, as you will remember from their leaked emails, were scheduled to be paid three minutes ago."

Within the first five minutes of its appearance, the post had been shared ten thousand times, and the pressure on the banks' networks had doubled.

* * * * *

"The irony of that is wonderful," Asim said as the returns from the unsuccessful ping attempts unfolded on his screen. "Making sure the government is telling the truth."

"It's about to become unable to tell either truth or lies," Fihr said. He looked at his watch. "If this is right--"

"Which it shouldn't be, it's a mechanical movement--"

"--then the government has thirty more seconds in which to make its voice heard."

* * * * *

Automatically, Fikri initiated a new script. This one reached out through satellite links and undersea cables to a small server farm in California. A cluster of several thousand Raspberry Pi machines, tiny computers consisting of only a single circuit board, came to life. They did so almost without sound. No fans rattled, no drives buzzed. The machines had no moving parts except the electrons surging about inside their chips. They began running their own version of Fikri, identical to the one ticking away in the warehouse in Manama, but with different targets.

The website of the Ministry of Defense was the first to succumb to the new cyberattack. One by one, the rest of the government's public sites followed. Then the overseas cluster, which had been designed by one of the imam's Indian supporters for that very task, reoriented itself and began going after the IP addresses of the Bahraini government's communications networks. These were not hidden or secure. They couldn't be. Email can't be sent to a machine that conceals its existence. The California cluster didn't bother trying to hack the email accounts, but contented itself with overloading the system with page requests. At the very instant the Bahraini police and military needed to communicate securely, they had to waste precious minutes waiting for messages to load, if they came through at all. Protestors sprang up out of nowhere around them while officers tapped at the computers in their cars and raved and swore at the reports that weren't reaching headquarters.

The two versions of Fikri consulted with each other. The California system took over the management of a number of machines in Bahraini internet cafes, which had suddenly become unresponsive to their users. Fikri was running in the background on those computers, too, where it had been placed by members of the underground. It had been so easy to install the program without anyone noticing, and it gave them additional resources while also making the source of the attack more difficult to locate.

* * * * *

One of the government's counter-terrorism squads blocked off a side street in front of a meandering taxi. Soldiers with rifles surrounded the vehicle. Some of them pulled the driver out of his car and sandpapered his face against the pavement while the rest tore the taxi to bits. They needn't have gone to quite that length. What they were looking for was shoved casually in a pocket behind the front passenger seat, in among the magazines left behind by previous fares. It was a worn, scratched tablet running an old, old release of the Android operating system. It was also running Fikri. But the officers couldn't tell that from looking at it, and they couldn't crack into it on the spot, either. All their technology gurus had been able to tell them was that one of the machines making an attack on their email network was in a car moving around the city. At least they assumed that it was in a car, given the cellular position they triangulated for it. Now they had the machine, which was attacking them even as they struggled to unlock its password protection. One of the squad leaders wanted to take it back to a lab for forensic analysis, but the commander on the spot overruled him. He picked up the tablet and smashed it against the side of the taxi until the road was covered in splinters of Corning glass. Then he ordered the driver hauled off for questioning, justifying his actions to his subordinate on the grounds that easing the attack on their systems at such a critical time was more important than tracing the perpetrators, whom the taxi driver would no doubt identify under interrogation.

The argument ended when an exceptionally large raindrop splattered against the commander's shoulder and covered both participants with brown slime. Not slime, they realized a few seconds later. Dye. A brown dye, thinner and more fluid than mud. The squad commander looked up and took the next drop in the face. He screamed as the chemicals seeped into his eyes.

From several of the surrounding buildings, protestors were raining little balls of dye and paint down on the police. Their thin rubber shells shattered immediately on contact with the firmness of the ground or a human body, covering the officers in spatters and splashes of half a dozen different colors. Drab colors and nauseating colors, not gay ones. Entirely harmless and completely humiliating. Bahrain had no mud to throw at the hated agents of the state, so its citizens substituted paint instead. It not only annoyed the police, it distracted them as well. While they were threatening to fire back at the teenagers on the balconies above, two men from the gathering crowd rushed them, knocked over a soldier, and hauled the taxi driver off into the safety of the mob. The soldiers, infuriated that their prey was escaping, opened fire on the retreating rescuers and killed three people before their commander could stop them.

* * * * *

Other squads met the same fate. They raced back and forth across Manama--as quickly as they could move in a city where most of the traffic was at a standstill, anyway--in search of the computers that were overloading their networks. They found nothing but outdated tablets in the backs of cars and in waste barrels and on the roofs of abandoned buildings, all connected to cellular networks, all on timers, all incessantly pinging government servers. No one was operating them. In some cases, no one had even been seen near the spots where they were deposited for several days. They had been programmed and left to do their job while also acting as red herrings to confuse the police, who would waste time hunting them down in a futile attempt to terminate the attack. The special units confiscated dozens of them, but the pressure on their networks did not lessen. The one time a police technician did manage to break through the password protection on one of the tablets, it proved to have been cross-wired and fried itself almost before he could jerk his hand away.

Then the Prime Minister attempted to make a phone call to a cabinet minister and couldn't get through. An aide came pelting up, breathless, to inform him that the security services were tapping as many phone conversations as they could under the circumstances, and that analysis was showing an increasing number to be nothing but ambient noise.

"The director suspects that the protestors are turning on a large number of disposable phones and letting them run for the purpose of jamming our cellular network," the aide added.

The Prime Minister could only stare at him.

*****

The soldiers had grown angry at being held back, at being isolated in the middle of an angry crowd without orders or direction, and began to take the initiative. Clouds of tear gas glowed radiantly in the orange light of the setting sun.

A police commissioner was attempting to induce part of the crowd to disperse. He reasoned. He cajoled. He promised to devote his personal attention to reforming his department. He offered to intercede with the Minister of the Interior. Eventually he lost his patience.

"You are ordered to disperse!" he shouted through a megaphone. "By His Majesty's decree, participation in street brawls is no longer permitted. I command you to lay down your banners and return to your homes!"

One of the protestors stepped out in front of the crowd, a broad man with wide shoulders. He halted halfway between the commissioner and his fellow citizens and threw back his head. Without assistance, his voice rose above the hum of conversation, silencing the policemen and the demonstrators alike.

"I am forbidden to invoke those whom ye invoke besides God, seeing that the Clear Signs have come to me from my Lord; and I am commanded to bow in Islam to the Lord of the Worlds."

Above their heads, a muezzin filled his lungs and let out his evening cry once again. "God is the greatest!"

17

"Time to welcome back an old friend that you've almost forgotten about," the Major said.

The three Marines looked up, bleary-eyed. Their faces were caked with dirt and their clothes, of the shabby variety to begin with, were now suitable in every way for a party of wandering tramps. The two Iranians were asleep on the floor of the van. The pace the Major had set, after their experiences in prison, had exhausted them.

Powers was the first to bite. "What friend would this be, sir? Hot water?"

"Cold water?" Brassey added. His remark was greeted with a chorus of approval. Heat was easy to come by in Iran. Cold, on the other hand, was as difficult to find in the high mountains as in the desert.

"The color green, gentlemen," the Major replied with a shake of his head. "Marine green!"

Brassey leaned forward to look out the window. "Well I'll be damned," he said.

Ahead of them, the curves in the road straightened out and the Sefid Rud flowed through the paddy fields that lined the floor of the Manjil Gap. On their left the town of Rostamabad rose in terraces above its course. Instead of scrub and dry streambeds, there was a full-flowing river irrigating an expanse of land measured in square miles, not square feet.

Real plants whisked by them, not bits of dessicated shrubbery with two leaves and a flower clinging to the topmost branch.

"That's--a change for sure," Powers commented.

Ramirez closed his eyes again. "It won't last," he said, making a negative gesture with one hand.

The Major chuckled. His eyes dropped to the speedometer. It wouldn't do to be caught again, now that the highway patrols had served their purpose and provided him with an alibi. The van--their third vehicle in as many days--was almost too responsive at times and he was tempted to behave as if he were behind the wheel of his Jaguar. Javed's network of connections was nothing short of astonishing. Why did the CIA never think of getting to know the Bahais better? he wondered. The answer, of course, was that the CIA hadn't managed to pull off a major operation since replacing the last shah on his steel throne, from which he was ejected anyway after giving his people additional cause to loathe the United States government. They simply weren't bright enough anymore to be original. "What were you saying, Lance Corporal?"

Ramirez lifted one eyelid. Then his mouth gaped open. "Shit."

The Manjil Gap had closed up again and the freeway was wedged against the river between two cliffs that hardly left room for both. The paddy fields were gone. In their place was a forest that swept down the mountains and threatened to push the few houses that lined the banks right into the water.

"There are trees in Iran!" Ramirez exclaimed. His surprise was more genuine than exaggerated.

"All the moisture that comes down from the north gets trapped on this side of the Elburz Mountains," the Major explained. "This part of the country is actually quite lush. It's only a narrow strip, though. You could walk across it in a day or less and then the rest of the region is desert."

Powers nudged Brassey aside and squinted at something in the distance. A broad band of dark blue haze stretched across the horizon. "Sir, that looks like a body of water ahead."

"Oh, that's nowhere near us," the Major said. "It must be at least thirty miles away."

"But it is water?"

"Last time I checked the map it was."

"Damn, we made it to the Gulf!" Brassey was ready to applaud at the thought.

"Not unless my sense of direction is seriously screwed up," Major Martin retorted.

"But, sir--if it isn't the Gulf--"

"It's the Caspian Sea."

"To get to the sea"--Powers frowned as he worked it out in the air with his hands--"we'd have had to have turned around and gone north again."

"Did you really think we were going to keep heading south with fifty thousand troops barring our path?" the Major inquired. His mouth twisted up on one side in a grimace. "I may be crazy, but I'm not suicidal."

"And that explains it," Brassey said. "You're what a British NCO I served with would call a right clever bastard, Major."

"I still don't get it," Ramirez protested.

"The traffic stop," Brassey explained. "We stopped on purpose so the Iranians would think we were heading south instead of northwest. And as soon as they figured that out and redeployed a couple of divisions between us and coalition naval forces in the Gulf, we turned around and started heading northeast, hundreds of miles away from where we attacked the prison van. We've been handing them clues to our whereabouts and then leaving them to chase their tails the whole time."

"Well, yeah, but why?"

The Major threw both of his hands in the air in mock exasperation, then seized the wheel again just in time to avoid a collision with a stray goat. "We can see the Iranian border ahead of us and there isn't a soldier anywhere in sight. Why not?"

* * * * *

"Would you like a drink?" Randall asked.

"Sure. What do you have?"

The congressman bent down and inspected the inside of his office refrigerator. "Not a lot. Beer and Jack Daniels for voters. Pellegrino for the aging seniors who drop by every now and then--and that includes my more venerable colleagues." He straightened up. "If you have the palate for it, I do have a Laphroaig thirty year-old single malt hidden away for special occasions."

"I'd like to try that."

Randall poured two glasses of the whiskey, diluted it with just a trace of water, and put the bottle away. No ice. He passed one glass to his guest and sat down opposite him.

"Cheers," he said. They sipped at their drinks.

"Congratulations on getting firmly back in the closet," Holloway said.

"Congratulations on putting me there. I haven't said thanks, by the way."

"Is that the kind of thing you should be thankful for?"

"I don't know. But it seems okay right now."

"It's your life, after all."

"Yeah, it is. I think we owe each other an explanation, though."

"I agree."

"Because--not that I'm being ungrateful here--but I don't think you went to all the trouble of perjuring yourself just for my sake, or for the sake of a principle."

"I didn't. Although those were compelling extras. You've never had to listen to Kyle Scott Bradley go on for an hour about equality and activism when every word he says makes it clearer and clearer that he hasn't got a clue what he's talking about."

"Sounds like what happens at an all-night sitting on the Hill."

"Anyway, Bradley is oblivious to reality. The rest of us aren't. We have to live our lives in it." Holloway paused. "I have to live in it, too, just like everyone else. And what he doesn't realize is that reality bites back. He met his husband in the cozy, safe confines of the Harvard community. The rest of us--well, we have to look harder, and sometimes that doesn't work out very well."

"Like how?"

"Like if you get chased down by three guys twice your size who see you as a piece of ass to use and throw away."

Randall took a longer sip of his drink. "I remember."

"The feeling never goes away, does it?"

"Nope."

"And is this your response to it?"

"How do you mean?"

"Making yourself so established and powerful that it cancels out the fear you once felt."

"Maybe. What's your response?"

"I didn't have one. And that feeling probably won't ever go away, either."

"So what happened?"

"Someone who did have an answer came along and beat the shit out of the problem."

"A knight in shining armor?"

"Not that far off, actually. His name was Martin. He was a major in the Marines." Randall's free hand clenched on the armrest of his chair. "He's the one that got in trouble for telling kids to fight back if they were bullied. And then

Bradley ended up being the one to break the story about him going to Iran to help that couple that was sentenced to death. He's still over there."

"Yes, I heard about that. So this fighting major beat up your attackers?"

"That's right. And then he cleaned me up and we spent the rest of the night talking about it. And everything else."

"What then?"

"Then--he called me a week or so later. He wanted to know if I would do a favor for him. I said yes. Heck, I owed it to him--and I trusted him. He's good at that. I can see Marines following him under fire. Anyway, we met for coffee and he asked to borrow my phone. He plugged it into his computer and uploaded a recording to it. Afterwards he handed it back to me and that was all."

"Did you ask him what it was?"

"Yes. He told me to go ahead and play it. I did. I couldn't believe it. I asked him if it was real. He said no, right out. He didn't try to pretend it was or be subtle about it. But then he asked me if it was believable--if, as an intern for Bradley, it was something I could picture him and Elliott doing. Of course, I said. Absolutely.

"And that's when he smiled. I think he liked my answer. So he said that Bradley and Elliott were trying to set you up, and that you had asked him to do something about it. If you tried to take the issue public, it would at best be a game of he-said-she-said, and your career would be ruined just the same. Which was what the two of them were hoping for. In order to expose them without getting you as well, he had to attack them from the inside. All I had to do was hang on to the recording until some enterprising reporter came looking for a source to talk to."

"And you didn't find it an odd request?"

Holloway finished off his drink. "Sure. But I understood his reasoning, and I agreed with him. I like his principles. I feel more sympathy for him and you than I do for the narrow little community for whose interests Bradley and Elliot claim to speak."

"The personal over the abstract." Randall got up and walked across the room. He stared out the window of his office at the traffic below.

"There are two things you deserve to know," he said.

"One I can already guess at. You and Adrian Meyers really were having an affair."

"Hardly an affair. We get together every now and then. Neither of us expects it to go anywhere, but it's fun."

"Until you get caught."

"Until we got caught. Bradley didn't have an elaborate scheme to blackmail me. He just threw a private investigator out there to see what he could dig up that his precious husband could use--and the guy got lucky." He shook his head. "For half a minute I actually thought I might have to go along with their game. And then I thought of an alternative."

"Major Martin."

Randall came back to his chair. "Matt Martin isn't just someone I know. We were roommates for four years. College." He stared at the coffee table. "You and I--we remember being bullied. Matt was never bullied. In part because he steamrolled anyone who tried to push him around, but more because he always had an air about him that deterred people from trying to take advantage of him in the first place. I was always happy for him when he got promoted, but I always wondered how it kept happening. He's a brilliant soldier, none like him, and every enlisted Marine I've ever met who worked for him admired him--and yet his superiors always suspected him of laughing at them or sneering at them behind their backs. I guess in going to Iran he finally decided to break the mold once and for all. But this isn't the first time he's protected me."

"He'll screw over the whole gay rights movement if necessary to keep you safe?"

"Pretty much. He won't budge on a principle for anyone's convenience. He never liked Bradley anyway. I've heard Matt call him a weakling at least half a dozen times, not to mention other names. And when I told him about the photos--and this shows you just how unconventional he is--he didn't get angry. His face lit up like a Christmas tree and he started laughing and dancing all over the room. He couldn't sit still. In two seconds this whole plot fell together in his mind. He understood how to protect me and reverse Elliott's threat so it recoiled on him without even thinking."

"So you two kind of grew up in the closet together."

"And it wasn't a very big closet at that." Randall laughed, half wistfully, half contemptuously. "You know what I find ironic? Painful, but ironic? He's always been the victim. He was never quite as not out as I was, and the few of our friends who knew about him were always pitying him. That he couldn't serve in the Marines openly. And that was the story of his life up until a few years ago, until DADT fell by the wayside. All that time, no one ever called him a hypocrite for hiding that he was gay. But me--I've spent my entire tenure in the House having my sexuality questioned, with the implication that I'm self-loathing and delusional for voting my party platform and my constituent's wishes instead of my sexual orientation. No one ever called me a victim. And yet Matt had to hide his sexuality to get to his present rank just like I did."

"Why did you both do it if you both resented it?"

"Because we both wanted something that was more important to us than being able to walk down the street holding hands. He wanted to serve in the Marine Corps. I wanted to serve in Congress representing the town where I grew up. To do so, we would both have to play it straight. We both made a choice to give up a desire for a dream. And we've lived with that choice for all its faults. But the rest of the world ignores that parallel. One of us got praised and the other got attacked."

Holloway said nothing.

"Anyway, that's why we don't mind playing dirty tricks on Bradley and Elliott, who never had to make that choice," Randall said, sitting back again. "What's your reason?"

Holloway got up and went over to the magazine rack by the office door. He came back with a copy of the *Washington Blade* in his hand. With Randall no longer fair game, the paper had abruptly switched targets. The lead story was about another HRC director being forced to apologize for transphobic comments.

"My great-grandfather marched with the Wobblies. My grandfather marched with Martin Luther King. My uncle marched with ACT UP." He tossed the paper down. "This isn't what they marched for."

* * * * *

The last section of chain link snapped under the jaws of the clippers. Price handed the tool back to Javed and waited.

It had taken hours to get this far. Inching their way back from the trees and foliage along Taleqani Boulevard, dressed as beggars, their equipment hidden under her chador and Javed's rags. Finding the right spot where a shrub grew against the fence and slipping under its cover in the growing dusk at such a rate that no one would notice their movement. Timing the patrols inside the fence, which fortunately only came by every half hour. Cutting the fence itself once they were sure of their timing. Waiting for one final patrol to go by, just to make sure.

The lights passed. Javed peered through the leaves and the links. He saw the soldiers leaning back in their seats, relaxed. Their weapons were slung. The jeep was moving slowly enough that he could hear one of them making a ribald joke. The others laughed. Then their voices and the sound of the engine gave way to gradual silence.

He nodded once.

Amanda Price wiggled through the gap in the fence, ignoring the sharp ends of the wire, and stood up for the first time all afternoon. She felt her irritation and impatience vanish. This was her territory. Bushehr Airport might be six thousand miles or so away from home, and she might be standing on a part of it controlled by the Iranian Air Force, but it was an airport all the same, and as a pilot that gave her all but divine rights when within its boundaries. Or so pilots think. She had tried to explain this concept to Javed, but she wasn't sure that he had fully understood the idea.

The Bahai joined her with his tattered pack. To their left and right, the perimeter road stretched out, bare in the reflected light from the rest of the city. Five hundred feet ahead of them, there was a bulge of hardy trees that looked like the beginning of a small forest. They covered the distance in less than two minutes. Javed bowed his head in thanks; Price went on a few yards through the trees and and found herself standing on the edge of a broad taxiway. The asphalt had been turned the color of sand from exposure to several decades of dust storms, but it was a taxiway all the same.

She checked that it was clear in both directions and nodded to the guide. They sprinted across it, diving into the belt of trees that lined the other side of the taxiway. Another fence barred their path. This one had barbed wire strung across the top. That was easy enough to anticipate. Price pulled a small rug from under her chador and threw it across the wire. The strands creaked under her weight as she scaled the fence and lowered herself to the ground on the other side. Javed followed, taking the lead.

In what seemed an act of supreme charity, love for nature, or just plain foolishness, the Iranians had not only lined the taxiway with trees to serve as a windbreak, they had surrounded the concrete hangars with them as well. Price remembered the aerial photographs she had studied earlier that morning. The foliage stood out in dark clumps against the uniform tan of the background. Something in her stomach had unclenched when she realized that. Walking up to a hangar surrounded by trees would be easy. The risk of being spotted and shot would be minimal.

Of course, they had to find one particular hangar in a field of a dozen from the ground in the middle of the night, which was less easy. Javed's particular skills were required for that task. Or at least they were until Price realized that the hangar towards which he was heading was lit up from the inside. That made their navigation simpler, but also reminded her that she wasn't quite safe yet.

Javed motioned to her to halt. From behind the shelter of her tree, she could see into the hangar at an angle. Two technicians were walking around inside, their sleeves rolled up, fiddling with various bits and pieces of equipment. They were less than twenty yards away. Ten, maybe. She judged the distance. Javed caught her eye and shook his head.

They sat down in the shadows and waited.

* * * * *

"Go," the Major whispered.

The Marines stepped around the corner of the building and sauntered casually down the deserted pier. Kadivar was in the lead, in case anyone questioned their presence. The Major and Jan were behind him. The three infantrymen followed, their pistols cocked beneath their clothes.

At the end of the pier, a small trawler rocked against the wooden pilings. It smelled of fish, and worse. The port of

Bandar-e Anzali is the center of the world's caviar trade. Accordingly, the vessels anchored there reek of blood and entrails and the eggs of Caspian sturgeons in addition to more common marine odors. The one the Marines were approaching was no exception to that rule.

    A watchman was sitting on deck, shaving long curls off a piece of juniper. He looked up at the newcomers. His expression shifted, becoming one of worry, not suspicion. A large party of visitors might mean trouble with the customs authorities, or refugees trying to buy a passage out of the country. Either would be inconvenient, but not dangerous. He put down his carving--and his knife, the Major noticed--and stood up. Kadivar engaged him in conversation. The Marines fidgeted, straining to catch the Persian words they couldn't understand even when they did hear them.

    The discussion grew animated. Kadivar was adopting a more belligerent tone. The sailor, incensed, clambered across the gunwale and onto the pier to continue the argument at shorter range. Jan threw in a few vigorous words over his lover's shoulder. As for the Major, he appeared to take no interest at all in the three-way debate the Iranians were having. He pulled a pack of cigarettes from his pocket and extracted one with no apparent haste. Then he tried to strike a match to light it, but the phosphorus wouldn't catch. Each attempt he made was wilder and more impatient, until, on his last try, his hand shot out and seized the startled sailor by the throat. The man started to make a noise, but the Major dug his fingers into the sailor's nerves and he dropped onto the wooden planks, unconscious. Brassey and Ramirez grabbed him and dragged him aboard the vessel. The Major and the rest of the group followed.

    "Get below, out of sight for now," the Major hissed. They followed his orders in silence. Powers opened the duffel bag he'd been carrying and began to unpack the last of their equipment.

In the darkened galley, the Major pulled out his satellite phone. The screen glowed for a minute, then turned black again. He set it on the table and stared at it.

18

"How many arrests?" Fihr asked, rubbing the sleep out of his eyes.

"Officially? Over ten thousand so far. That doesn't count the ones the police contented themselves with beating up and then throwing back to the crowds to take care of."

"Ten thousand prisoners. Where on earth are they putting them all?"

"Ten or more to a cell where necessary." Junayd pointed at his computer screen. "The few they've released are already crying foul play to the world and denouncing the 'primitive' and 'barbaric' conditions in Bahraini jails."

"Any jail is barbaric. And we're circulating their statements through our mailing lists?"

"Of course. And getting a good response on Twitter. Today looks very promising."

"Any new instructions from the imam?"

"Haven't seen him this morning."

"That's odd. I thought he would be up all night waiting to see if the momentum held."

"He sleeps sounder than we do."

"Well, I'll go look in, see if he's awake yet." Fihr turned and walked out of what passed for their operations center.

He was back in two minutes. "He's not in his usual room."

"Is he in the courtyard?"

"No, I checked it on my way back. He's always out there for morning prayers."

Junayd shrugged. "When have we ever been able to predict what he's up to? Try to find him, though. I need to know when he wants us to execute the next stage of the plan."

Fihr pulled out his phone and sent a text to all the members of the underground network. "Is Ra'd bin Mazin with you?" it read. A string of "no" replies tumbled into his hand in the next thirty seconds.

"He doesn't seem to be with any of our people," Fihr said. The air whistled through his nostrils as he drew deep breaths, trying to calm himself.

"Suppose he went out and didn't ask anyone to go with him? There are plenty of people in Manama who would be glad to help a blind scholar across the street, or take him wherever he wanted to go."

"Yes, but why?"

Fihr's phone vibrated again. He looked down at the screen. It was showing a text from Asim. "I saw him leaving an hour ago with one of the hackers who used to work with us."

"He's gone," Fihr said, holding the message up so Junayd could read it.

"So he stepped out for prayers elsewhere. That's not surprising, given the scope of today's plans. He probably wants to commemorate the occasion or ask for special guidance."

"That's not what it feels like."

"You think he's been lured out by the police?"

"Not necessarily. Why would he call one of our associates who's been out of the loop instead of one of us, who he knows he could trust?"

"Maybe he thought he could trust someone else too?"

"Or perhaps he thinks we trust each other too much."

"Why so pessimistic?"

"I don't like how this feels," Fihr hissed, throwing himself down in front of his computer.

* * * * *

Ra'd bin Mazin looked around at the congregation inside the Al Fateh Grand Mosque. Or, more precisely, he made the gesture of looking around at a congregation he could not see. It was packed to capacity, the spheres of light in the rafters gleaming off every inch of the polished marble floor that was not covered by prayer rugs. Between floor and ceiling, the Kufic quotations marched around the walls in an endless geometry of worship. He knew the hall possessed these attributes, even if they were invisible to him. To a blind man, the world that is is very much the same as the world that is to be. Both must be taken on faith.

He rested his hands on the front of the minbar again and leaned forward.

"God is merciful," he said into the stillness. "He has revealed Himself to us as a merciful Lord. He judges, but He does not demand a great deal from us in order for His judgments to be in our favor. That is a sign of His mercy and His compassion. Likewise, He enjoins us to show mercy to our fellow men. That is the essence of the law, for with mercy and forbearance all other virtues become more readily attainable.

"And it is also a sign to us that the state and its rulers are not within that law. The true Lord of the Worlds has ordered us to be just to one another, and has Himself set the example in His own dealings with humanity. Has the state followed this example? Has the king followed this example? Have you ever observed that the state is merciful and just in its dealings with us? Is it an act of mercy to kill believers and leave their bodies lying in the streets to demonstrate the worthlessness of human life compared to the value of the abstract idea that is government? Is it an act of mercy to hide a man away in the dark for the rest of his life, to torture his mind and his soul with isolation, because he raised his voice in defense of his fellow man?

"This is not mercy. It requires no scholarship, it requires nothing but a just heart, to look around us and realize that the rule under which we live is not a merciful one.

"And if it is not, then it cannot be the rule of a merciful and compassionate Lord. Nor can such a Lord wish for us to live under such conditions.

"But because He is gracious, He has gone farther than we in our limited imaginations might conceive. He has given us an injunction to mercy and justice--but He has not constrained us to follow these paths alone. We are free to choose between good and evil, and we are answerable not to one another, not to a human ruler, but to Him alone. He who made the worlds could have created us in such a way that we never desired to do evil, or in such a way that we would always raise up just and honest rulers to arbitrate our disputes. He chose to do neither, though both courses were well within His power. In His greatest act of mercy, He gave us freedom.

"His gift is one that we do not have the power to reject. He has written the law, and no man can alter it, not the Apostles of God themselves. We are to be free. We are to follow His laws as we best understand them, but we are not to force another to follow them according to our interpretations. To do so would contradict both His word and His intent. If, as single believers, we cannot bind one another, no government, even though it be composed of believers, can bind a society.

"The law is the work of God, immutable and eternal beyond the duration of any state. Were there ten thousand states in the world, or none, the law would remain the same. The community of believers will continue so long as there is one man on earth who will bear witness. If an individual is merciful towards his fellow men, he will consider the effect of his actions on the community before he takes them, thus regulating himself without the need for force or a formal consensus. No external law, save that of God, can bind man. No other law is necessary for a true believer.

"Consider also that even in sin there is mercy."

In the back of the hall the crowd stirred. Half a dozen men in black robes, with sticks in their hands, were pushing their way through the worshipers, who didn't notice the intrusion until they were already being shoved aside from behind. Their attention was on the imam and his words. As for the newcomers, their attention was on the imam as well, but in a different way. They had just found the mosque's usual imam tied to a chair in his office and swearing with vigor.

"God is oft-forgiving. Having given us free will at our creation, in His greatest act of compassion, He has further demonstrated the truth of His nature by holding out forgiveness to us for those errors into which we may fall while exercising our free will. He who created the law is not bound by it, unlike man, whose laws cannot show mercy if their impartiality and strength is to be believed. If a man breaks the law, but repents of his deeds, God will forgive and redeem him. Why should we not do the same? If we see an idolater, a thief, a murderer, who are we to usurp the position of the King of Mankind and punish him for his deeds? For all we know, he may yet repent. He may have repented already, and been forgiven by the Merciful, the Compassionate. Were we to attack him then, we would be guilty also. And if we knew that he had not yet repented, but attacked and abused him, thinking that we could force him to repentance, we would be doubly guilty. We would be depriving him of the will that God had given him. We ourselves would become thieves.

"Sin itself is a sign of God's mercy, for without mercy, the double mercy of forgiveness and free will, sin would not exist. So rather than condemning, let us offer patience to those who err. Rather than force, let us meet them with forgiveness, anticipating the work of the Most Great. Rather than anger, let us offer them understanding, for the same potential for error exists in every one of us, and if we lead by example, they may learn mercy from us and turn to God to seek His compassion.

"If it is within the power of God to bind us fast with laws, and yet He chooses to let us go free, then we cannot make ourselves greater than God by saying to others, 'You have committed a crime; we will punish you.' The question of whether we can judge becomes irrelevant. We should not judge. If we had the power, we should not exercise it."

The noise in the mosque was growing. The intruders were almost at the base of the minbar and cries of annoyance followed after them.

"And if you and I as individuals should not do more than offer forgiveness to our fellow believers, neither should a group of individuals. If they call themselves a state, a government, a parliament, that does not alter the fact that they remain mortal men whose need for mercy is as great as ours. And if they try to compel our obedience, asserting that their wisdom is superior to ours, we should not retaliate against them. Instead, we should avoid compounding their lack of understanding by setting aside their orders. If we cooperate with them, and they lead us into sin, we must answer for our own actions, but they must answer for both theirs and ours. It is an act of mercy on our part to disregard their demands, so that they may not be called upon by the Lord of the Worlds to account for crimes they would not have committed without our aid. It is an act of mercy towards a ruler to disobey him."

The minbar shuddered as two of the black-robed men broke through the front ranks of the audience and dashed up its steps.

"Disobey your rulers, but do so out of mercy. Disobey them, but with a heart that is empty of anger and full of faith. Disobey them, but do so out of faith, not out of mere perversity. Disobey them, but do not fight them. Acknowledge their free will, their membership in the community of believers--and in doing so, leave them to go their own way with neither your submission nor your opposition. Disobey, and in doing so, remember that God, the Merciful, the Compassionate, is a better ruler than any man. Violence--"

Whatever Ra'd bin Mazin had intended to say about violence was lost as the stick in the hand of the leading intruder came down on his head. He staggered and clutched at the front railing of the minbar for support.

"You lie!" the man screamed, striking him again and again in the ribs. "Authority on earth is ordained by God for the execution of the law and the punishment of unbelievers!" The imam swayed, but did not turn around. He lifted up his hands to the crowd and tried to continue his sermon. His attacker, enraged, grabbed him by the waist and threw him off the platform.

The four men waiting below did not so much as try to catch him. Instead, they struck down those who did, and the marble pavement, brought thousands of miles to a land where it did not belong, split the imam's head open like one of the dye packets the protestors in the streets were flinging at the police.

Those in the front rows saw the blood well out from under his body. They drew back in shock. Few Muslims in history, whatever their politics, had been so bold as to commit murder inside a mosque. Fewer still had been brave enough--or depraved enough--to do it with their own hands. And these men had not only done it, but stood and gloated over the body, praising God for death rather than life.

* * * * *

Fihr's phone buzzed again.

"Oh, no," he moaned. "No, no, no, no, no…" He flung himself out of his chair towards the nearest computer.

"What's happened?" Asim, who had just come in, asked.

Fihr was flipping open a dozen new tabs at once, checking live feeds, blogs, Twitter accounts. He didn't bother to respond at first. His eyes never left the screen. Then he suddenly shuddered and let them drop.

"What's going on?" Junayd echoed.

His fellow hacker looked up. "They killed him."

"Who killed who?"

"The imam."

"Our imam?"

"Our imam," Fihr hissed. He clutched the edge of the table as if he wanted to throw it right through the wall in his fury.

"Oh, God," Junayd said. A minute later, he added, "You were right."

Fihr set his jaw and said nothing.

"How did you find out?" Asim ventured.

In response, Fihr handed him his phone. Asim didn't recognize the name of the sender, but the message on the screen was clear enough.

"This morning Imam bin Mazin asked me to accompany him to the Grand Mosque. He said he wanted to deliver a special sermon. With the help of one of my friends, we locked the regular imam in his office and the leader of the underground took his place in front of the crowd. He asked me to film his words. Halfway through his address, members of the Haia burst into the mosque, discovered the switch, and attacked him. They threw him off the minbar. He did not get up again."

There was a video clip attached to the email.

* * * * *

The video of the imam's death was viewed more than a million times in the first two hours after it was posted to Youtube. Then Google stepped in to remove it, citing violations of the site's terms of use. A flurry of angry emails and tweets received no reply beyond an official statement that it was inappropriate content and had been taken down for that reason. The protests from Bahraini activists that it was an important example of the oppression that they suffered went unanswered. Their demands to know if the Bahraini government had pressured Google to take it down were also ignored. A dozen other users re-uploaded it immediately and kept doing so each time it was removed, engaging the largest octopus on earth in a grim struggle for the awareness of mankind.

In Cairo, in Islamabad, even in Tehran, broadcasters cut into their regular programming to air the video, complete with commentary by distinguished scholars and policy experts. From Morocco to Bali the feed was picked up and retransmitted, encapsulating the resurgence of the Arab Spring, and all the reasons for it, in five minutes of inspiration and twenty seconds of horror.

Except by Al Jazeera. Callers across the Middle East demanded to know, hours after the video was common news fodder in the rest of the world, why they had not seen it on their own televisions via the largest Arabic network in existence. The studio at first declined to comment. When call volume increased, its switchboard was disconnected altogether.

About seven hours after the video had gone viral, Al Jazeera's news team finally made a statement to the effect that militant protestors had temporarily seized possession of the Al Fateh Mosque early that morning and staged the murder of one of their own number to make it look as though the Bahraini government was using foreign bullies to intimidate religious scholars into greater orthodoxy. The video, the newscaster asserted, was a complete fabrication. He also added that the police were investigating a link between that group of protestors and a radical anti-Islamic group in the United States. The network then returned to coverage of local football matches, not bothering to the give the rest of the Bahraini revolution the time of day.

The Emir of Qatar, who had his own revolution to cope with, was in no mood to listen to balanced accounts of what the Saudi religious police were up to. He might have to call them in soon enough himself. And he owned Al Jazeera, so his word dictated coverage. If he said there was no revolution, then, as far as the network was concerned, there was no revolution and they wouldn't cover it. They had done the same during the Arab Spring 1.0.

* * * * *

"What do we do now?" Asim asked.

Fihr pulled his head out of the sink and wiped his face off. "We carry out the rest of the plan. And now we have a bigger target."

* * * * *

In a dorm room in Berkeley, a sleeping computer woke up and decided to go hacking.

Its screen was dark, but in its memory cells, Fikri was running and waiting. A string of numbers arrived via satellite from halfway around the world. The program processed them, connected to the appropriate DNS server, and began sending page requests.

So far, the Bahraini underground had only used Fikri on their own machines, overshadowing its real purpose. It had been designed as the world's first peer-to-peer DDoS system. The imam had gotten the idea from NASA's SETI@home software, which farmed out the raw data from space telescopes to private enthusiasts for processing on their own computers. A hundred thousand users ran the program, which put their spare computing resources to work analyzing radio signals for signs of extraterrestrial life.

Ra'd bin Mazin had suggested to his hackers that they apply the same technology to revolution. A conventional DDoS attack would seize control of machines against their owners' will, using viruses and malware. But a peer-to-peer DDoS network would secure the consent of its participants before acting. It would bring together activists from all over the world to use their combined computing power to shut down any government network through sheer excess demand. It would be a genuine and very effective way to contribute to social change without personal exertion or risk, just as the bittorrent networks were an unstoppable protest against oppressive copyright laws. Instead of signing a petition, or clicking "like" on a Facebook page and forgetting about it thirty seconds later, users could contribute their unused processing capacity--and Fikri didn't require much capacity to send pings and page requests--to really accomplish something. The power of collective action and distributed action over the state and centralization.

So Fihr and Shihab and Junayd and Asim had written the software in the intervals between their blogging duties, and sent it out through their mailing lists. And it had been downloaded and installed already by over twenty thousand users. They let the program run in the background on their machines, and when the Bahraini underground fed target IP addresses into the system, it attacked those addresses automatically, coordinating its efforts with other iterations of the program across the network. Response had been particularly strong among college students. At MIT, an enterprising team had hacked most of the campus computer labs and installed Fikri on those machines. Its success was given an added boost by its popularity in North America. When it was midday in Manama, it would be night in the United States and Canada, meaning that many unused computers would be ready and available to pour their resources into a DDoS attack.

And now the capacity of the global Fikri network was to be tested for the first time on a new target.

* * * * *

It took two hours, but the Al Jazeera website crashed in the end. It was not built to withstand a global attack. The constant increase in pressure as Fikri applications around the world came online, combined with higher visitor numbers from locals wanting to find out what coverage of the revolution it was actually offering, led to its failure just before dusk.

The point of the attack shifted. Al Jazeera technicians in foreign areas were scrambling to erect new and better firewalls around their systems, to prevent at least the subsidiary websites from going down. Some of them were already close to overload. They patched every hole they could find, negotiated frantically for more emergency bandwidth with their network hosts, and braced themselves to isolate and block communications from any address that might pose a threat.

And nothing happened.

At a command from the underground, Fikri turned inward rather than outward. The Al Jazeera affiliates were allowed to continue making fools of themselves in front of a worldwide audience. All the machines that formed the peer-to-peer network, which by this time included thousands of smartphones running a mobile version of the software, began pinging a list of addresses that linked back to no obvious URL. Internal addresses. The parts of Al Jazeera's network that it used for its own communications--and for organizing broadcasts and transmitting content. The satellite relays were useless if the transmitters on the ground didn't have any information to feed them, and with the network saturated with traffic, the newsroom would be unable to get updates or video feeds or to coordinate its activities with other departments in the same building. It was a subtle attack, aimed at something unprotected and yet vital. Even as a corpse, Ra'd bin Mazin could still reason better than the Emir could.

In an hour and a half, Al Jazeera went off the air for thirty seconds. Fifteen minutes later, its broadcasts were interrupted for a full two minutes. They would continue to be sporadically cut into for the rest of the night.

* * * * *

A hundred Bahraini soldiers lay dead on the ground in Manama. They were the unlucky ones. Thousands of their comrades had gotten away with desertion, and were still getting away with it. They took off their armor, handed their rifles to someone in the crowd, and joined the ranks of the protestors. Entire units had refused orders to fire on the dissidents with gas and rubber bullets. Memorably, the members of one troop had turned and aimed their weapons at the captain who, from behind the safety of his vehicle, had commanded them to fire on the civilians with live ammunition. He had run for his life and the soldiers had laid down their arms and dispersed. Other officers, with more stubbornness or less flexibility, had drawn their weapons and opened fire on their own men. It was a useless gesture, as a Beretta pistol only held fifteen rounds, and not all of those would be guaranteed to hit their intended targets. And then? The officers and NCOs who had tried to compel obedience did not live very long after they began killing. That was not the way to earn the respect or obedience of men who were sickened by the government's violent response to dissent.

The Royal Bahraini Army was royal no longer. It had been halved in size during the course of the day. The soldiers felt affronted, betrayed, and threatened, not only because they were being forced into action against friends and neighbors, but because the government's unequivocal support for the Haia placed them in jeopardy, too. It was well known that across the border, in Saudi Arabia, even the royal palaces and government offices were not exempt from the jurisdiction of the mutaween. They were disinclined to tolerate a purge of their own ranks by outsiders. So they took the imam's advice and walked away from their posts, drifting through the streets, going where they pleased. As for the soldiers who remained on duty, they often proved reluctant to act and difficult to command. They held back their officers and proved themselves to be useless as a countervailing force against the revolution. The police were another matter. With their tradition of institutionalized brutality, they had been unaffected by the problem of desertion--but there were not enough policemen to pacify the city, not without the army to help them.

* * * * *

"They're coming!" Junayd yelled, pounding up the stairway. "He did it again, that bastard!"

Asim froze in his seat, the old panic returning. Then his reflexes took over. He leaped up, his wheeled chair flying out from under him, and went chasing after Junayd.

He found him on the roof, staring west through a pair of binoculars into the glare of the setting sun. "Who's coming?" he demanded. Junayd didn't answer. Asim grabbed his arm and shook him roughly. "Who's after us? Who?"

Junayd handed him the binoculars. "Look for yourself!"

The building beneath them was old and dilapidated, but it was tall and stood on a slight rise in the ground, one of the few geographical features of any kind that Bahrain possessed. It was also well outside Manama, near the western extremity of the island. And Junayd's binoculars were powerful. Asim swept the horizon with them, looking for anything unusual. He found it.

Ten miles away, or more, there were troops massed in a line across the King Fahd Causeway, the road that linked Bahrain with Saudi Arabia. Troops in Saudi uniforms.

King Hamad had called for help again.

19

The beggar stopped and looked around him. The arc lights were bright on the other side of the fence, and his shadow stretched away in a long, bold blot across the bare dirt. He was quite noticeable, but that was a good thing. Anyone else nearby would have been equally noticeable. They would have stood out in the light just like he did, and he could have seen them coming. There was no one.

He fished around in a bag hanging from his shoulder and brought out a dead mongoose, freshly killed. Under his breath, he said a prayer. He drew his arm back and lobbed the mongoose over the fence with a precision borne of long practice.

There was a flash of sparks and a crackling sound on the other side of the fence. Two seconds later, an explosion rang out, accompanied by a cascade of smoke and the smell of ozone as a transformer exploded. The old city of Bushehr went dark. The beggar turned and shuffled off.

* * * * *

Amanda Price sensed through her closed eyelids that there was no longer light streaming from the hangar entrance. She opened her eyes cautiously. After having kept them shaded for the past hour, they adjusted to the blackness of the night at once. Beside her, she felt Javed stir.

The airport, like the city around it, had been blacked out. In the distance, she heard a faint rumble and cough as the Iranian technicians worked on starting a backup generator. Judging by the noise, they were having trouble with it. That was all to the good.

The two maintenance techs had wandered out of the hangar and were gossiping about the power shortage. She listened to their voices and decided that they weren't worried about the accident. Apparently power outages in Bushehr were nothing out of the ordinary. According to Javed, local humorists blamed them on the nuclear plant, which was so good at producing electricity that the government had never bothered to connect it up to the local grid, wanting to keep all of the energy for themselves in Tehran.

One of the men lit a cigarette. The flare would have ruined his night vision at that range, Price thought. She rose on the balls of her feet. Javed was already moving. Following his lead, she slipped through the trees to the hangar wall, then sidled along it until they both reached the corner.

The technicians were not more than fifteen feet away from them and had their backs turned.

Javed took off. Price was an instant behind him. Out of the corner of her eye, she saw him jump on the back of the airman nearest him and imitated the move. Hers went down with a sound more like a bleat than a gurgle. She felt his jaw break his fall--and break under the force of it. Before he could do more than grunt, she stabbed him with one of the Major's hallucinogenic injectors. *Where on earth does he find these things,* she wondered before pushing the thought aside.

Cold steel touched her skin. Javed was passing her a pair of handcuffs. She dragged the man's wrists behind his back and snapped the cuffs on him while Javed gagged him. Leaving him to get the bodies out of the way, she turned and sprinted into the hangar.

And stopped almost immediately.

The slim, upturned nose gleamed in the ambient light. It tapered away in a series of gentle curves, rounder and thicker than she remembered. In fact, all of its lines were less curvaceous and more angular, more rakish than she had anticipated. The sharp, squared-off intakes were a complete departure from the original. The canted double tails, too. All the same, the effect was pleasing. It looked even faster than its predecessors.

A couple of weeks ago, when the Major had showed her a photo of the plane, no Westerner had ever flown the Saeqeh fighter. In five minutes she would become the first.

She dragged the chocks out from under the wheels. The checklist listed that as one of the last steps, but she didn't have the time to follow it literally. Instead, she grabbed the landing gear pins and pitot tube cover and stuffed them into her jacket. She'd find somewhere else for them later. Off to her right, Javed was straining at the starter cart, an old and reluctant dinosaur acquired by the Imperial Iranian Air Force back when the Shah was still carrying on at Maxim's. There was no time for a thorough preflight check, either. She'd thought to bring a flashlight, and by its light checked the wing roots and hydraulic actuators in as short a time as possible. Nothing was cracked or damaged. That was to be expected. The Iranians wouldn't be taking risks with a prestige product like their first indigenous fighter. She turned off the flashlight and joined Javed in pulling the cart over to the aircraft.

The Major had given him a manual explaining how to connect the ground power and air hose to the aircraft, but Price helped him do it anyway. She'd done it before. The Saeqeh was close enough to the T-38's she'd flown that everything was in exactly the same position. The difference here was that it had to be done fast, without double-checking.

The cockpit was still open. Rather than waste time finding a ladder, she grabbed the rim and pulled herself up the side of the aircraft. Everything on the panel looked familiar enough. Price strapped in and balled up her discarded chador behind her for extra cushioning. No time to connect a G-suit; besides, she wasn't wearing one and didn't plan on needing one. She flicked on the battery but not the lights. The engine instruments were still analog rather than digital, thankfully. The aircraft didn't have a full fuel load, but it would be enough. She nudged the throttles open and turned on the fuel pumps. Praise be to the engineers who designed this as a training airplane, she thought, and raised her hands over her head. Fist into open palm as the start signal, just like the Air Force flyboys did it. From here on, there was no other way out but the one in front of her.

Javed turned the key on the starter cart and the old engine clattered its way into a steady roar. Price cringed and hoped that the noise would be mistaken for one of the auxiliary generators that had been going on across the airport since the blackout began. They were counting on that. Behind her, the right engine began to wind up. She stared unblinking at the RPM gauge. The instant it hit fourteen percent, she punched the start button with her left hand.

The engine's whine changed pitch as the fuel flow ignited, then quieted, running steady. Her finger sweated on the start button for the left engine, but she couldn't touch it yet. If she tried to start the left turbine as well before thirty seconds had passed, it would interrupt the air supply and she might lose both. And there wasn't time to take that risk. She counted, her eyes glancing from her instruments to the hangar entrance--still empty--and back. Thirty! She signaled to Javed and he flipped the diverter valve inside the engine housing over. The left engine spooled up. She pressed the starter, and in eight seconds, just like the book said, it was ticking over smoothly.

On went the electronic display. The abbreviations, for some silly nationalistic reason, were in Persian, but a gyro and an altimeter look the same the world over. On went the generators. Price waved to Javed one last time. She saw him disconnect the starter cart and tug it away. The Saeqeh was free now. She slammed the canopy shut, pumped the controls and felt them move freely through their range, and only at this late moment flicked the lights on. A lighted aircraft departing openly would cause less suspicion at first than a darkened one. Pulling the brakes, she let the jet roll forward.

Outside the hangar, she glanced over her shoulder. She saw Javed's dim form dart back into the belt of trees. And all at once she missed him. It was because of him and his cousins all across Iran that she was about to make history.

She pushed the throttles forward.

Two Iranian guards, coming to see why there was an aircraft starting up during a blackout, had to throw themselves flat on the taxiway to avoid getting clipped by her wing. She didn't look back. She knew they wouldn't fire at her. It would never cross their minds that their airplane was being stolen. They would run to their officer to find out what was going on and complain about the reckless pilot, and by that time--

The twin runways at Bushehr are long. Price swung the Saeqeh onto the closer of the two and reluctantly brought it to a stop. One last check. Throttles to full military power. The gauges trembled but showed nothing out of the ordinary. Nosewheel steering off. Brake release. Throttles to afterburner.

The Saeqeh gathered itself underneath her. At a hundred and thirty-five knots, she eased the stick back. At a hundred and fifty, the plane came alive. At a hundred and sixty, it lifted off the ground. She pulled a switch and the gear came up. Before a third of the runway was behind her, she was already edging the aircraft into a gentle left-hand turn southwards. Its lights rose in the sky, framing the twin suns of the tailpipes as the Iranians on the ground looked up, watching the departure, the brightest thing in a dark night.

Then, abruptly, the lights jerked and fell towards the ocean. They went out.

*****

The screen on the Major's phone lit up. He grabbed it off the table in the galley before it started to vibrate and pressed the button to view the message it had just received. The text consisted of only five words, but the expression on the Major's face when he read them was ecstatic. He leaned back and laughed long and silently. Then he rose and made his way to the bridge, where his Marines were lying concealed.

He tapped Ramirez on the shoulder. "Time to put those childhood skills to work again, Lance Corporal."

*****

The trawler's captain came pounding down the pier, his heavy boots making a noise like shots rather than like footsteps. He was shrieking in a mixture of three languages and had invoked God by at least a simple majority of His hundred names before he reached the end of the pier. At that point his language became even more colorful. His boat was chugging happily away into the darkness without lights. His thirty years of experience at sea allowed him to make out her shape against the night sky, but it was growing more indistinct every second. The trawler had to be at least a mile away by this time, maybe farther. The captain stepped sideways to get a better view, tripped over something large and squishy, and gashed his forehead open on the rough planks as he fell.

He swore again and wiped himself up with a large, fishy-smelling cloth he carried about with him, kicking at the pile of rope or whatever it was that had tripped him. The pile groaned. The captain stopped cursing and listened. It groaned again. He sat up and rolled it over, and found himself looking into the face of his own watchman, bound and gagged.

"Get the police!" the captain hollered at his mate, who was standing in the middle of the pier with a stupid expression on his face. "Go! Go!"

The police, already attracted by the captain's screaming and the unusual noise of a boat departing so late at night, were nearby. They were on the spot by the time the captain managed to get his crewman untied.

"Where's your boat?" the police sergeant inquired sarcastically.

"Stolen!" the captain spat. "Bahman, here, was on watch. I found him tied up. See the marks on his wrists!" He thrust the unfortunate sailor's arm at the policeman to underline his point. Bahman himself howled in pain as his stiffened, chafed limbs were jerked around.

"All right," said the sergeant, pondering this. "Who did it?"

"How in the name of--"

"There were six of them," the sailor burst out, talking over his captain's profanities. "Two of them were Iranians. The other four were Americans. Americans!"

"Don't talk nonsense," the policeman snapped. "There are no Americans in Bandar-e Anzali."

"But it's been all over the news!"

"You mean the American marines trying to get away with prison breaking? Ridiculous. They're heading for the Gulf. They're at the other end of the country. Now, who was it that stole the boat?"

"Americans! I swear!"

"How could you possibly know they were Americans?"

"They spoke English!"

"And I suppose you do? I've known you for years and you've never spoken a word of it. You've been hiding your gifts all this time, is that it?"

"I know what it sounds like." Bahman dug around in one of the pockets of his jacket and brought out a worn cassette tape. He held it up for the officer's inspection. Under the rays of his flashlight, the writing on the cover read "Freddie Mercury."

The policeman was interrupted before he could form an adequate retort. "Sergeant?" his colleague called. He was standing a few paces away, shining his light down on the pier, looking for any marks or evidence that might have been left behind by the thieves. Something round and shiny gleamed against the dark wood. The sergeant abandoned his questioning of the watchman with a grunt and bent over to take a look at it.

It was metal, about an inch and a half in diameter, engraved and enameled on the visible side. An outer band of blue encircled an inner field of red, on which was a gold globe with an anchor through it and a bird standing on top.

"I've seen that before," the patrolman said. "When I was in the army. It's the American marine insignia."

* * * * *

The local police captain was dizzy from the sudden changes in elevation he was going through. His call reporting the presumed theft of the boat by Americans was being kicked upstairs at a rate he'd never experienced before in his career. Someone wanted this information confirmed very badly.

The commanding general of First Army Headquarters in Tehran came on the line. "You say that four Americans and two Iranians stole a boat in Bandar-e Anzali less than an hour ago?" The captain could hear the stress in his voice, and sympathized.

"Yes, sir. They tied up the sailor on watch and gagged him while they went aboard the vessel and waited. Then they dumped him back on the dock before departing. He heard them speaking English among themselves. When my men examined the pier, they found a coin or medallion there bearing the eagle, globe and anchor emblem of the United States Marine Corps."

"A coin?"

"Yes, sir. I have had a photograph of it emailed to your office."

There was a pause on the other end. The captain could hear the general yelling at his staff in the background. A minute later, the yells subsided. "We have the picture here. Your identification is correct. Now, this is important--you've interviewed that sailor thoroughly by now, I assume? Did he hear either of the Iranians speaking English?"

"No, he did not. One of them conversed with one of the Americans in a different language that our witness thought might be Arabic, but he wasn't sure."

"What was the course the trawler was last seen taking?"

"According to the boat's captain, due north, or slightly northwest."

"That's all I needed to know. Congratulations, Captain, you may have actually found these bastards." The general slammed down the phone and looked at the map in front of him. "Slightly northwest from Bandar-e Anzali--they'll be in Azerbaijan by morning. Get a reconnaissance flight out there now!"

* * * * *

The Air Force, when queried, sent the general a very nasty reply to the effect that one of their pilots had defected from Bushehr with a valuable pre-production fighter plane and that they were busy deploying their forces to shoot it down before it reached a nation friendly to the United States. Given the resulting reshuffle of their air operations, and the need to maintain constant patrols, they regretted to inform the general they could not help him. Preventing Iranian technology from falling into American hands, they implied, was more important than chasing after a couple of convicts who were outside Iran's territorial waters by now. First Army Headquarters, rather than waste time arguing with the flyboys, diverted two of the old Super Cobras that were loitering near the Azerbaijani border and sent them after the trawler instead.

The helicopters spread out along the last known path of the vessel, sweeping the surface of the Caspian with their infrared sensors. One went north, the other south. The observers kept looking up from their scopes to do visual scans of the sea. There was enough starlight for that, and it never hurt to double-check.

It was the southbound helicopter that picked up the first contact. Off to port, a bright point of light warmed into existence on its screens, hot against the background of cold air and colder water. The observer plotted the course of that spot on his map. If it was the trawler, and it had come from Bandar-e Anzali, then it lay on a direct line between Anzali and the Azerbaijani port of Neftchala. That was highly suspicious. He radioed the information back to headquarters in Tehran, which was coordinating the search.

"Have you made positive visual identification yet?" First Army wanted to know.

"We should have that in another forty seconds," the pilot radioed back.

The glow swelled on their sensors. It was a ship, all right. A trawler, very like the one that had been described to them. Pilot and observer both looked left as they came up on it. The pilot eased off the throttle and let the helicopter sink to a bare hundred feet above the water. The moon peeked out from behind a cloud. They could even see the colors on the ship's funnel and superstructure.

The pilot pressed the transmit switch on his radio. "Confirmed. We have the stolen vessel in sight." He read off the coordinates.

"Hail it and order it to return to port."

"It's not responding to my attempts to make contact."

"Can you determine how many people are on board?"

The helicopter swung around and took up a position astern and well above the trawler. The observer fiddled with his infrared scope, fine-tuning it. "From the heat signatures there appear to be six people on board. One on the bridge, the others below."

In Tehran, First Army had already checked the vessel's position against those of the Navy's patrol boats in the Caspian. None were anywhere near the trawler. "You are ordered to sink the vessel if it does not respond to your instructions to reverse course."

The trawler did not respond. The helicopter pulled back to a reasonable distance and let a salvo of rockets fly at the boat. From such a stable firing position, it was impossible to miss.

The wrecked hull burned for a short while before sinking. After it was gone, little flames still floated on the surface of the water, feeding on the oil that had leaked from the hull. The pilot of the helicopter, surveying the scene from high above, reported no life jackets or survivors in sight.

*****

There was a military roadblock outside of Choobar. The van pulled over behind an empty produce truck and waited.

From the opposite direction came army trucks filled with soldiers, dozens of them. The soldiers were dirty and obviously sleeping as best they could during the journey. The road was a decent one, so that much was in their favor. With the trucks came the smell of forest soil and crushed pine needles, mingling with the scents of fish and salt drifting up from the Caspian.

The convoy passed, and the military policemen who had held up the traffic got back in their car and moved on. They didn't stop to glance at the occupants of the waiting vehicles.

The van started up again and pursued its way north towards Astara. It turned up into the hills above the town and began climbing the grade into the mountains, past ponds, scattered houses, small fields. The road began to fold over on itself more often. Clearings gave way to forests. Pavement turned into dirt and then rutted dirt. The van rocked to a halt and its engine died.

"Everyone out," the Major ordered, his voice low. "Marines, keep your weapons handy."

He took the lead himself. Brassey and Ramirez spread out on his flanks. Powers stayed with Kadivar and Jan, right behind the Major.

"How far, sir?" Powers asked in a whisper.

"A mile at most. Keep as quiet as you can."

That was difficult, since the trees around them were dropping leaves everywhere, but the Marines were trained to cope with such conditions. The two Iranians did their best to imitate them. The ground rose, dipped, rose again, dipped again. As if to make things more complicated, the Major wasn't cutting straight across the ridges, but was taking them obliquely instead. Which made scaling them much more work.

They crossed another dirt track, and the slope started to angle down once more. Off to their right, a couple of lights glittered through the trees.

"Kashfai," the Major breathed in a voice so quiet it was hardly perceptible above the rustling of leaves in the background. He gestured to his Marines. They edged to the left.

In front of them, the forest came to an abrupt end at a two-lane road. The Marines regrouped.

"Cross one at a time," the Major instructed them. "Get into that belt of trees on the other side and stay there. It's narrow. Do not go beyond it. Do not split up yet."

One by one, the six men sprinted across the pavement, those on either side of the road covering them as they ran. No cars interrupted their crossing, but none of them regretted taking precautions anyway.

The Major consulted a very dim GPS unit, then turned and led them away to the right. The trees around them were getting thinner, and they could hear the sound of rushing water. There were more lights nearby, on the same side of the road. The Marines walked carefully. They passed the lights and breathed easier.

Again, the Major changed direction. Where the trees stopped, so did he: on the edge of a shallow river. There was a broad stretch of water-worn rocks between the little troop and the river itself, but on the other side the trees came all the way down to its edge.

"Take Kadivar and Jan with you," the Major ordered Brassey. "We'll cover you. Don't fall."

The river was shallow and slippery, exactly the sort of stream that makes falling while crossing in haste easy, but Brassey was strong and Jan was stronger, and they were across it in no time. The rest of the Marines followed.

The ground changed slope again and led them up into more forest. In spite of the cover, the Major set a very slow pace, stopping and listening at short intervals. His wariness communicated itself to the rest of the team. Without him saying anything, they knew it was almost time to make their final run.

They crossed another dirt road. It was like being back in Virginia, the Marines thought, except more dangerous.

Then the Major halted. The group closed up on him and looked across the border into Azerbaijan.

There were scattered trees on the other side of the border as well, but between them was a wide swath of cleared area hemmed in by two fences. The Azerbaijani fence wasn't much, a broad-gauge mesh tacked to posts about the height of a man. The Iranian fence--the nearer one--was more intimidating. The posts were taller, and there were crosspieces strung with barbed wire across the top of each, making them look like stunted, vicious telephone poles.

"Time to cut our way to freedom," the Major whispered. "Sergeant Brassey, you've got the strongest hands." He passed the sergeant a wire cutter. Brassey nodded, slung his rife, and rose from his crouch, but Jan stopped him and said something in Farsi.

"Sir?" Brassey asked. The Major turned to Kadivar, who exchanged a few words with his lover and then translated for the Major's benefit. The Major shrugged.

"He says that he can see this is a case for strength, pure and simple, and he wants to do it. He says he can do it faster than you." Major Martin looked from Jan to Brassey and back again. "All right. Both of you go. You can cover him while he works." He nodded and they were gone.

The Marines stood in a semicircle, weapons ready. If a border patrol came along, the two men at the fence would be out in the open and plainly visible. The only solution would be to shoot their way through the opposing force.

"They're through," the Major said softly. His voice held a note of surprise. He hadn't expected Jan to be able to work so much faster than Brassey.

In less than a minute, the Iranian made short work of the Azerbaijani fence as well. Even before Brassey had finished scrambling through it after him, the Major was ordering his men into action. "Ramirez, take Kadivar and go now!"

The two of them threw themselves at the hole in the fence. Ramirez got stuck and Kadivar hauled him through. On the Azerbaijani side, Jan was still cutting, enlarging the gap to make the passage easier. The instant Ramirez spun and dropped into position, his rifle facing Iran, the Major took off. He pushed Powers ahead of him and followed through with a final lunge than landed him on his face in the dirt, but bounced right back up. "Move!" he hissed. "Get away from the border!"

Everyone took his advice.

They skirted a small pond and several farm buildings. Fortunately, no dog awoke to mark their passage with a chorus of yells. A couple of hundred yards farther on, they crossed a narrow bridge and found themselves on the edge of a paved road again.

Lights flashed in their faces. The Marines raised their weapons, but the Major waved them down. A late-model Chevy Suburban pulled up next to their group. The driver lowered his window.

"Major Martin?" The Major nodded. The words had been spoken in English. "Welcome to Azerbaijan, sir. If you and your party will just climb in back, I'll have you in Lankaran in half an hour. Oh, and if you wouldn't mind losing the guns? We didn't pay extra for those."

The Marines tossed their rifles into the bushes. It took Kadivar what seemed like an agonizingly long time to get Jan to throw away his trophy pistol, but he succeeded at last. They climbed aboard. The driver threw the Suburban into sharp reverse, skidded around a hundred and eighty degrees, and took off to the north.

"Sir, who is this ride courtesy of?" Brassey asked.

"Oh, one of the oil companies," the Major answered vaguely.

There was no nighttime traffic in southern Azerbaijan. The Suburban didn't stop rolling until it pulled up at the

Lankaran International Airport, right behind one of the hangars. A heavy Sikorsky helicopter sat on the tarmac, both turbines screaming, its lights illuminating the entire parking ramp as well as the garish markings on its sides. The Major shook the driver's hand, then led his troop over to the helicopter. No customs or airport officials were anywhere in evidence.

The Sikorsky rose straight up and set a course for Baku. Two hours later, it put them down at the international airport in Azerbaijan's capital. It landed on the executive ramp, rather than at the heliport. As Powers climbed out, he swore he saw a pair of airport police turn and very ostentatiously walk away from the helicopter, so as not to notice what was going on. Major Martin noticed him looking.

"Bribery is so cheap in Azerbaijan," he called out cheerfully above the rotor noise.

Powers shook his head in amazement.

A Gulfstream G650 was sitting on the ramp next to the helicopter. The pilot frowned down at the shabby party approaching his aircraft.

"You're late," he said to the Major. His tone made the simple comment into an accusation.

"Iranian police," the Major explained.

"We have a flight plan to keep."

"Then stop talking and start keeping it." The Major pushed him aside and ushered the two Iranians into the interior of the aircraft.

Ten minutes later the Gulfstream floated off the runway and turned for Spain.

* * * * *

Price saw the lights of the bridge ahead and eased the stick back a mere fraction of an inch. The Saeqeh nosed up and shot across the causeway at over three hundred knots. She wondered if the jet wash had knocked any of the soldiers marching along it off their feet. Probably not. She hadn't been able to stay as close to the surface of the Gulf as she would have preferred during the pass due to the tall streetlights that rose tower-like from the bridge's centerline. That was easily remedied now. She nudged the plane down again until it became indistinguishable from the surface of the ocean, at least as far as radar was concerned.

So the King of Bahrain was having to run to his fellow monarch for help again, was he? Nothing unusual about that. He couldn't call on the US Navy to help him put down a rebellion, although even that was possible, given the current commander-in-chief's leanings. But it would make for an interesting conversation when the Bahrainis and the Saudis and the Americans all started arguing about why and whether an American jet had been overflying a Saudi invasion. The Saeqeh's blue-and-yellow markings and its twin tails made misidentification inevitable. In the meantime, the tricky security situation on the ground was doubtless making it hell for the Bahrainis to monitor their airspace properly, and that was all to her advantage.

She edged over towards Bahrain itself, using the bulk of the land to help her hide. It would block the radar from any Qatari or American patrols to the east, and return a confused signal to any Saudi scanners to the west.

Eight minutes later, she was feet-dry over the Saudi desert and no one had spotted her. There was nothing in this part of the world except the distant city of Al Hofuf, which she had just passed some forty miles to starboard. She flew on southwards, into the Rub al Khali. The ground began to rise gently, forming a broad plateau cut through with an ancient alluvial delta.

The Iranians, of course, had been right, she reflected. The Saeqeh did have a lower radar signature than the new American Super Hornet. It was a much smaller plane. Did those scientific sailors at Boeing really think that they could shrink an entire aircraft just by making a few of its parts out of plastic and giving it a coat of paint? A metal object sixty feet long was going to cast a bigger shadow than one only forty-seven feet long. Five hundred square feet of wing was going to reflect more energy than two hundred square feet. Simpletons.

She couldn't decide whether to shut her instruments off or not as she strained to keep track of the ground by moonlight alone. Her eyes needed to be at their most sensitive now--but she also needed the altimeter. Damn liquid crystal displays, she thought. For low-level night flying, old-fashioned dials were by far the best. They didn't leak excess light to mess up your night vision. The tiny GPS unit strapped to her leg, its screen turned down to the lowest possible brightness setting, was almost invisible by comparison.

And it told her she was almost there. It was still too dangerous to use her radio, so she had to watch the ground and not take her eyes off it. Six miles more...five...four...

Two white lights blinked into existence ahead and off to her left. They weren't in line. Price snapped the plane over, bouncing into and back out of ground effect as she did so, then flung it the other way. Now the lights lined up. She dumped power and dropped the flaps. In this aircraft, the gear had to wait till the very last second. She risked letting them down a hair early. The first light passed underneath her and she held the nose up, feeling the Saeqeh sink, sink until its wheels touched the earth and nearly shook her out of her seat.

She didn't dare lean too heavily on the brakes. A burst tire now would be a disaster. The aircraft bumped and rattled, and came to a halt. The engines were at idle. They didn't seem to have suffered from debris, which meant the ground must have been somewhat clean.

But she didn't pull the throttles back all the way and let the turbines die. Instead, she just sat there.

A truck pulled up on her left. Men in heavy jackets--the Rub al Khali is frigid at night--piled out of it and began unreeling a hose attached to a tank in the back of the truck. One of them left the group and came forward to peer into the cockpit from as close as he could safely get. Price smiled. She waved at him through the glass.

She'd conceived the entire plan the instant the Major had explained his idea. His thought had been for her to draw the Iranian Air Force off, then drop the jet in the desert and be picked up by one of his friends in the Emirates, for which she had a valid tourist visa and pre-booked departure flight. But the Major didn't know that her Uncle Jack worked for Saudi Aramco, heading up an exploration team. He had access to vehicles and maps and ground-moving equipment--and the Aramco compounds were the only places in the entire kingdom that were off limits to the religious police.

What if Uncle Jack could top up her tanks and she could get the aircraft out of the Arabian Peninsula altogether? What if she could eventually fly it home?

Her uncle, who had his own adventurous streak, had been delighted to help. Machining the proper fitting needed to refuel the Saeqeh from old plans for the Northrop F-5 turned out to be easy. With the maps and information at his disposal, picking a landing site had also been simple. He and his crew had gone out and cleared it of all large rocks and other potential debris, then sat back and waited for her to show up. It was all concealed beneath the umbrella of oil exploration and looked innocuous to the paper-pushers in Riyadh. She'd kept in touch with him by satellite--all under Major Martin's nose. Price didn't feel like answering the Major's questions. This was her venture. She also didn't want him telling her that her side trip risked interfering with his operation.

The fuel gauges on the right of the instrument panel were going up in a very satisfying way. At first she'd felt uncertain about whether the jet could handle a hot refueling, but then she recalled that astronaut Frank Borman had done it all the time to edge out his fellow pilots in unofficial cross-country races. She had remembered Borman's most famous words, too, spoken about the flawed design of the first Apollo spacecraft: "There's no question that it was a coffin, and I'd have flown it gladly." That was a feeling she could understand, and now she was living it out.

Her uncle was waving at her again. She saw his crew hauling the hose back to their truck. In front of her, the single runway light still burned in the distance. There was plenty of room for a takeoff, albeit a dangerous one. Price threw her uncle a mock salute as he stepped away. Then she pushed the throttles forward and the Saeqeh began to rattle down the makeshift landing strip.

There would be abandoned military runways and plenty of spare parts in Ethiopia.

20

The Saudi infantry battalion was making no progress. Ten thousand Bahrainis, arms linked, blocked the King Fahd causeway from rail to rail. When the American airplane had nearly landed on their heads, the soldiers had ducked, but the protestors had been too thoroughly jammed against one another to show fear. That embarrassed the Saudis and led to them buttstroking the civilians, but that tactic was also useless. There were so many demonstrators pushing forward from behind that every man who fell was replaced at once. The soldiers desisted and retreated towards the island of Um Al Nassan to regroup.

Somewhere on the Saudi general staff there was an officer with an agile mind, who, during the discussions on how to meet a Bahraini revolution with force, had proposed that they attach engineering units to the infantry. The engineers, in turn, were to be given tools designed to manipulate crowds rather than soil. Chief among these were military bulldozers with plow-like angled blades fixed to their shovels. They had traction and power that could knock down a house--or part a mass of human beings by thrusting them aside instead of back. The commanders in the field had received the idea with grim pleasure. No messy shooting, and if the dissidents didn't get out of the way of a moving vehicle, any accidents would be their own fault. The colonel in charge of the Saudi assistance force ordered one of the bulldozers to advance.

The crowd did not part for it. There was nowhere for them to go. It only nudged them at first, but as the demonstrators lost their balance and fell, first the blade and then the treads and body of the vehicle passed over their limbs. The driver was deaf to their screams. The general staff had foreseen the possibility of weakness in the drivers and ordered that they be equipped with noise-canceling radio headsets. As the bulldozer edged farther into the ranks of the protestors, those who were falling pressed against those behind them, until the men along the bridge rail could no longer keep their balance and began falling into the sea by the dozen.

* * * * *

King Hamad had no bulldozers in the courtyard of the Al-Qudaibiya Palace. The grounds crawled with hundreds of policeman and soldiers, who roamed the lawns under the glare of improvised arc lamps that had been hastily erected. They were accompanied by the few remaining members of the Haia squads that Saudi Arabia had loaned Bahrain. The street trash of which the squads were composed had turned coward in the end and fled to the one place in Manama that they reasoned must hold out against all odds, arming themselves along the way with the discarded weapons of soldiers who had deserted.

"Down, Hamad!" rang out thousands of voices in the streets encircling the palace. "Down, Hamad! Down, Hamad!" They meant it this time. Not just a transfer of power to a democracy, but the departure of all claims to power. No man spoke for the revolution or its aims, but the men and women of Bahrain built a wall of flesh around their ci-devant leader, trapping him and his soldiers in his palace, which was a clear enough expression of their will.

Metal beat on air. The kingdom's two Blackhawk helicopters configured for royal transport, accompanied by a pair of armed Cobras, circled the palace. There was only room for one helicopter at a time to land in the courtyard, out of any potential line of fire from the perimeter walls. The remaining aircraft slipped to one side and hovered as the first began to descend. The demonstrators waved their fists at it and jeered.

The sinking helicopter was not quite level with the dome when smoke began to pour out of its engine housing. The airframe trembled, then gave a screech that was heard even over the noise of the mob. Its transmission had frozen. Wobbling, the helicopter dropped into the courtyard with only the existing momentum of its rotor to hold it up. That wasn't enough. The crowd held its breath in expectation of the crash and was not disappointed.

The soldiers turned and ran, converging on the palace. There were screams, yells, sirens going off. To the crowd outside, the wreckage was invisible except for a trail of gray smoke rising up from the courtyard. Nothing happened. The soldiers began to return to the gardens.

Then the helicopter's fuel detonated with a puff of flame and sound that blew out the palace's windows and scattered glass like confetti all over the king's defenders, who threw themselves on the grass in an excess of caution.

The protestors to the west of the palace could not see it, but those on the northern and southern and eastern sides all could. It was a line of light, stretching from the second hovering helicopter to the roof of the Shaik Isa National Library on the other side of the highway. But it wasn't stretching from the helicopter at all, they realized. Helicopters do not have lasers in their tails. The light was coming from the library. Someone was training a beam on the Blackhawk. The crowd noticed and let out a roar of astonishment and approval as its members raised their hands, their fingers pointing in the direction of the beam.

The Cobra pilots saw the beam, too. They dropped out of their covering positions and wheeled towards the library, their gun turrets rotating to bear on whatever threat might lurk there. They weren't quick enough. A faint grinding sound, barely perceptible in the chaos, came from the Blackhawk. Its spinning tail rotor, nearly invisible by virtue of its speed, became visible. Unable to stabilize itself, the helicopter started swinging around its own rotor in a wild loop, pulled by the torque of the dual turbines. The pilots killed the engines in an attempt to slow the motion. That took away any chance they had of remaining airborne. The Blackhawk slewed out of control and went sliding across the sky as it fell. It crashed through the perimeter wall of the palace, tearing the grounds open to the crowds in the streets. The crew scrambled free. The engine housings had not been injured, and so the aircraft did not explode on impact the way its companion had.

Inside the compound, the soldiers clustered around the gap in the wall, but did not dare intrude into the streets. The protestors were not so reticent. Ignoring the airmen working their way out of the wreck, they slowly closed in on the breach. The soldiers menaced them with their weapons, but the officers held them back. They knew it was a lost cause. They couldn't hold the palace now, not with the chance of immediate evacuation gone and a fifty-foot hole in their defensive line. Behind the rows of guards, the demonstrators could hear a loud argument going on. It ended with a gunshot.

A man in a Bahraini captain's uniform stepped out in front of the soldiers and turned to face them. "Stand down!" he ordered. "Do not oppose the crowd, but do not surrender, either."

There was muted applause from the nearest protestors. A few of them advanced to the wall and stepped through the rubble. The soldiers backed away and let them pass. By twos and threes, the revolution began to seep into the last stronghold of the government.

On the other side of the palace, two black Cadillacs shot out from a rear entrance and headed for the main gate. Between them was an armor-plated Mercedes. The policemen manning the gates swung the steel grids open a fraction of a second before the speeding convoy arrived, then ran for their lives.

From the windows of the front vehicle came a steady spray of bullets. Without being attacked, without being fired upon, the king's bodyguards were firing on the crowd anyway, to clear it out of the way as one would clear a field of grain with a scythe. To them, the people encircling the palace were stalks of grain, nothing more. The suppressive fire broke the first several turns of the human chain that girded the palace, but the links behind those held firm. The Cadillac plowed into a wall of bodies, its mass arrested immediately by the greater mass of the Bahraini people. Behind it, the Mercedes was forced to brake to a stop. The second Cadillac swerved to avoid hitting the royal car, skidded, and collided with the reinforced concrete of the gatepost.

The men in the lead car kept shooting. Those from the wreck behind them climbed out of their vehicle and joined the fight, adding their firepower to the massacre. The streams of automatic bullets the bodyguards poured into the mob killed everyone in its front ranks--but when they died, they sank down on the spot, having nowhere else to go and exposing the thousands of living citizens behind them. More healthy, angry men and woman than the royal guards could kill with an arsenal. And they didn't have an arsenal, only half a dozen clips of ammunition apiece. A dozen if they were lucky. One man pulled a grenade out, slipped on the blood he'd shed, and fumbled his throw. The grenade rolled under the foremost Cadillac, where it burst, ruptured the fuel tank, and killed most of the bodyguards, who had formed up around the vehicle to make their last stand.

Those who survived staggered back to the king's Mercedes. Their ammunition was gone, so they drew knives and daggers and prepared to kill as many of the king's subjects as they could.

The crowd parted just enough to let a group of new arrivals through. On the edge of the graveyard created by the bullets, they stopped and began to throw things at the bodyguards.

Not bullets, not grenades, not even stones as suggested by the Quran, but balls of paint and packets of dye. Soldiers who could not see could not fight. The demonstrators blinded them, then quietly walked up to them, took their weapons away, and tied their hands. They pulled the guards back into the crowd and waited.

Five minutes passed. Ten. Fifteen.

The rear door of the car opened. King Hamad stepped out. The fringe of his brown robe touched the ground and was instantly dyed scarlet.

There was nothing regal or noble about his round, scared face and stumpy form. To his credit, perhaps, he didn't cower, either. He stared around at the dead and wounded, at the crowd that had transformed him from a pampered billionaire to a man standing alone in a hell he'd built. The mob stared back. Ripples of silence radiated out in circles from the spot where the former ruler and the formerly ruled faced off.

An old man emerged from the crowd. He stepped around the piles of dead with great caution and respect, but his eyes never left Hamad, and he did not stop moving until no more than a yard separated them.

"I am Ahmed bin Mazin," the old man said.

Hamad did not respond, but the fear in his eyes deepened. His accuser nodded.

"God spares your life, as my grandson spared the life of the spy you sent among his men, because He alone rules, not you or I."

* * * * *

"I didn't realize his grandfather was still alive," Asim said.

"Alive and eloquent, to hold half the city spellbound like that."

"So what did they do with the king?"

"Took him to the causeway and turned him over to his friends the Saudis, who, having no instructions on how to deal with such a situation, pulled back to await further orders from Riyadh." Junayd chuckled. "I don't think he'll be back, regardless of what our neighbors decide to do."

Asim stretched. "So we've won."

"We will never win." Fihr came into the room and stared down at the dancing lights on their screens. "There is no such thing as winning."

Junayd shifted in his seat uncomfortably. "I know you loved him, but--"

"What happened to our Facebook page?" Fihr asked.

"I'm sorry?"

"What happened to our Facebook page?"

"It was taken down earlier this morning."

"And the other pages? For our blogs? The imam's essays?"

"Most of those have also been taken down or temporarily blocked."

"Why?"

"'Violating community guidelines,' they say. The same blanket excuse that they use every time they censor something."

"Meaning that advocating the overthrow of an oppressive government is considered too dangerous to be allowed by their policies, which promote the least common denominator of mediocrity."

"Pretty much."

"How can we have won if the ideas we fought to make heard are still being suppressed?"

"We got rid of the immediate threat."

"The immediate threat is not the only threat there is."

"So this is why you're brooding over not winning."

"The internet is the natural tool of revolution. Forget that governments try to censor it. What happens when those who build it and use it start censoring themselves?"

"Hey, it's still easy to build a website and make your voice heard. It's just not as fast and accessible as going through one of the existing platforms."

"And what happens when hosting services refuse to sell you server space? When transmission companies refuse to provide bandwidth? When ICANN bows to legal pressure and hands your domain name over to thieves with civil service badges?"

"You can't get the internet without it having to flow through points where someone can control it. If there were no suppliers, there wouldn't be an internet, and there certainly can't be things like Facebook."

"On the contrary, there can be."

"How do you propose to do that?"

"We just did it with Fikri."

"The social functionality of distributed computing? A peer-to-peer network running in the back of existing resources is one thing. But everyone who's tried to build a true peer-to-peer social network has come up short so far. There's not a framework for the technology, for one thing. It's still necessary to run some functions on a server to provide any kind of reliable speed or routing."

"Then get rid of the servers."

"Sorry?"

"Get rid of the servers. Put all the functionality of a server on each and every computer, so that each one is an independent node on the global network, subject only to the control of its user and not a corporate policy or a law."

"That's a pretty tall order."

"But it's possible."

"Yes--if you could invent a markup language that would surpass all others in convenience. And it would have to be small. Tiny. Compressed. Or it would never fit on a single machine, or run at acceptable speeds."

"All for the better. Focusing on building such a network would fix the bloat problem. Programmers have gotten lazy. We were never taught to build for efficiency; our instructors always told us that the hardware would be equal to anything we could construct. Even Fikri is messy in some regards. And to the end user, the bloat makes no difference in usability--but it makes a difference to us. Not size, but simplicity. Simple software is a revolution in itself. It requires fewer people to build, and thus less organization and coercion."

"Taking the imam's reasoning into the electronic world now?"

"It was always there to start with."

"You still have an insoluble problem. Even if we did write a code that could run the entire internet without a single server--even the nameservers, if you want to go that far--our code would still run through wires and satellites under someone else's control. And whoever controlled the conduits would still be capable of censoring the traffic."

"That's not insoluble. The solution is quite easy."

"Take the network off the wires altogether?"

"Yes."

"Impractical. Besides, how would you connect machines?"

"Peer to peer again--physically this time. Each computer would contain its own shortwave transceiver. It would be independent of all others and could talk directly to any machine in range without a go-between. If it needed greater power to reach farther, it could use the surplus bandwidth of a friendly machine nearby, just as Fikri does."

Junayd whistled. "I'll believe it when I see it done."

Fihr sat down, opened a new text window, and began typing.

"You can't seriously mean to start coding this now!"

"Hamad is gone. So is Ra'd bin Mazin. But I can't forget there's a revolution out there. Can you think of a better way for me to pursue its broader goals?"

Junayd thought about this while the sound of keys being tapped filled the room.

21

"Since it clearly wasn't you who were in the boat that the Iranians blew up," Josh Cranford said, "who or what was it?"

The Major brushed a speck of lint off the trousers of his service uniform. "Space heaters."

"Space heaters?"

"Turn them to the right setting and wrap them in a couple of blankets, and they look enough like a human body to fool a helicopter's infrared sensors."

"I'm surprised you found some in a country that's mostly desert."

"Those we brought with us from Dubai," the Major admitted. "Our guide's network of co-religionists, relatives, and fellow smugglers was excellent, but I didn't want to put too much pressure on their ingenuity."

"And after planting the heaters--"

"We put the watchman back on the dock, put on life vests, and slipped over the opposite side of the boat to get underneath the dock. Corporal Ramirez stayed on board to set the trawler on her course and swam back to meet us when he was finished. All we had to do was keep quiet and not splash around."

"And the entire time the police were stomping about on the pier looking for you, you were right underneath them."

"It was a hilarious situation," Major Martin said. He looked pleased.

"Sitting in ice-cold water while a trigger-happy cop is searching for you one story up sounds a bit less than hilarious to me."

"Marines are a strange breed."

"I've noticed. Yours seem a bit subdued, though."

"It's the suddenness of the change. One minute we're on a boat about to leave Iran by sea, the next we're cutting through a border fence, the next we're on a luxury jet heading for home. They were almost as unsure of what I was planning as the Iranians were, and they're still a shade confused. Thanks for arranging the last stages of the trip so well, by the way."

"It helps to own part of an oil company heavily invested in Azerbaijan. They like doing the larger shareholders favors. Speaking of transport, where's this pilot of yours who's queer and yet not queer? I want to meet her."

"Ethiopia."

"Ethiopia? Was that in the plan?"

"No," the Major said. "She pulled a fast one on me. I got a call from her a few hours ago saying that she'd decided to keep the Saeqeh and was taking it south to refuel before flying it across Africa. Like you, she also has connections in the oil industry, except hers are familial. And she didn't tell me in advance so I wouldn't thwart her desires."

"Devious."

"And admirable in a devious sort of way. I hope she gets it back. Even if not, the fact that she stole an Iranian jet while the CIA sat on its hands and whined about its lack of data will bother those armor-plated asses for a good ten years to come."

"I smell spy-on-spy rivalry. You like bothering people, don't you?"

"When they deserve it, absolutely."

"'Bothered' would be a mild word to describe how the Iranians feel about you right now. Or most of the gay community back home." Josh held up his phone and scrolled through the feed. "They celebrate your ingenuity and the liberation of Kadivar and Jan, but they deplore that you acted without official sanction." He tossed the device to the Major. "That's about what the consensus amounts to."

The Major shrugged. "It's hard to argue with results. As I said to you before, there are two men alive today who wouldn't be without our efforts. Nobody can spin the saving of human life out to make it look like a trivial accomplishment."

"No, they'll have to give you that at least. I wonder, though--" He paused.

"You wonder?"

Josh jerked his head in the direction of the two Iranians, who were dozing in the rear of the plane. "If anyone ever had a good case for asylum, it's them. They shouldn't have too many problems."

"But they will have some."

"Yes, they will have some. And that's the issue."

"Meaning that they shouldn't have any?"

"You risk your life to snatch them away from death in order to bring them to a culture that, even if it feels benevolently disposed towards them, will still lock them away for years while it plays games with them. And when they get out, as members of a still-controversial minority, they'll be subjected to all sorts of official and unofficial behavioral expectations they're not used to, right after they escaped from a society whose expectations are what got them in trouble in the first place."

"Oh, I have no illusions about our actions providing them with true freedom," the Major agreed. "It's incremental. It's the best we could do at implementing the principle. They won't have it any more in the United States than they will in

Iran--but they will spend the rest of their lives remembering that it wasn't the gay community that got them out of Iran. It was their fellow men. We created two individuals here."

"Two individuals with the idea that they can set aside the habits of society and culture anytime they like."

"As you pointed out, they were already predisposed to understanding that, given their treatment in Iran. All they have to do now is to look beyond their specific case and find the general principle involved. When men tie each other's hands, they all suffer."

"How delightfully ironic," Josh mused.

"Explain."

"Isn't the argument for the existence of government and society in the first place that they provide human beings with things they could not obtain individually? That members of a society sacrifice some of their freedoms for greater safety, individually and as a whole?"

"That's the argument, yes."

"And yet, as you've just demonstrated by your success, the evidence contradicts that hypothesis. The larger society would have sat by while Kadivar and Jan died. They're alive because you ignored that society."

"True."

"So safety does not result from numbers or a surrender of freedom of action."

"Correct."

"But freedom of action isn't very merciful sometimes."

"On the contrary. Freedom and mercy are the same thing."

Josh blinked. "Even if you exercise that freedom through a brutal action?"

"Yes. Because the most compassionate and understanding thing you can do for another human being is admit his right to act as he pleases, even if you view his actions as despicable. Can you think of any gesture of respect for humanity that is more significant?"

"Well…"

"Which brings us back to where you began," the Major continued relentlessly. "In neither the United States nor Iran will these boys find that kind of understanding. Both cultures will box them up and try very hard to cut off anything that sticks out of the boxes."

"Then what was the point of the exercise?"

"They're still alive. Maybe one day they'll have a chance."

One of the pilots came down the aisle from the cockpit. "Excuse me, sir," he said, addressing the Major, "but we have Potomac approach control on the radio. They're refusing us permission to land at Dulles."

"Did you file your flight plan before departing Madrid?"

"Yes, we did."

"Then get back in the cockpit and fly the airplane."

The pilot visibly struggled with his inner feelings. "Major, we can't land at Dulles or anywhere else in the United States. They've told us not to land. Where would you like to divert?"

"Nowhere. I intend to go to Washington, and I'm going there."

"Can they do that?" Josh interrupted.

"The controllers can tells us not to cross their airspace, yes, but such instructions are highly dubious under international law. Besides, when it comes down to it, they're not the ones flying the airplane."

"Sir, we can't--"

"No, you won't, which is a different story." The Major stood up. "Get back to your seat and I'll come talk to them."

In the cockpit, the pilot was trying to charm his way past the controllers and getting nowhere. Major Martin took the copilot's headset and put it on. He silenced the pilot with a gesture before pressing the transmit button.

"Potomac approach, this is Gulfstream three-zero-alpha. We are a humanitarian flight on a properly filed flight plan in accordance with international regulations and we intend to land at Dulles as per that flight plan. Please advise accordingly. Over."

The controllers came back with the same snappy reply they'd been feeding the pilot for the past few minutes. "Gulfstream three-zero-alpha, you have fugitives on board and are not authorized to enter United States airspace. We advise that you divert to the nearest available airport or return to your point of departure."

"Potomac approach, we will be landing at Dulles shortly; please contact us as necessary. Out." The Major took off the headset and handed it back to the copilot.

"Great, what am I supposed to do with this situation?" the pilot demanded.

"Land the damn airplane."

"They'll revoke my certificate."

"We'll cover any fines," Josh said from behind the Major's shoulder.

"And in the meantime?"

"Ignore anything they say that isn't landing instructions. Shouldn't you be starting your descent about now?"

"Yes, but--"

"Do it."

The pilot shrugged, took a deep breath, and put his hand on the throttles.

The radios crackled again. "Gulfstream three-zero-alpha, be aware that you are not permitted to enter US airspace, and if you proceed on your present course you will be intercepted by air defense."

"Translation, please?" Josh asked.

"They're going to send up fighters to frighten us. Probably F-22s from the 1st Fighter Wing at Langley. The Air Force can't ever use them in combat, so they like to send them up to take on defenseless aircraft sometimes. It's the only fair fight an F-22 will ever see."

"I don't really want to see it, much less be in it!" the pilot snapped. He was sweating now.

"No one is going to shoot us down and you know it. Stay on course. If you have to, play the medical emergency card. I'll be back in a minute."

"Arguably, this wouldn't have happened if you hadn't sent out that press release the minute we left Spain," Josh said as he followed the Major back down the aisle, past the started Marines sitting up front.

"Why do you think I sent it out at that particular time?"

"To provoke the Iranians? To let them know you got away with it?"

"And to force the ostensibly pro-gay United States government to pick a side. They knew we were coming, flight path, time of arrival, everything. Either way, it was a losing situation for them. Set aside regulations and precedent and do the humane thing, or uphold the regulations and admit where their priorities are. They chose to bluster about it. Fine. We can deal with it."

"You may have just pushed too many buttons all at once."

"Did you think I wasn't prepared for this?" the Major asked. His satellite phone was already in his hand.

"So what are you going to do about it?"

"I'm going to call in our air cover."

* * * * *

The two F-22 fighters flashed past the Gulfstream with ponderous grace, one on either side of the larger aircraft. The shock wave generated by their engines was audible and loud in the business jet's cockpit. They circled around behind it and dropped into position off its tail, one of them covering the Gulfstream, the other one covering its companion.

"They are, in fact, threatening to shoot us down," the pilot said. "Who would have ever thought it?" He was past the stage of being nervous and had started being sarcastic instead.

"Keep flying," the Major said.

"While you update Facebook?"

"While I save your ass."

"I don't have a threat warning receiver on this bird."

"Good, you'd probably panic even worse if you did. Now shut up."

The Gulfstream continued to descend. The fighter pilots began to show signs of irritation.

"All right, this has gone far enough, I think," the Major said, slipping his phone back into his pocket. He reached for a headset again.

"Three-zero-alpha, if you attempt to enter the ADIZ you will be shot down!" the pilot on the other end was shouting.

"Cyclon flight, this is three-zero-alpha. Check your six," the Major said into the microphone.

"What's that supposed to do, scare him off?" the Gulfstream pilot jeered.

"Wait for it," the Major replied, cocking his head as if to listen.

Astern of the G650, the rearmost fighter throttled back and dropped away in a curve. The pilot saw what the Major was referring to immediately. Another Gulfstream jet, an older one, but with the same big oval windows as all Gulfstream models, was flying a few thousand feet below the larger jet, keeping pace with it.

"Cylon flight, be advised that the aircraft you see is carrying a full passenger load of journalists and photographers," the Major's voice said over the radio.

For a blessed minute, there was silence as the F-22 pilots talked to Langley on a different frequency. Then the pilots punched their throttles forward and they roared past the Gulfstream, shaking everyone on board as they did so, before fading away ahead of it.

"They're so predictable," the Major said indulgently as he gave the copilot his headset back again.

"There's a press plane behind us?"

"Watching and listening to everything that went on."

"How the hell did you pull that one off?"

"It was simple. I intended for the controllers to try to stop us. I knew that if we weren't cooperative, they'd probably run crying to the Air Force for help. So I arranged for a charter plane and a bunch of reporters to make sure there was no interference."

"No, I mean, how did you keep the F-22s from seeing the press plane?"

"One, they weren't looking for it. Two, it was going in the opposite direction. Three, it was flying on top of the waves the whole time, blending into the background clutter. I only called them into action after the F-22s were already on our tail. Even if their radar was any good, they still can't see behind them. The press plane floated up nice and easy into their blind spot for the big reveal."

The pilot shook his head and listened to the radio traffic. Potomac approach was suddenly being cooperative, if sullen.

"They won't forgive you for that," Josh said, fastening his seat belt.

"I doubt it."

"Any more tricks left?"

"No. Now we just go home and get arrested."

"You think they will?"

"I'm sure they will. Me, anyway. The rest of you--well, you might get off."

"But we might not."

"That too."

"I think you're enjoying the ambiguity of our position."

The Major chuckled. He was satisfied with his work.

The Gulfstream's nose breached the twelve-mile limit and it entered American airspace.

Also by this author:

Hyperdrive

L'Affaire Famille

Totum Hominem

The Bettor

Made in the USA
Lexington, KY
08 April 2019